HOW WE
HATED

Copyright © 2024 by Lauren Runow.
All rights reserved.

Visit my website at www.LaurenRunow.com

Cover Designer: Enchanting Romance Designs

Editor: Jovana Shirley, Unforeseen Editing, www.unforeseenediting.com

No part of this book may be reproduced or transmitted in any form or by any means, electronic or mechanical, including photocopying, recording, or by any information storage and retrieval system without the written permission of the author, except for the use of brief quotations in a book review.

This book is a work of fiction. Names, characters, places, and incidents either are products of the author's imagination or are used fictitiously. Any resemblance to actual persons, living or dead, events, or locales is entirely coincidental.

No copyright infringement intended. No claims have been made over songs and/or lyrics written. All credit goes to original owners.

CHAPTER 1

Dalton

I walk into first period and slump down in my seat with a big thud, kicking my legs out in front of me and hitting the person sitting there. Trish—a girl I've had a relationship or two with—turns around to see what just hit her and gives me a shy smile when she sees it's me.

With my ball cap tugged low, I give her a slight grin, wondering to myself if she'd be up for another go-around sometime soon, when Marcus—a guy who's like a brother to me—kicks my foot out of the way as he walks by.

"Come on, bro," I say with a questioning tone.

"Some of us need to get through. Stop taking up all the space around here," he replies.

"That's what happens when you're my size and expected to sit in these tiny-ass desks, which I know you know nothing about," I taunt back.

HOW WE HATED

He flips me off as he sits down in an open seat a few rows up.

At five foot nine, Marcus might be small compared to my six-two, two-hundred-pound frame, but the guy can run like no one else on the football field, so he's all good in my book.

I sit up in my chair, feeling every muscle ache after the ass-kicking we just got before school. Yes, it's the first day of school, and our football coach still called for practice at six a.m.

Most players are worried about getting a scholarship to play, so it's worth everything we have to do, but I already know I'm going to Stanford for college. It's the same place my dad went, so I don't really have a choice, which makes days like today extra pointless.

Even if I didn't already make the team with a full-ride scholarship, my parents give the school so many hundreds of thousands of dollars a year, so why would my tuition be any different? I'm sure the school just treated my scholarship as their thank-you for all they give.

Kind of stupid if you ask me, but no one ever really asks for my opinion, so what's the point?

I knew—or I guess I should say, the school knew—I'd be going there from a very young age even though I live thousands of miles away in a small-ass town called Leighton River.

My parents started their tech company, TimeLand, with three friends from here after they all moved away for college. The company blew up—creating a gaming app that's on every person's phone nowadays—so they all moved back to Montana because they didn't want to raise their kids in California.

I ask all the time why I have to move there for college, but I get the same response from my father.

"Moving to California made us appreciate what we have here, so you will follow in my footsteps, go to Stanford, and prepare to take over this company one day."

Blah, blah, blah.

What we have here in Leighton River is a whole bunch of nothing.

The bell rings, and I sigh with the beginning of another school year.

"Okay, class, everyone take your seat," Mrs. Anderson says from the front of the classroom.

She goes over all the same boring shit we have to listen to every teacher say at the beginning of the year.

Yes, we get it. *Turn in your work on time. No cheating. No plagiarism.*

Thank God this is my senior year, and this is my last first day in this school.

I drop my head back, already bored as hell, and we're only ten minutes in.

"Throughout this class, you will be assigned a class partner—and, yes, it will be the same person all semester long. Not only will you be checking in on each other, making sure they are turning in assignments, but you will also have projects that you will be finishing together," Mrs. Anderson announces.

I sit back and watch as everyone looks around the room, trying to figure out who their partner will be. When Trish turns around to me with a simple raise of her eyebrows, my lips tilt up in a grin.

HOW WE HATED

Well, maybe this semester is looking up after all.

"Now, don't go trying to choose who your partner will be." Mrs. Anderson raises her finger to make a point. "Just like in real life, we don't get to choose who our co-workers are, so these assignments will be teaching you just as much about English as they are about learning how to work with people you might not know very well or even like very much."

She grabs a bucket from her desk and holds it in the air. "Everyone will pick one number out of this bucket, and this will decide who your partner is."

She sets it on the front corner desk, and I watch as the bucket is passed back to the other kids sitting in the row after each person takes their number.

When it's my turn, I grab a number and see I got eleven. Having no clue what that means, I fold it up and place it on my desk. I take these few seconds to close my eyes to get a brief moment of sleep until the bucket makes its way around the entire classroom.

"Does everyone have their number?" Mrs. Anderson asks, and the class mumbles their response. "Who has number one?"

Two people raise their hands, and she asks them to state their names, which they do. Then, she goes down the list until she gets to eleven.

I hold up my hand, not paying attention to who else in the class does too. Before she even asks, I say, "Dalton," in a tone that tells her I'm bored and over this already.

"Natalie," I hear someone else say from a few rows up, and I instantly cringe inside.

You've got to be fucking kidding me.

LAUREN RUNOW

I drop my hand with a slam on my desk probably harder than necessary, but having Natalie as a partner absolutely will not work.

Marcus turns to me with his eyes wide, and I shake my head with a laugh.

Just my luck that I get Natalie Spencer, the only person in this entire fucking school I stay as far away as possible from. Well, her and her brother, Thomas.

If you've heard of the Hatfield and McCoy family feud from the 1800's then you'll understand why this is not humanly possible for us to be partners. To say our parents despise each other is the understatement of the century.

We spend the rest of class listening to Mrs. Anderson explain how the partner assignments will work and what our first assignment will be together. Once it's over, I grab my things and head to her desk.

"Mrs. Anderson, there's one slight problem," I state firmly.

She looks up from her desk, and I watch as her eyes move to what is going on next to me—or rather, I should say *who* is standing next to me.

Mrs. Anderson holds her hands up. "Don't ask me to change partners." Her tone lets us know right away that this is final. "I know your families have history, but I don't care. This is supposed to mimic real-life situations, and I think it's perfect. I guarantee, at some point, you will have a co-worker you won't like, and there's nothing you will be able to do about it. Treat this the same way. Figure out how to make it work."

She gets up and walks away without listening to a word I have to say.

HOW WE HATED

I look at Natalie, only to see her huff off.

Fucking great way to start my senior year.

I head out of the classroom and go straight to the area we all hang out at during passing periods.

Marcus is telling a story, and everyone covers their mouth, saying, "Oh shit," when I walk up.

"And here's the unluckiest guy in school now." Marcus acts like he's going to punch me in the stomach but stops short.

"Ha-ha. Not funny," I deadpan.

"I think it's hilarious!" Marcus laughs.

Maya—who's been considered *one of the guys* since we were little because her dad, along with Ben and Eli's, all started TimeLand with my dad, so we all grew up together—comes up and puts her head on my shoulder, trying to comfort me. "You'll be okay. At least we know she won't bite."

I push her off me as she falls into a fit of giggles.

"You all suck—you know that?" I point to them.

Marcus and Maya are two peas in a pod, high-fiving each other, while Eli is looking like he couldn't care less as he grabs his phone from his back pocket and starts to type something out.

I plop down on the couch we had our parents buy for the school that sits in the hallway entrance where the area is bigger so we'd have a place to chill during passing period. Ben is leaning up against the arm of the couch, flirting with a freshman, I presume. I push him out of the way so I can put my arm on the rest, like it's supposed to be used.

Maya stares at Ben for a brief second before she sits down next to me, and we meet eyes. She doesn't say anything. Just smiles. I give her a fake cheesy grin back.

This is her thing. No one can be mad long. She won't allow it. She says life is too short for anger. She's been this way ever since she lost her mom seven years ago. I know it's a good outlook to have, but sometimes, I just want to smother her happiness.

When it doesn't work, she shakes her head and places her hand on my knee, using it as a crutch to help herself up.

"I'm off to Spanish. *Adios, amigos!*" she says cheerfully, making me want to throw a wadded-up piece of paper at her with the way her cheerleading skirt bounces from side to side, looking as joyful as she is.

I drop my head back on the couch and close my eyes, hoping to just lie here the rest of the day. When the warning bell rings, I let out a frustrated sigh, slap my hands on my knees, and make my way to standing so I can head to my next class—Econ.

I'm the last person to walk in, so I look for any empty seat available, only to see Natalie is the person right in front of me.

Looking up to the ceiling, I mouth, *Why?*

Then, I sit in the chair just as the final bell rings.

I don't mean to hit the seat in front of me, but of course, this is not my day, so when I do, Natalie turns around to see me sitting there. When she rolls her eyes, all I can think of is how I feel the exact same way.

CHAPTER 2

Natalie

I jump out of Thomas's truck after he pulls up to our house. Yes, he's a year younger than me, and, technically, we are supposed to share the truck, but I let him drive us to and from school. The truck is constantly breaking down, and since he's the one that actually fixes it, I figured it's more his anyway. I don't mind him driving us around though.

I've never been so thankful that he's not a talker because there's nothing I want to say anyway. Today, I'm very happy for his blasting stereo that sometimes drives me crazy. Now that we're home though, I know my luck is about to change.

I'm not in the house for two seconds before my mom, Tracy, asks, "How was the first day of school?"

"Fine," I state as I walk straight to my room to change.

HOW WE HATED

There's only one thing that will help this mood I'm in, and it's Brandy, my horse, so the quicker I can get out to her stable, the better.

When there's a knock on my door, I don't even have to think twice about who it is. "Yes, Mom?"

My tone doesn't hide a thing, and she's quick to call me on it as she enters my room.

"What's wrong, baby? Did you have a bad day?"

I question telling her about my assigned partner in English. The last thing she and my Pops want is me hanging out with someone from the TimeLand crew, especially Dalton. I know I can't get away from it though, so I might as well get it out now.

"They assigned partners in English today." I plop down on my bed with my shoulders slumped.

Mom sits next to me. "It can't be that bad. You've always worked really well with other kids. Why did this upset you so much?"

I look at her, hoping she sees the anguish in my expression. "Because I got assigned to partner with Dalton Wick."

Her eyes widen as she takes it all in. "Oh …" is all she says.

"Exactly. *Oh*. Pops is going to flip. And, yes, we both went straight to the teacher after class, but she insisted that nothing will change, no matter what our family history is."

Mom takes in a breath and lets it out slowly. "Well, I guess that's real life."

I throw my hands up in the air as I stand up. "That's exactly what she said. Can't you guys call the school and complain?"

"I can try, but it sounds like the teacher has already made up her mind. I see what lesson she's trying to teach you."

"Really? The same lesson you guys and the TimeLand crew have been working on since before I was born?"

She stands up and places her hand on my shoulder. "That's different."

"No, it's not." I grab my boots from the floor and shout over my shoulder as I walk out of my room, "I'll be out with Brandy."

"Go see your dad in the barn. He's going to need your help with the baby pigs. A few more were born today."

"Okay," I yell back.

Hearing more babies were born today does lift my spirits a little. That's the best part of living on a ranch—all the babies that are born seemingly year-round.

We can't afford the staff we need so my brother and I have our duties that have become our biggest contribution to the family business. For my brother, it's herding the cattle; for me, it's helping with any of the newborns.

First though, I need to go to Brandy.

As I enter the stable, I call out her name, and she instantly perks up from her stall and looks at me. There's a reason she's my best friend. I know that sounds sad, but it's the truth. There's no drama with her, and she's always happy to see me.

I walk up to her and place my palm on her face, then my cheek against hers. She nuzzles into me, and just like that, the stress of the day floats away.

"Hey, girl," I say, running my hand down her mane.

HOW WE HATED

"You want to get out of here?"

She huffs and moves around, showing me she knows exactly what I'm saying.

I grab the saddle and place it over her, getting everything ready to head out for my favorite part of the day—the time where it's just her, me, and the land surrounding us. Normally, I go for rides later in the day, but I can't wait that long now.

Once she's all set, I open the stall door and walk her out of the stable. I put my foot in the stirrup and jump up, then swing my leg around until I'm securely sitting on the saddle.

With a kick of my heel, I say, "Come on, girl."

She instantly starts off, and within seconds, we're racing down the hill, through the stables, and past the barns to where our cattle are held. It takes a few minutes to get through our two-thousand-acre ranch to the back by the river. The first part of our ranch is still actively running, but a large portion back here has been left empty for the past twenty-five years.

My Pops never comes out here because it's too devastating to him to think about what this place used to be, but I love coming out here because there's no one else around. I feel like it's my personal sanctuary.

Brandy and I race through the rolling hills of the now-empty land, feeling like we could run forever, as free as we could possibly be.

Our property line is marked by a narrow river. Even though downstream, where the river gets much wider, is a popular place for people to hang out, our ranch is so big that no matter how far you look right or left, you'll never see a single soul.

Well … maybe one. Across the river is the Wick property. Thankfully, their monstrosity of a mansion is up higher on the hill, so I don't have to see it from here, but every once in a while, I'll see Dalton back in these hills. Of course, he's never cared to even notice I'm back here too.

I dismount Brandy and walk her to the stream so she can get a drink of water.

When I look off to the hills above our ranch, all I see are the houses that now dot the land that once was covered in just trees. The sight always saddens me, so instead, I push the thought out, especially after my partner incident today, and go about my routine of brushing Brandy to help calm any bad emotions that pop into my mind.

Here, with her, is my Zen place.

I know my time is slipping away and my dad needs my help, so I mount Brandy again, and we make our way back to the ranch and the barn, where my Pops still is.

After I hop off of Brandy, I tie her to the fence and enter the barn, which has the few ranch hands we have, working in the area. I head toward the back, where I'm sure he is since that's where the babies are kept.

"Hey, Pops," I say when I see him pouring some feed into the containers.

He's obviously had a rough day just by the way his clothes are covered in mud, yet he's working like he's as clean as can be. He's the hardest worker I've ever met. His biggest fear is losing this ranch, but sometimes I wonder if the ranch is even worth saving if it means he works his life away just to keep it.

HOW WE HATED

He walks up and places his arms around me to give me a hug. No matter what he's doing, he always stops to give me a hug. "Hey, sweetheart. How was your ride?"

I hug him back not caring if doing so gets me dirty. "It was good." I say nothing more, not wanting to think about my day any more than I have to.

He goes back to what he was doing. "Your mom said you have something to tell me. Something about a partner at school?"

I inhale a breath and let it out slowly, not happy my mom told him anything, but honestly not surprised. These two have this amazing bond, and I swear they are like one soul, split into two bodies.

"In English, we have to work with the same partner all semester, and we chose them randomly by drawing numbers."

"Do you not like who you got?" he asks sincerely while continuing his work.

"You're not going to like who I got either," I state matter-of-factly, making him stop in his tracks and look at me.

"Yep. She assigned me to Dalton Wick," I state clearly, ripping off the Band-Aid.

Our eyes meet, and I watch as his jaw tics.

My Pops is an honest, hardworking man who is loved in this community, but there's one thing he hates—in all capital letters, H-A-T-E-S—the Wick family and, subsequently, the other three founders of TimeLand.

The damage Mike Wick, Dalton's dad, inflicted on our ranch and our family will never be forgiven.

He stays silent as he finishes pouring the feed and crumples up the bag before throwing it in a barrel he uses as a trash can. When our eyes meet, I can tell he's upset, but he just shakes his head like he's still in thought.

"Well, I'm sure Mom has dinner waiting on the table for us. What do you say we head in?"

"You're not mad?" I ask.

"Sure, I'm mad. You know how I feel about them. You know how his dad's actions have affected our entire family. The last person I want you or Thomas having any contact with is him."

I bite my bottom lip, dread pulling low in my stomach as he wraps his arm around me.

He continues, "But I also know that school is important, and who are we to tell the teacher how to do her job? Our family issues shouldn't decide how she runs her classroom. In life, sometimes, you have to do things you don't want to do, but that doesn't mean it doesn't get done. You'll have to treat this as one of those things."

I lean my head on his shoulder. "This is cruel and unusual punishment though."

He laughs. "Now, I agree with that." He kisses my forehead. "Let's not think about it for now. I'm sure whatever Mom's cooking will help us forget. Remember …"

"Don't ever bring the drama of life to the dinner table," I say before he can, making him chuckle.

It's one of his mottos of life. Family dinnertime is sacred in our house, and he always says there should never be anything that ruins our special time together.

There are many things we don't have, but no matter what, good food is always on our table. A perk for being

HOW WE HATED

the producer of said food and not having to purchase it at the store.

I grab Brandy's reins, and we walk back to the barn to put her away before heading inside. With every step, I feel slightly better about my day. My dad always has a way of making any problems I have seem to melt away. At least for the time being.

CHAPTER 3

Natalie

Thankfully, Mrs. Anderson didn't make us do anything with our partners today, so I slide out of English class with a smile on my face, only to remember Dalton sits behind me in Econ for my second period class.

When I meet up with my closest friends, Susie and Ashley, in the hall, they can tell I'm already annoyed, and it's barely nine a.m.

"Oh no. What happened now?" Susie asks as she holds her arms out to give me a hug.

I hug her back with a slump of my shoulders. "I was just thinking how happy I was to make it out of English without having to talk to Dalton, only to remember he sits behind me in Econ."

Susie shakes her head. "It's really too bad you two hate each other so much because I would give my big left toe to be his partner."

HOW WE HATED

I squint my eyes at her for her *left toe* comment. She shrugs.

"I've heard guys say they'd give their left nut for something, so I figured it kind of fit," she says with a laugh.

"You're crazy." I nudge her out of the way to get to my locker.

"My words might be, but not my thoughts. How do you not see just how fine that boy is?"

I grab my Econ book, shut my locker, then lean my back against it. "He is not cute," I state as clearly as possible.

Ashley laughs. "Yeah, okay. Keep telling yourself that, and maybe, one day, you'll actually believe it."

I eye her, and she smiles a big, cheesy grin.

"I agree with Susie. Many girls at this school would give their big left toe"—they high-five at the saying—"to be his partner. So sad such an awesome experience is wasted on you."

"Don't you guys realize just how fake he is?" I plead.

"Fake?" they ask in unison.

"Girl, there's nothing fake about that body of his," Susie says slowly as she shakes her head from side to side.

"He literally drives a big, lifted *work* truck, yet he hasn't worked a day in his life," I state, emphasizing the word *work*.

Susie sighs. "He doesn't need to work. Remember, he's worth millions?" she says, enunciating every syllable in the last part.

"And that's the problem. Money isn't everything." I stand up straight and head toward my class. "See you later." I wave over my shoulder, feeling defeated that they both seem to like him and everything he stands for.

Well, I don't.

Thankfully, these are the only two classes I have to share with my archnemesis this year. As I walk into Econ, I pray he was able to switch seats with someone so we can go back to ignoring each other like we have for the past eleven years that we've been in school together.

When I get to my row, I look up, only to see Dalton already sitting there, turned around, talking to the girl behind him.

I roll my eyes and sit down in my chair, hoping he doesn't notice that I just arrived.

The bell rings, and when he turns forward, I feel my hair being flicked to the side.

"Hey," I say as I grab it and smooth it down with my hand.

"I don't want your long brown hair on my desk," Dalton says with a glare.

"Then, you ask politely for me to move it. You don't just touch my hair without asking." I turn back around with a huff, only to get shivers down my spine when I feel him get too close.

"Most girls want me to touch them. Too bad I'll only ever touch you to get your hair away from me. As far as possible away from me," he whispers.

I grip my desk to turn me around faster when our teacher, Miss Hernandez, asks, "Are you two done? I'd like to get the class started."

I glare at Dalton, who has a grin on his face as he sits back in his chair with his feet stretched out in front of him so far that he's invading my space.

HOW WE HATED

After I close my eyes and take a deep breath to calm the fire building inside of me, I smile at Miss Hernandez. "Sorry, it won't happen again." For good measure, I kick his foot that's next to mine in a silent *sit your ass up* motion.

Miss Hernandez—who is a new teacher here and just graduated from college herself—laughs it off, probably remembering the days of having to sit in similar desks herself, and starts the class.

"Everyone, open your books to chapter one," she says as she writes *Introduction to Economics* across the whiteboard. "In this chapter, we'll go over things like microeconomics, macroeconomics, and what the differences are, as well as the global economy and financial planning. I thought it would be interesting to start the class off with something local since it's such a huge deal in Leighton River. Let's talk about TimeLand, which falls in the technology and economics category."

Eli—one of the TimeLand kids, who is sitting one row over from me and a few desks up—snaps his head up when she says *TimeLand*. I've never seen him have such a reaction to the company his dad helped create. Is he finally seeing them for what they are—an addictive death trap?

I've always been one to interact in class, so I don't hesitate when I say, "Technology is ruining our world."

"Not with this again," Dalton says with a huff behind me.

I don't bother to turn around to address his comment before I continue, "Technology might make life easier for some, but our bodies are made to move. Sitting is becoming the new version of smoking because of the negative effects on our health."

"Okay," Miss Hernandez says. "So, you don't think the technology to make milking cows easier has helped your ranch produce more?"

"Burn," Dalton fake coughs into his hand, but I still pay him no attention.

"Actually, it's caused some harm to the cows, and it ups the level of bacteria, so no. I wish it would go back to the old-school way of doing things."

"Well then, let's talk about the technology that has made getting your farm products easier to the people of Montana. I'm new to this area, but in my research, I learned that your ranch provides products pretty much all over Montana," she states.

I want to say, *We used to supply all over Montana*, but I keep that to myself. Pops is a proud man, and it's sad that no one in our community really knows just how much he's had to cut back. Only the places he used to supply know, and that's because there was no way of getting around not telling them.

Pops has kept the running of the ranch tight-lipped, and I'm not going to be the one to spread his business, especially in front of people from TimeLand.

"If you're talking about transportation to drive the goods across the state, then I'll give you that," I respond. "When transportation became more readily available is when my great-grandparents really grew the ranch."

"That wasn't the only technology. What about refrigeration?" she asks.

"These are all very old things that were great inventions for their time, but that's not what I'm talking about. I'm talking about the new addictive devices that everyone carries around in their pockets or the fact that

HOW WE HATED

some crazy-high percentage of people work, sitting at a desk, behind a computer. That's what is ruining our society."

"You do realize you have a phone in your back pocket too," Dalton snaps back.

I don't give him the satisfaction of turning around, but still state, "Yes, that I use as an actual phone to communicate with people. I don't play with all the games and apps." I inhale a breath. "All I'm saying is, people have gotten away from what really matters. Most people wouldn't have a clue how to raise, slaughter, and cultivate their own food. When all the technology crashes, what will people do?"

"It's human nature; we'd figure it out," Dalton says snidely.

I laugh and turn to him because this is just too good to not see his reaction.

"You? You'd figure it out? Do you think you're big ole truck will suddenly do the work for you? Have you ever even mowed your own lawn or, God forbid, taken out your own trash at home?"

His face is stoic, and I love that I've gotten under his skin.

"If you had to slaughter a pig, would you know what part of the pig you should actually eat?"

Again, he doesn't respond. He just stares at me as his jaw tics ever so slightly.

Yeah, that's what I thought.

I turn back around. "My point exactly."

Miss Hernandez goes back to her lesson, obviously feeling the tension rolling off of Dalton from this conversation, and I couldn't be happier.

CHAPTER 4

Dalton

The second week of school started without a hitch, and I'm looking forward to our first football game this Friday.

I park my truck in the back of the school by the football field since that is the first place I am in the morning and the last place before I leave at night. Technically, no one is supposed to be back here, but until they tell me no, I look at it as my own personal parking spot.

Yes, I know my parents are ridiculously loaded, but, no, I don't drive a fancy car. I love my '94 Chevy truck that was my grandpa's when my dad was my age. Of course, we fixed it up a little with new wheels, and we put a six-inch lift on it, but it still has some original parts, including the country-style upholstery that almost feels made out of wool, as well as manual windows and

HOW WE HATED

door locks. It's a damn good thing I'm tall, too, because reaching over to unlock the passenger door would be a pain in the ass if I wasn't.

The one thing I wouldn't change is the paint. Every dent and scratch were put on this truck by my grandpa so I left them there as my way of keeping his memory even more alive.

Fall might be right around the corner, but it's not here yet, and under all that football gear, it might as well still be the dead of summer with how hot and sweaty I get during practice.

I toss my pads and bag in the back of the truck before I fling my door open and climb inside. My body aches with every move I make, so I take a second to just sit and let my muscles relax a bit before I reach forward and crank the engine.

The loud roar of the engine piques my senses—that is, until the speaker system I have set up behind my driver's seat kicks on and really smacks my ass awake again.

Morgan Wallen's "Last Night" comes over the radio, and I turn it up even louder than it already was. I sit and let the music run through my veins to bring me back to a calm place before I put the truck in reverse and pull out of the parking space.

I mindlessly drive around the school until I'm stopped in my tracks due to a huge trailer parked sideways with dirt everywhere, blocking my only way out.

You've got to be shitting me.

I throw the truck in park and hop out to see what this mess is all about.

"Hello!" I yell out when I don't see anyone around. "I need to get out of here, and you have the entire area blocked."

I look up just as I see someone sauntering out of the Future Farmers of America, or rather, the FFA area without a care in the world.

Natalie.

She's putting her gloves on nonchalantly, slapping them together as she walks to the building to grab a shovel, completely ignoring the fact that I'm standing here.

I drop my head back as I let out a loud sigh. *Why is the universe fucking with me this week?*

I shake my head and turn to face her. "You've blocked me in." I point to the mess she's created.

Not only does she not respond, but she also doesn't even flinch at my question.

"Hello!" I wave my hands in the air.

Nothing.

Biting down the anger brewing inside of me, I swiftly move toward her.

"Are you going to just sit there and ignore me?" I bite out.

She fights a grin as she removes the earbuds she had hidden behind her hair.

"What do you want?" she asks like she hasn't a clue in the world what's going on.

"What do I want?" I huff at her. "I want you to move your shit, literally. It smells like absolute crap back here, and you've also completely blocked the only way for me to get out."

"Well, there's a reason people don't park back there.

HOW WE HATED

So"—she sidesteps me and goes back to what she was doing—"that's not my problem."

Completely dumbfounded at the audacity of this girl, I fight back the urge to scream at her while she goes about her business, putting her earbuds back in and walking toward the trailer that's full of manure.

She thinks she's putting one over on me, but she has no idea who she's messing with. Two can play at this game, and I'm about to place a checkmate on her ass.

I walk past her and head straight to my truck.

One of the things I wanted on my truck was a massive aftermarket steel bumper. My father thought it was ridiculous, considering I wouldn't actually be using the truck for work purposes, but right here, right now, I know I got it for this exact reason.

"Lil Bit" by Nelly and Florida Georgia Line is playing on the radio now, and I turn it up even louder. The two fifteens I have in the back, where a second-row passenger seat is supposed to be, will get anyone's attention, no matter how much they are trying to ignore me.

Breaking out my big wheel and saying, "Let's roll," like the song suggests, brings on a totally different meaning, but it fits perfectly as I slowly roll forward, pushing her entire trailer, including all the things she had resting on the side to the ground. Slowly, I rev the engine, using my bumper to clear a path for me to get through.

I watch as Natalie comes running up, screaming something, but the music is so loud that I can't hear a word she says.

She approaches my passenger door and slaps her

hand on it, but I just look at her and point to my ear, like I can't hear what she's trying to say, continuing to slowly move forward to push her trailer out of the way.

I have to bite back my laugh when I see a vein practically pop out of her forehead because she's so pissed off.

I don't know why she's so mad. I'm not being a total dick about what I'm doing. Believe me, I could ruin her shit in point-two seconds by just running it over completely, but that's not me—I'm not a total asshole, even to her.

Right now, she's getting what she deserves. Anyone who fucks with me gets fucked with right back. I ain't no bitch, and I surely won't back down.

She's just getting a taste of the real Dalton, which, hopefully, she'll remember when we have to partner in this bullshit English class.

I think she's given up as I make more progress, moving the trailer out of the way—until I notice her jumping up on the trailer and onto the pile of dirt until we're face to face, and she puts her hands on the hood of my truck.

"Stop the truck!" she screams, but I can only tell by reading her lips and by the way her face is beet red.

I spare her throat from having to yell—and, really, mine too—and turn down the music.

"I'm not going to stop. It's cute and all—you trying to stop me—but you do realize you're standing on a pile of shit right now, right?"

She crosses her arms. "No, I'm staring at a pile of shit," she responds with a raise of her eyebrows.

HOW WE HATED

I laugh out loud and press the gas pedal slightly harder. She loses her balance and falls back on her ass, still within the trailer, just as I'm able to push through far enough to be able to make it out to the normal parking lot.

I roll down my window and wave my hand out the side. "Thank you!" I taunt.

When I look in the mirror, I see she's flipping me off. I know most people would be mad at that, but I laugh as I turn my music up loud again, feeling somewhat pleased with myself that I was able to get out of the back lot and royally piss her off at the same time. I'd say I've done my best work tonight on both accounts.

Leighton River is about as small of a town as you can get, so it's not long before I'm home, and I see my sister's car in the driveway, which lifts my spirits a little more.

It's funny how when she lived here, we seemed to fight all the time, but since she moved out, we've gotten even closer. I'll never admit that I actually miss having her around though.

Once I enter our house and put all of my gear in the mudroom, I walk around the foyer to see her curled up on the couch with her laptop in front of her as she practices sign language.

"What's up, sis? You're still learning ASL?"

She closes her fist and holds it out, bobbing it up and down—meaning yes.

I plop down next to her on the couch. "*No hablo ASL*," I tease, saying it in Spanish—the language I chose to take in school. I look at the video she's mimicking. "I didn't realize you had to take a language in college too."

She smiles. "You don't have to, but I want to continue. I enjoy learning it, and I want to be able to teach it to my students once I become a teacher."

I shrug. "Yeah, sounds cool, I guess. What are you home for?"

She talks as she signs the words she's saying. "Mom and I are going to dinner. Dad had some meeting, so she wanted to have our once-a-year dinner."

She rolls her eyes because that's about all we get from our mom. We both know it's a joke, but we still go along with her plan.

"And what am I, chopped liver?" I hold my arms out to my sides.

"No, we just know you'll go for a run, then down a protein shake before you shower. Then, when you get out, you'll eat the rest of the leftover steak you guys had for dinner last night."

My eyes widen. "There are leftovers?"

She laughs. "See, we were right. There was enough for either the two of us or you. We figured you'd want it more. Now, go for your run so I can get some practice in before Mom gets home"—she looks at her watch—"which should be any minute, so scooch your booch out of here." She slaps my thigh with the back of her hand.

I hold up my pointer finger. "Fine. But only because you're leaving me the steak." I get up and head toward my room.

"You stink, by the way," she yells out to me.

"Good to see you too, Leslie," I reply with a laugh. Funny how some things just don't change.

CHAPTER 5

Natalie

I've never been so pissed off in my life as I am now, watching Dalton drive away. Picking myself up off the dirt pile, I stomp down to the ground and dust my pants clean just as my brother, Thomas, approaches.

"What happened to you?" he asks, staring at my clothes.

"Dalton Wick is what happened," I state as I pat myself off some more.

Thomas takes in the situation—the trailer cocked to the side and dirt spilled out into the parking lot—then looks at me, rage filling his veins.

"What. Did. He. Do?" he asks, barely able to contain his anger.

Like me, he hates anyone involved with TimeLand, but we both have a special place in our heart for the Wick family. The unfortunate thing is, he has to play

HOW WE HATED

football with him. The whole *be a good teammate* is hard when you can't stand the sight of said teammate.

We all have learned to be civil with each other over the years, but him moving my trailer out of the way like that pushed things too far, and I can tell my brother feels the same way. Only thing is, I know how to move on, but he doesn't.

I pick up my rake from the floor and get back to business. "I'll handle it."

"How are you going to handle it?" He gives me an *are you kidding me* expression before continuing, "He thinks he's some god who can get away with anything around here. It's time we put him in his place."

I throw my rake on the ground, realizing I'm finally able to take out my frustration about the situation with someone who will fully understand. "You're right. You're totally right. But, you see, I have to do an English project with him all semester. So, what am I to do? Fail English? That can't happen. The teacher already told us she won't let us change partners. I tried. Believe me, I tried. We both did. Now, I'm stuck with that total loser, and there's not a dang thing I can do about it. We know firsthand how that family gets away with anything they want. If I want to pass my class"—I stare him to make sure he's paying attention—"which I do, then I—we—need to figure out how to get along for just a few months. Then, we can move on with our lives."

Thomas has no clue where my rant came from and is looking at me like I'm a crazy person. "What are you talking about?"

"Ugh!" I push past him. "English. Partner. Him. Nothing I can do." I break out the bullet points for him to understand.

"I was just talking about the mess he made and how he could have broken the trailer—Dad's trailer."

I shake my head. "I know, but there's more to it. Just help me clean this up so we can go home. I'm over today."

"That fucker will pay for this," he says as he picks up the rake I dropped earlier.

"Fine." I blow him off. "Just keep me out of it and do it on the football field so it's not so obvious."

Later that night, I borrow the truck to go pick up some supplies I need for school. As I drive through town, I see Dalton's truck parked on the side of Trish's house. Still fuming over what he did earlier, I pull over and back up so I'm parked right in front of it. Why the dumbass parked here and not in front of her house I'll never know, but I sure am glad he did.

In the past, I could just ignore his presence and try to move on from the destruction his father had caused my family, but now, he's taken it too far. What he doesn't know is, two can play at this game.

The good thing about having an old farm truck is, it's equipped with towing capabilities because it's not uncommon for our trucks to get stuck in the mud and we have to use one to pull the other out. The tow straps are kept in the toolbox attached to the bed of the truck, so I climb out and grab it, hoping I'm not seen.

I might be a girl, but I've worked on the ranch my entire life, so I know exactly what I'm doing when I

HOW WE HATED

crawl under Dalton's truck and attach the tow strap to the hook that's at the front. Of course, he left the truck unlocked because no one's going to mess with it here in Leighton River—that is, until he messed with me first.

I open the door and climb in to put the truck in neutral and make sure the wheels are pointed straight ahead. Once it's set, I slide out of his truck and shut the door as quietly as I can before I run to my truck, put it in drive, and slowly press the gas pedal to get both of us moving.

The tow straps are thirty feet long, so it takes a little while to get his to roll, but once it does, an absolute jolt of a thrill races through me at the fact that I'm towing his beloved truck.

Knowing there's no one to press the brakes or steer it in any direction, I can only go straight, but it's perfect because the road takes a turn up ahead. When I get to it, I'll turn, and his truck will continue straight right into a marshy mess.

I laugh at the thought that his pretty bumper is what allowed him to move my trailer today, and now, it's going to plow through this fence. The steel bumper will take out the old wood fence without really damaging the truck. The fence, on the other hand, will be ruined, but the Wick family can afford to fix it.

With his big tires, driving the truck out of the marsh will be easy as pie, but getting to the truck will be another story. If there's one thing I know for a fact about Dalton, it's that he doesn't have work boots in his truck, so his precious Nikes will be ruined with him just trying to get to the truck. Never mind the mess it will cause on the inside as he steps in to drive it away.

I get the truck going at a good pace, just in time for the turn in the road.

Gripping the steering wheel tighter, I turn the corner and slam on the brakes. Just as I hoped, his truck goes up the curb, right through the fence, and into the marsh.

I laugh so hard until I feel the truck start to pull at my rear end because I'm still attached to it. I press my foot on the brakes as hard as I can, hoping it keeps my truck from moving any farther.

Thankfully, between me pressing the brakes and his tires getting stuck in the muck, his truck finally stops about ten feet in.

That's when something catches my attention. I glance up the street and see Dalton racing down after me.

I hop out of the truck and climb under to disconnect the strap from our truck and climb back in, putting it back in drive and racing away before he gets to me.

Seeing his face as I drive away is priceless. I've never felt so vindicated in my life.

Dalton

That bitch!

I stare in shock as I watch Natalie drive away.

When I see my truck in the marsh, I'm so pissed off that I could seriously lose my shit on anything that steps in my path.

HOW WE HATED

"What just happened?" Trish asks.

I have to close my eyes and take a deep breath so I don't take it out on her. When she invited me over, I figured, why not? When I got here, I could tell I wasn't really into it—into her anymore. I was just explaining to her how I had to go when I looked out her living room window and saw my truck start to roll down the street.

I wave my hand at her, hoping she gets the drift to go back inside. I'm too mad for words, and I know anything I say right now will just make the situation worse.

I glance down at my brand-new white Nike Air Max shoes and curse under my breath. Kicking them off, I remove my socks as well, leaving them in a pile on the street, and hike up my pant legs.

As I make my way to my truck, mud and tiny plants wrap around my toes. With every step, my feet get heavier and more caked on with the disgusting organic matter.

When I make it to my truck, I fling the door open and hop in, trying to get everything off my feet before I place them on the floorboard.

I grab the keys from my pocket and crank the engine. The mean roar sounds like a kitten's meow compared to the rage flowing through me.

I put it in reverse and back out of the marsh, through the fenced area, and back onto the street. I hop out to grab my shoes and socks, then lean down to figure out how to remove this strap Natalie attached to the front of my truck.

Once it's off, I pick it up and throw it in the back of my truck.

"Is everything okay?" Trish asks.

"Not now," is all I can get out as I hop back into the truck and drive in the direction Natalie just drove.

This town is not that big, and she'd better hope I don't find her.

There was no way she was just randomly driving around, looking for my truck, so she must have been coming into town for a reason. I search a few parking lots, and that's when I see her truck parked at the Alamo shopping center.

As I turn into the parking lot, my tires squeal when I press the gas much harder than I should have.

She's nowhere to be found, so I hop out, grab the strap from the back of my truck, and lean on her truck with my arms crossed as I wait for her to come out of whatever store she's in.

It's not long until Natalie exits the store with a huge grin on her face and a small bag in her hand. When she sees me sitting here, she stops in her tracks.

That's right, sweetheart. You should be shitting in your boots right now.

She approaches me with a smug expression on her face, then looks down and smirks at me. "Nice feet."

She opens her truck door, not giving two shits that I'm standing here.

I hold up the strap she used to tow my truck. "What the fuck is this?"

She grabs it from my hand nonchalantly, like I'm handing her an ice cream cone and not the thing she used to just tow my truck into the marsh.

"Oh, thanks. I was wondering how I was going to explain to my brother that it was gone."

She walks to the back of her truck to put it in the toolbox as I watch, stunned.

HOW WE HATED

"What the fuck, Natalie?" I yell, knowing there's nothing else I can do in this situation.

If this were her brother, I'd beat the ever-living shit out of him. But she's a girl … so I stand here, helpless, as she acts like nothing happened.

"Paybacks are a bitch. Maybe next time, you won't push my trailer out of the way," she responds smugly.

I point to my truck. "You could have caused real damage."

She steps right up and gets in my face. "And you could have caused damage to my dad's trailer—the trailer he needs for the ranch—which he was letting me borrow when you pushed it out of the way. The only difference is, we don't have the money to buy a new one, so any damage you caused would have been much worse than any little scratch on your precious truck."

I'm speechless.

Rage races through me as I stare into her eyes, seeing my same anger glaring back at me.

She takes a breath, then steps back. "Thanks for the strap. I hope you don't get an infection from being in the marsh in your bare feet. There's some nasty skin-eating stuff in that water—that's why it's fenced off."

My eyes open wide, and I instantly start cleaning the dry mud off my feet. When I hear her laughing, I glance up and realize she was just fucking with me some more.

I clench my jaw as I watch her get back in her truck and drive away, leaving me standing here like a fucking idiot, feeling more pissed off than I've ever been and knowing there's not a damn thing I can do about it.

CHAPTER 6

Dalton

The next day, the crew and I are all walking out of practice toward the parking lot when my phone dings with a message. I look down to see I have a Snap add request from Natalie. Curiosity gets the best of me, and I hit accept. Instantly, I'm hit with her phone number, asking me to call her.

"Ha." I laugh out loud as I tuck my phone back in my pocket.

After the shit she pulled last night, she's high as a kite if she thinks I'm calling her. It took everything in my power to not smack her across the head as I sat behind her in Econ. Thankfully, she acted like I didn't exist, and I played right along. She's dead to me for all I care.

If she really wants to ask me a question about our assignment, she can message it right there.

HOW WE HATED

Maya—who always gets a ride home from Ben after her cheerleading practice even though she does have her own car but says she'd rather ride with him—turns to me and asks, "What was that?"

I sigh. "Natalie. We have that stupid project we have to do together, and she wants me to call her."

I glance at Ben who's stifling a laugh. Yes, they all got a kick out of my misery when I told them what happened last night.

I flip him off which just makes him laugh harder.

We get to where all of our vehicles are parked next to each other. As much as I hate to admit it, Natalie wasn't wrong yesterday about how I shouldn't have been parked back there to begin with. I don't mind fucking with her, but someone else could be working back there today, and the last thing I need is getting stuck for real.

I throw my gear in the back of my truck and open my door.

"Come on. You have to change your attitude on this, or you'll just make the situation worse. I'm sure it will be fine," Maya, ever the optimist, says.

I raise my eyebrows at her. "Do you remember who you're talking about, or what she did to me last night?"

"Don't you remember in junior high when Thomas tried to fight all four of us at once?" Ben asks Maya. "He would have gotten his ass kicked if the principal didn't break it up, but he didn't care. He was all in. That's the level of hatred he has for us. Why? I'll never truly get it, but hey, they can get on with their bad selves with that bullshit."

"Well, I think it will be just fine," she says as she opens the door to Ben's truck.

"Fine, huh? If it's so fine, then why aren't you friends with her?" I ask with a sarcastic tilt to my head.

"She's always had something against me. I don't have any hard feelings against her. But being friends and being partners in school are two completely different things," she volleys back.

I shake my head. "Either way, I have to deal with her and her bullshit. Which means I'll probably have to deal with her brother at some point too."

Ben slaps my arm. "Speak of the devil."

He points to where Thomas is heading toward us. He always showers at the school after practice, so he's already in his Ariat jeans, belt buckle, and cowboy hat. He's the epitome of small-town farm boy.

I square my shoulders and narrow my eyes at him when I see he's heading straight toward us.

"You!" he yells out, pointing his finger right at me.

Ben, Marcus, and Eli all turn their attention toward him and move closer to me.

That's right. You fuck with me, you fuck with them too.

"What was that shit you pulled yesterday?" Thomas growls out.

"Correction: I didn't pull the shit. I pushed it out of the way because it was blocking my exit," I say with a smirk on my face.

Marcus lets out a sharp laugh, which only makes Thomas angrier.

"You could have hurt her." Thomas gets up closer to my face.

I stand up straighter, making sure he sees just how much bigger I am than him. "No. I was going, like, two

HOW WE HATED

miles an hour. But you can back the fuck up before I have to hurt you."

I'm still pissed off about what she did last night, and I have no problem at all taking it out on Thomas. Her, I can't hit, him, I can.

"You're such a fucking coward." He gets so close to my face that I can feel his breath on my chin. "Just like your old man. But I get it. You let your big, fancy *fake* work truck do something for a change. How did it feel, actually using it for what it's made for rather than driving it around like the poser you are?"

My blood starts to boil with how much he is in my space, but I don't let him see it. "Don't be jealous that my truck is better than your filthy piece of shit."

"At least my piece of shit is dirty for a good reason. I use it for an honest day's work. Work that feeds this entire community and everyone else around us."

I narrow my eyes at him. "Are we done here, or did you have a real reason for coming over here?"

He shakes his head and backs up. "Yeah, that's about right for all you TimeLand crew. Whenever you want to know what it's like to be real men, doing actual manly work, you just let me know. Until then, have fun pretending to do so on the football field."

"What the fuck did you say?" I step toward him.

"I said, you all have no clue what being a real man is. You drive around in your fancy cars, run into each other with big, bulky pads to protect you"—he shrugs his shoulders, like he's pretending to be scared—"then run off and hide indoors in your tech world. Just like my dad said about your dad. He was a computer nerd back then and is raising you to be a pansy ass now."

That's it. I might not agree with my dad all the time, but there's no fucking way I'll let anyone talk shit about me in any way.

I rush toward him and swing my fist to smack him square in the jaw. He falls to the ground, and instead of letting me take another swing at him, Eli jumps in and yanks me off him.

Thomas gets up, ready to fight, but Eli just towers over him with a glare. I'm a big dude, but next to Eli even I look small.

"Don't even think about it," Eli bites out.

Thomas opens his arms out wide. "You might have gotten me this time, but watch your back, techie. This shit ain't over."

I don't pay him any more attention as I turn around and shake out my hand, hoping I didn't break it.

"Ooh!" Marcus sings as he dances around like he's getting ready for a fight. "You smacked the shit out of him."

I open and close my hand a few times, seeing the pain it causes me isn't too bad so it can't be broken.

"You think it's going to be just fine now, Maya?" I ask over the top of Ben's truck.

She shakes her head. "Well, maybe you shouldn't have hit the guy."

"He deserved it," I grunt out.

"Yeah, but it doesn't mean you should have done it." She laughs,as she slides in Ben's truck.

Ben walks toward me with his hand out to slap mine in the same goodbye greeting we've done for years. "You good, bro?"

I slap his hand. "Yeah, I'm good."

HOW WE HATED

Marcus and Eli nod their heads in goodbye, and we each get in our vehicles with the little bit of adrenaline still rushing through us.

Natalie

"Where have you been?" I hold my arms out in question when I finally see my brother arrive at his truck that's parked near the FFA back lot.

"I had to handle some business." He hops in the truck and unlocks my side.

Without a word, he starts the engine, puts the truck in reverse, and places his hand on the back of my seat to look behind me.

"What happened to you?" I ask when I see his jaw is red and swollen.

"Nothing."

"Nothing, my ass. Did you just get in a fight?"

He puts the truck in drive and leaves the parking lot while turning up the music. "Don't worry about it."

I reach over and turn it down. "Don't give me that. Who did that to you?"

He turns up the music louder as his way of saying, *Back off*, so I do. He can be just as stubborn as my father, so there's no reason to bother when he gets like this.

Of course my thoughts go straight to Dalton. He's the only person who Thomas would get in a fight with. I didn't tell my brother what I did last night. I know he would have bitched at me for what could have possibly happened to his truck, so it just wasn't worth it to tell him.

I'm not surprised if he tried to handle the situation by himself, but by the looks of it, it didn't go too well.

I lean back in my seat and pick up my phone to see if Dalton responded. Of course, it shows as *Read*, but no response. We have to decide something tonight for our project, and him not answering me makes it impossible to do so.

I sigh. *Why do I have to put up with this nonsense?*
I send him another Snap.

We have to decide on our subject tonight.

I stare at my phone for a while, waiting for it to show as *Read*, but of course, it doesn't. By the time we get home, I'm even more annoyed I'm stuck with him and ready to just go ride Brandy and forget about the anxiety he's causing in my life.

CHAPTER 7

Dalton

I sit down in my seat in English class, absolutely dreading the idea of having to work with Natalie today. When I look a few rows over to where she is, she's already staring a hole through me.

Fucking fantastic.

Yes, she sent me a Snap, giving me her number, and, yes, I ignored it. I was hoping, in some cosmic way, I would wake up, and this would all have been a dream, but no such luck.

After the bell rings, Mrs. Anderson gets our attention. "Morning, everyone. I hope you all were able to talk to your partners and decide on a topic for the interview."

I close my eyes and curse, *Fuck me*, to myself.

I grab my phone and open the Snap she sent last night that I never looked at. After what I did to her

HOW WE HATED

brother's face, I was not ready to listen to her bitch about it. When I see she was asking about the assignment, I feel like an ass.

Her expression proves I've already more than pissed her off, so I give her a cheesy, sarcastic grin to sew up the start to another fucked-up morning.

We were supposed to pick a topic that we would interview each other about. It had to be the same subject, like favorite food or how many siblings we had, but our answers had to be something totally different than one another. So, if we both only had one sister, that wouldn't work, or if we both liked pizza the most, that was a no-go. The goal was to learn about life through someone else's experiences.

The problem is, we have to answer ourselves for the other person. Mrs. Anderson says this is how she'll make sure we are each holding up our end of the bargain—which I've already failed.

As the teacher starts down the rows, asking partners what their topics are, I look at Natalie with wide eyes, and she starts moving her hand in a weird way over and over again. I squint my eyes, thinking she's crazy, then finally catch on to what she's doing.

My older sister, Leslie, knows sign language, and as I take in the movements she's making with her hands, I try to remember what Leslie taught me. I put my hands under my desk and try like hell to work my way through the alphabet she taught me last year.

When I get to *H*, I notice it's the same sign Natalie started her word off with.

When I look back to Natalie, she rolls her eyes as she spells out what she's trying to say for the tenth time.

"Natalie and Dalton," Mrs. Anderson calls out. "What topic did you guys choose?"

Thankfully, Natalie speaks up. "We're going to do hobbies. Dalton's is running."

My head snaps up as I turn to her in shock. *How did she know I liked running?*

"Okay," Mrs. Anderson says as she writes it down on her notepad, where she's keeping track of everyone's topics. "And, Dalton, what is Natalie's?"

I try to visualize what she was trying to say in my head that started with an *H*, and when I take a few seconds too long, Mrs. Anderson calls out again, "Dalton, do you know what Natalie's hobby is?"

I close my eyes and say the only thing that comes to mind. "Horses?" My tone proves I'm unsure, but when I glance at Natalie, the way she closes her eyes and drops her head back in relief proves I at least got the answer right.

Mrs. Anderson moves on to the other students, and when she's done, she reminds us that the hobby papers are due Thursday, which we should have started by now.

After class, I walk to Natalie's desk to stop her before she heads out.

"Hey." I grab her arm slightly.

She rolls her eyes, which I'm learning is her favorite gesture when it comes to me. I guess it's better than flipping me off.

"Thanks for saving us today," I say sincerely.

I'm not a total dick. We would have been screwed if she hadn't spoken up.

"Look, I don't want to have to do this either, but guess what. We're stuck. The least you can do is reply back to me."

HOW WE HATED

"I know. That was a dick move. I forgot we had to do something for today." I place my hand on my chest, trying to show I genuinely mean what I'm saying.

When she sees my knuckle that's cut up from yesterday, her eyes go big in recognition though she blows me off.

"Whatever. I have to get to class."

She storms off without another word, and I let her, knowing I kind of deserved it today, but only for not doing the assignment, not for hitting her brother. He had that coming.

I get home after practice to an empty house. I shouldn't be surprised though. This is how my entire life has been. When Leslie lived here, we at least had each other, but now that she's away at college, I spend a lot of nights by myself.

I head to the fridge to see Mary, our maid, left me a plate for dinner.

I don't know what I'd do without her. She's been more of a mom than my actual mom, who is always off, gallivanting on trips with her girlfriends and spending my dad's money in any way she knows how. I guarantee that's the only reason she even married him in the first place. To my knowledge, they've never had a real relationship.

I close the fridge door, deciding to go for a run before I eat. Yes, I had football practice after school, and, yes, I still go for a run. The nanny I had up until

I got my license always said it was my *me time*, which I try to blow off as a bunch of bullshit, but deep down, I know what she said was true. It seems to be the only way I can get through all the fucked-up shit in my head at the end of the day.

With my AirPods in, blasting my workout playlist, hoping it will drown out my thoughts, I head out to the back side of our property for my run. Twenty yards down the path, and no such luck.

How did Natalie know I liked to run?

The thought is stuck in my mind on repeat, and no matter what song plays through my head, I keep going back to that.

No one else besides my family knows that I come back here, not even Marcus, Eli or Ben. I don't go running through the streets for everyone to see, so how did she know? Lucky guess seems pretty farfetched to me.

In this world where everyone knows who I am and who my dad is, it's been something that's only mine, but now that I know she knows, something inside me just feels weird, and I can't figure out why.

At first, I thought it was more of a violation of my privacy, like she was some Peeping Tom, but then I rolled my own eyes at that thought. Even I know she's not stalking me in some crazy way.

Then, what was it?

Why am I so bothered that she knows I like to run?

After I shower, I lie on my bed and go through my Snapchat app to find the message Natalie sent me with her phone number and finally decide to just come out and ask her through a text message.

HOW WE HATED

How did you know I like to run?

Bubbles instantly appear, so I keep my Messages app open and wait for her reply.

Oh look who decided to actually talk to me. OMG it's THE Dalton Wick. Stop me while I vomit.

Very funny. But seriously why didn't you say football or baseball?

There's a pause, and I watch as the bubbles appear and disappear for a minute or two before she responds.

Because running is something for only you. That's what a hobby is supposed to be. Football and baseball are with groups of people.

Then how did you know I ran?

Because I see you on the hills.

I pinch my eyebrows together. *She sees me? How can anyone see me? I run through the hills behind my house.*

Are you stalking me?

Get over yourself.

Then how do you see me?

LAUREN RUNOW

I ride my horse to the river. That's the back of our property. Your house sits on the hill that overlooks our ranch.

I didn't realize the ranch went back that far.

Yeah, well, it does. So, no, I'm not stalking you. We just happen to be in the same place. Brandy's gotten spooked by you a few times.

Brandy?

My horse. You should probably know her name at least since we're supposed to be interviewing each other about our hobbies.

There's a pause in our conversation, and I think it's over, so I put my phone down, thinking we'll talk later since I've at least done my job of giving her my number. Then, my phone dings again.

Why do you always run back there when the stadium has that new fancy track?

I think about what to say, then figure there's no reason to lie, so I tell her the truth.

I like to be alone when I run.

I pause, then type more.

HOW WE HATED

Well at least I thought I was alone. Why do you ride back there?

Same reason I guess.

Good. That's one thing we can put down for our interview. The faster we can get this done, the better.

When I get the middle-finger emoji back, I can't help but laugh as I throw my phone down and get ready to hop in the shower from my run.

I walk to the bathroom and close the door, but before I can turn on the water, my dad knocks.

"Dalton."

I let out a heavy breath. "Yeah, Dad?" *Can this not wait until I'm out of the bathroom?*

"We need to talk about getting that application ready."

"Dad, it's barely September. We have time."

Early applications are due the first week of November, and he's been riding my ass every day about it.

"Yes, but we need those letters of recommendation. Did you ask your coach yet?"

"Dad, you paid for the entire new wing at the school. I don't think I'll have a problem with getting in."

He turns the door handle, and I've never been so thankful that I remembered to lock the door.

"You can't live your life thinking I'll buy your way in. You need to earn it—"

I finish his sentence. "Just like you did. I know, Dad.

And don't you think I've been busting my ass to make sure I don't let you down?"

"Don't worry about letting me down. You'll be letting yourself down if you don't get a good education."

I sigh. "I know, Dad. Can I shower now?"

I hear him huff off and finally get the opportunity to turn on the water, wanting more than ever to wash all the stress away. The last thing I want to do is go to more school after I graduate. Yeah, I want to continue playing football, but every other aspect of going to college just doesn't sit well with me. I don't know what I want to do, but I know it won't be working for TimeLand in any capacity.

If only that was actually an option.

My dad started the company with his three friends, but since it was all his idea to begin with, he's the president and CEO, and there's nothing more that he wants than to see his son follow in his footsteps.

The idea of sitting at a desk all day, working on a computer, makes me want to scratch my eyes out.

I've never been the guy to sit and play video games or spend all day on my phone, yet my dad wants me to take over a company that is basically *that*. If I don't like to actually play the game, then why would he ever think I'd want to work on the backend of it?

In a perfect world, he'd have me start at the bottom of the company, learning all aspects of programming and design as I work my way up, so I know every side of the company before he retires and leaves it all to me.

The fact that he puts it all on my shoulders and not my sister's frustrates the hell out of me too. She's two years older than me, and she goes to a local college to

HOW WE HATED

get her teaching degree. My parents think it's noble that she wants to work with kids. I think it's sexist that they think I have to have the corporate job since I'm a guy while she can do whatever she wants, knowing she'll have a trust fund behind her the entire way.

When I step into the hot water, I can't help but stand there and let it wash over me, wishing it would wash my dad's words off me, too, but, no, they keep replaying in my head.

"You have to go to Stanford."
"You have to take over this company."
"You have to keep my legacy alive."

Well, fuck that. What about my legacy?

He's never cared about me a day in his life. To say I've had a normal upbringing would be a huge laugh. The only time he even talks to me is to make sure I'm on track for his plan or to make sure I'm making him look good on the football field, like I'm his fucking trophy boy. He was never able to play football, so it's like he's living the life he wanted in high school through me.

I've heard him talk to people about me and how I play, like he's bragging, yet he's never once said those things to my face. I've never heard that he's proud of me or that I do a good job. No, it's always things that I need to do better.

CHAPTER 8

Dalton

It's finally Friday, and I can't wait to play our first game tonight. Coach has us all amped up to play and I'm itching to catch that ball to run it in for a touchdown. Coach says I'm the secret weapon this year, and I'm locked and loaded for sure.

We have a rally after lunch, so only four classes to go, and the game is on.

After I walk into my first period class, I slide into my seat, leaning forward to whisper in Trish's ear, "Looking good this morning."

I sit back and watch her blush as she turns to face me, tucking her hair behind her ear.

"Thank you."

The bell rings before I can say anything else, and like the good girl she is—at least in class—Trish turns to face the front of the room.

HOW WE HATED

"Okay, class, since it's Friday, I thought I'd give you time to work in class with your partner on the next assignment," Mrs. Anderson says to start the day.

The hobby paper was easy since both of us can write about horses or running without having to really talk to each other. I'm praying this one will be the same way.

"For the next assignment, you'll be conducting interviews with each other. I want you both to learn things about one another that aren't obvious. This is your time to dig deep. Talk to one another and see where your conversation leads. That's the best way to really find out who someone is," Mrs. Anderson says. "It might get loud in here, so you're welcome to go sit in the quad outside the door, but don't leave this area."

Everyone is quick to move to meet with their partner. That is, everyone, except Natalie and me. Both of us stay seated, dreading having to work on this project.

I lean back in my chair with my eyes staring up at the ceiling when Natalie finally comes over and hits my arm.

"Get up. If we have to do this, let's at least get out of this damn classroom."

I sit up in mock shock. "Did the ranch princess just cuss?"

She glares at me. "Shut up." With a roll of her eyes, she turns toward the door and heads out of the classroom, expecting me to follow her.

What sucks is, I totally have to, especially when Mrs. Anderson raises her eyebrows at me, silently asking why I'm still sitting here.

With a huff, I drag my large frame out of the small desk and head toward the quad, where I'm sure I'll find her waiting with a pissed-off expression.

As I approach the picnic table she's sitting at, I see her staring down at her phone, so I throw my notebook in front of her to, yes, be a dick and startle her. I get the satisfaction I was looking for when I see her jump. When she narrows her eyes at me in anger, a wee bit of happiness rushes through me.

I know it's childish, but I have to find some kind of joy in this fucked-up partnership we've found ourselves in.

"So, what's the plan?" I ask once I sit down and stare at her for a moment.

"There is no plan. We're just supposed to talk. She says that having an open conversation is the best way to find out about the other person," she responds.

"Okay, so talk."

She shakes her head. "About what?"

"I don't know. You're the girl. You're supposed to be the talkative one."

She lets out a harsh laugh. "Are you serious right now? You think just because I'm a girl, I should be leading our conversation?"

I shrug my shoulders. "That's seems to be my experience with girls, so yes."

"Your experience?" She levels her eyes at me.

I lean in closer. "I know you would love to have an experience with me, but sorry, not going to happen."

"Fuck off." She shakes her head, and I can't help but laugh.

"Wow, two cuss words out of you. I thought you were this goody-two-shoes girlie girl who was a total kiss-ass and told on anyone who was up to no good."

"And I thought you—wait, actually, I know you are

HOW WE HATED

this playboy asshole who can do no wrong because your daddy owns this entire town." She rolls her head in a *I know I'm right* way.

I just lean back and blow her off. "You don't know shit about me."

"And you don't know shit about me, so don't pretend you do."

"I don't need to pretend. You've made it very clear to me since we were in elementary school that you didn't like me." I pause and get a little closer to her to make sure she hears me clearly. "Give me one reason why."

"One reason for what?"

"Give me one reason why you hate me."

She doesn't back down and gets closer to me, trying to prove she's not afraid of me. "I can give you ten."

I open my arms up wide to the sides. "Well, there's no better time than the present."

She holds up her hand and starts counting on her fingers. "You're selfish. You're an asshole. You think you run this town. You think you can do no wrong. Your family has ruined this community."

I stop her there. "Ah, there it is. You can say all you want about me, but how would you even know this stuff unless you actually knew me? But that last one, that's your real problem. It's with my family. Not me."

"You're all one and the same, so why does that matter?"

"Really? So, I'm my dad, my sister, and my mom, all at the same time? And what about everyone else? It wasn't just my family that started TimeLand. Do you really think we're all exactly the same people?"

"Yes, I do."

I nod my head slowly, squinting my eyes like I'm trying to understand her. "So, Eli and Ben are just like me?"

"Ben, one thousand percent. You both are just party boys who don't give a shit about anyone but yourself."

I cross my arms over my chest. "Oh, really? Then, what are your thoughts of Eli?"

She waves her hand dismissively. "Eli is Eli. He never says anything anyway."

"So then, he's just guilty by default?"

"Exactly."

"Then, fine. What do you have against Maya?"

Maya is the sweetest person alive, so I'm dying to know what Natalie has to say about her.

She sighs and rolls her eyes, knowing she has nothing to say. "Fine. There's nothing wrong with her." She's quick to move on. "But you guys are some of the cockiest assholes in this town. Just like your parents."

I lean in again. "Well, sweetheart, you're wrong. I'm nothing like my parents, especially my dad, so maybe you shouldn't pigeonhole people to a certain category before you actually give them a chance."

"Oh, like you didn't do the same with me? I saw you trying to get Mrs. Anderson to change partners, so don't give me that bullshit line."

"I knew you"—I point at her—"hated me." I point at myself. "You and Thomas have made that very clear over the years, so I just went along with it and hated you guys too. Believe me, you didn't make it difficult at all. I wanted to change partners because I didn't want to deal with your drama due to that fact."

"You're so full of shit. Don't try to blame this all on me." She tries to blow me off.

HOW WE HATED

My lips tilt up in a grin as I reach out my hand to her. "Hi. I'm Dalton Wick. I don't think we've actually met."

She crosses her arms and purses her lips. "Are you kidding me right now?"

I jerk my hand slightly to make sure she sees it, still holding it out for her to shake. "I'm not kidding. You've never actually met me. You have this preconceived notion of who I am in your head. And I'm fine with that. I don't give a shit if you like me or not. But I won't let you sit here and think things of me that aren't true. Now, are you going to shake my hand and move on with this nonsense, or are we going to sit here and fight the entire period and not get anything done?"

She begrudgingly shakes my hand as she whispers under her breath, "Whatever."

"Okay, now that we have introductions out of the way, tell me why you're being such a bitch."

Her eyes widen so big that I swear they might blow up into balloons that will float away.

I can't help but laugh, then slide my head forward slightly with my eyebrows pulled up. "I'm kidding. Relax. I promise I'm not the asshole you've made me out to be in your mind."

"Then, fine, tell me who you are so I can write this interview." She opens her notebook and gets her pen ready to take notes.

In thought, I drum my fingers on the picnic table. "I like to cook."

"Lame. Next."

"Lame? Really? Do you cook?"

"Yes, of course I cook."

"Yeah, but how many guys my age do you know who like to cook?"

"Whatever. I'll write it down. *He. Likes. To. Cook,*" she says slowly as she scribbles it on her paper.

"Then, give me one better about yourself," I bite back.

"I'll give you one. I help grow the food that you like to cook."

"Oh, please. You don't grow my shit. I go to the market to get the food I cook with."

"And where do you think they get the food to sell? Huh? From my family's ranch. But you're too busy in your tech world to even realize that."

"That's what it is, isn't it? You're just bitter because my family brought something bigger to Leighton River than your family's ranch. I've always been told of the bitterness your father has toward my dad. Looks like the apple didn't fall far from the tree ... literally."

She narrows her eyes at me. "You're such an ass."

I hold my arms out to my sides. "Who knows? Maybe I am, but unless you actually give me something to work with here, we won't be able to finish this assignment, so suck it up, buttercup. You're stuck with me."

She places her pen down and folds her arms over her notebook. "Why did your parents and everyone from TimeLand move back?"

I let out a frustrated breath. It's the ultimate question I get from anyone new I meet. Why would my dad and his business partners move their booming business from the center of the tech world in Silicon Valley, California, to the middle of nowhere, in Leighton River, Montana?

HOW WE HATED

I tell the same story I've told a million times. "They didn't want us kids growing up in California. They wanted us to have a stable childhood, like they had, where we played with dirt and were able to ride our bikes wherever we wanted. I guess that's not really possible over there. At least, that's what they say."

"Didn't they take into consideration what moving a company like that to this area would do?"

I throw my hands in the air. "You're kidding, right? You do know that the only reason we are sitting right here, right now is because my parents built this portion of the school so we could sit outside and eat if we wanted to or, you know, do projects like this and not be stuck indoors all day long? I think that's what they had in mind." I place my finger down on the table in front of us, making a point. "They've done a lot for this community."

She looks down and shakes her head. "Not all of it is good though."

"Like what? Name one thing they've done that's hurt this town and not helped it?"

To my surprise, she gets up from the table. "You'll never understand."

I watch as she walks away, heading toward the restroom, probably because she thinks I won't follow her there. Well, news flash to her: I wouldn't follow her even if she wanted me to.

CHAPTER 9

Natalie

Susie, my best friend since I can remember, knocks on my front door.

"Hey, girl," I say as I swing the door open.

She's dressed in Leighton River High gear, head to toe. Her face is even painted with *LR* on each side. The sight makes my shoulders drop instantly.

"I thought we were going to a movie."

"Nope." She pushes the door open and walks past me with a *get your shit together* attitude. "We're going to the game, whether you like it or not. Have some school spirit. You'll look back on these days and wish you had."

I know I should go support my brother, but even he understands why I don't like to go sit in the stands that feel nothing like football in our small town should.

I shut the door. "Doubtful. And why do you sound like my father all of a sudden?"

HOW WE HATED

"Because he told me I had to get you to the game so you wouldn't regret it later." She grins my way, and I can't help but laugh.

Of course my dad got involved. He talks about his days at Leighton River High as the best of his life. He doesn't understand that it's totally different now than when he was there. Kids are different.

Everyone in my class is addicted to their phone and couldn't care less about actually doing things outside. That is, unless there's a football game. This town literally shuts down every Friday night during football season. The only thing open is the gas station on Davis Street, the market, and the movie theater, which I'm sure is only due to some contract they have with the film companies. Even the bowling alley closes.

"Come on. You've had fun at these games. Don't try to act like you haven't," she taunts.

"Yes, when we were twelve, going to the game to see older boys hanging around was fun. Now, we're the older people, and there ain't any boys worth seeing," I tease.

"They're on the football field," she singsongs.

"Who won't even know we're there," I singsong back.

She grabs my letterman jacket, which I got for being the FFA president, and throws it at me. "We're going. Besides, we can get the lowdown on what's going on afterward, and then we'll be able to hang with the players."

"Yippee," I say sarcastically as I head toward the back room to tell my parents I'm leaving.

"Mom, Dad, Susie is forcing me to go to the game, so I'll be back later," I state.

Mom looks up from the puzzle she's working on. "We'll be leaving here shortly, too, to go watch your brother. Any plans afterward?"

I look at Susie, who shrugs. "Not sure yet. I'll let you know."

"Okay. Don't stay out too late."

"I won't," I respond.

Dad stands up and heads toward me, reaching into his back pocket to get his wallet. "Here, take some money and make sure to get some food afterward. I know you didn't eat much tonight during dinner."

That's my dad. Always watching out for me, even when I think no one's looking.

Even though my mom made one of my favorite casseroles, I just pushed it around on my plate, not in the mood to eat anything. All I could think about was how ignorant Dalton was about what his family had done to this community. To us.

I grab a twenty-dollar bill from him, then reach up and kiss his cheek. "Thanks, Pops."

We head to her car that's parked on the street next to our house. Once we're in, Susie grabs a tube and holds it up for me.

"It's not too late to paint your face too!" she suggests optimistically.

I laugh, and she shrugs her shoulders, putting the tube down.

"It was worth a try."

She starts the car as I buckle my seat belt, and we head to pick up Ashley, then go to the football stadium that, yes, TimeLand built a few years ago. Everything about it is high tech with full LED scoreboards that replay video and all. It's beyond ridiculous for a high school to have something this expensive, but that's the way TimeLand does things around here.

Out with the old and in with anything as high tech as they can get.

Once we've paid our way in—through an app, of course, because God forbid you actually pay cash at the ticket window, like normal people—we head to the student section, where a lot of our friends are sitting. We've already missed the opening ceremony festivities, so the crowd is hyped for the game, and it shows.

Seeing everyone lifts my mood slightly. We do have a good group of friends that I know I'll miss once we graduate.

I sit next to Ashley, who instantly turns to me like she just remembered something that she was dying to ask.

"Um, why did I see you sitting at the picnic tables today with Dalton Wick?"

I sigh and roll my eyes. "Believe me, it is not what you think. Remember Mrs. Anderson is forcing us to be partners? I don't know how I'm going to get through this."

"You're kidding, right?"

I eye her, and she raises her eyebrows, like, *What's the problem?*

"I thought you were all about Marcus lately?" I ask.

"I am, but you do realize you're complaining that you have to work with that?" She points to where he's standing on the field, talking to his coach, going over plays before the game starts.

Seeing him there with his hair in a tousled mess

and the way he's holding on to his pads around his neckline does make my heart do a little jump because of how good he looks, but I instantly remember who I'm actually looking at and shut that shit down fast.

"He … is a complete ass, and I want nothing to do with him."

"That's too bad because I want everything to do with that specimen of a human being," Susie says with a laugh.

I can't help but glance his way again and instantly regret it.

The referee calls for the team captains to meet in the middle of the field, and of course, Dalton is one of the three guys who heads toward the center of the field to greet the other team and do the coin flip.

"You can't tell me you're not checking out his ass right now," Susie leans in to whisper to me.

I give her an exasperated expression, making her laugh.

"Deny it all you want, but every other girl in this stadium is doing just that."

I sigh, knowing she's right with that statement, and, damn it, she's right about me too. But at least I know I'm not the only one.

"So, what's the plan for after the game?" Trish, who's sitting in front of us, turns around to ask.

I know she and Dalton have hooked up a few times, and her smug expression proves she heard us talking about him.

Ashley nudges me with her leg, signaling she saw how obvious Trish was being, but she still answers, "Everyone's going to Ben's."

HOW WE HATED

She doesn't ask Trish if she's coming, too, but knows whether we want her there or not, she'll be there. Where else would she go? It's Leighton River; there aren't many other choices of what to do on a Friday night, which is why I mainly stay home.

Ashley grabs my hand, and before I can say anything, she stops me. "You're coming."

I laugh out loud. "Um, no, I'm not."

"Yes, you have to," she whines.

Thankfully, kickoff catches all of our attention, and everyone hollers for the start of the game.

Once everyone is sitting down, Ashley nudges me again. "You're going. I need you there so I can talk to Marcus."

The two of them have been talking for a few weeks now, and we think he's finally going to make his move. She's been giddy this entire time, and I'm happy to see that she's happy, but …

"Then, what happens when you go off with Marcus, leaving me all alone? Because we both know Susie will already be off roaming around."

"You'll be just fine. Most of the school will be there too."

She's right. I've heard so much about these parties and the shit that goes down even though I've never been to one.

She squeezes my knee. "Come on," she begs. "Please come with me?"

When I see her puckered-out lips and puppy-dog eyes, I can't help but laugh.

I sigh. "Fine, but you owe me."

She does a little happy dance in her seat. "Yay." She looks back out onto the field, probably searching for Marcus. "I really think tonight's the night. He must have asked me three times this week if I was going to Ben's."

"It will be." I grin her way, honestly hoping they'll finally cross that line together.

CHAPTER 10

Dalton

I'm fucking hyped!

We won in probably the best game we've ever played tonight. Our defense was on point, and our offense, well, let's just say I scored three touchdowns before halftime. It was a great way to start the season.

We all race into the locker room, and I can't help but jump up onto Marcus's shoulders when we enter through the doors.

"Fuck yeah!" I yell. "I love winning!"

Marcus laughs at my antics as he heads toward his locker and starts to remove his pads. "You're heading to Ben's to celebrate, right?"

"You know it. It's about to be on tonight." I fling my locker open with so much force that it slaps open, then closes again.

"Can we not break the locker?" Ben asks sarcastically as he walks up. "Actually, on second thought, break

HOW WE HATED

whatever you need to break here *before* you get to my house."

I laugh and begin to remove my pads, feeling so alive that I can hardly contain how juiced I am.

"Is everyone coming over?" I ask Ben.

He shakes his head and chuckles under his breath. "Sure sounds like it." He pauses and stands up straight with his hands out to each side. "How come my house is always the place to go?"

I slap his shoulder as I walk by to head to the showers. "Because your parents don't seem to give a shit."

"Oh, they give a shit. Just not until the next day, when I have to clean everything up."

"Exactly. Until then, we get to do whatever the fuck we want," I shout over my shoulder.

After I shower, I throw on the clothes I brought with me, and then Marcus and I head toward my truck that's parked near the field.

I laugh as Marcus has to hold the oh-shit bar just to be able to climb in, but it's the perfect height for my tall ass.

Once I crank the engine, "Should've Been a Cowboy" by Toby Keith blares through the speakers in the back.

We head straight to Ben's property, which is part country, part mansion. His house rivals those in Los Angeles, spanning ten thousand square feet. Everything around it screams country living with multiple firepits, a volleyball court, horse stalls, white lights strung throughout the property, and a huge barn that has officially become our place to hang out.

Every Sunday our small crew hangs out in the barn, but tonight it will be more like the entire school.

I put the truck in park. We hop out and head toward the closed barn doors, but there's no hiding the party that's already letting loose, judging by the bass that's making the ground shake around us.

I slide the door open, yelling, "Let's party!"

Everyone turns my way and screams with my same enthusiasm. I feel like a god, walking through the area as everyone slaps my hand and congratulates Marcus and me on the win tonight.

We make our way to the back room, which is set up with couches and multiple TVs for us to hang out in. The music quiets slightly with the walls that surround us, which is nice because we can actually hear each other talk—a stark difference from the rest of the barn.

I look to my favorite spot, where I like to sit and chill, and am pleasantly surprised to see Trish, who just happens to be sitting right there. Everyone knows that's my spot, so seeing her there is like a neon-green sign flashing over her head, saying, *Dalton, come fuck me tonight.*

My night just keeps getting better and better.

I give her a wink, letting her know I noticed and know exactly what she wants, but before I head her way, I make my rounds through the crowd to say hello to everyone.

I head to Maya, who's sitting on the couch with Ben on the floor, lying between her legs. These two I will never understand. If someone were to walk in here and see them, they would instantly think Maya and Ben were together by the way they act, but no. Ben swears

HOW WE HATED

there's nothing going on between them and they're just best friends, and Maya ... well, Maya is the sweetest fucking girl I've ever met, so if she wants to put up with his friend bullshit, then who am I to question it?

Other kids from school surround the area, and I say what's up to all of them as I make my way to my spot—or I should say, to Trish's current takeover of my spot.

Eli is sitting in a chair, just taking it all in, like he normally does. At six-five, he's a beast of a dude and as quiet as they come. Any girl who tries to actually date him doesn't get far, as he seems bored with them almost right away. People don't understand him, but I get it. He's an old soul and over this high school bullshit.

When I get to Trish, I stand tall, cross my arms in front of me, and narrow my eyes at her in a serious but playful manner.

She tries to hide her grin as she says, "Oh, is this your spot?"

"You know damn well that's my spot."

She plays coquettishly with me. "Well ... I'm not sure I'm willing to get up. Maybe you'll just have to—"

I don't let her finish her sentence, and in point-two seconds, I swoop in, pick her up, and swing her around so she's sitting on my lap. She lets out a yelp in surprise as I settle her in so she's more comfortable.

"Ah, now, that's better," I whisper in her ear, my mouth lingering there for a few more seconds just to get a reaction from her as I watch chills cover her arms.

"Why, yes, it certainly is."

She gives me raging bedroom eyes, and my dick gets a chub instantly.

When she shimmies slightly against it, I know she knows it too.

I let out a loud laugh and nod my head.

Oh, yeah, I'm getting me some tonight for sure.

Ashley, a girl Marcus has been trying to hook up with, enters the room with Susie, and I am surprised to see Natalie right behind them. I might see Natalie and her brother at other parties, but neither of them has ever set foot in any of the TimeLand owners' homes.

I laugh at the so-called family feuds that all of our parents have had with Natalie's parents for as long as I can remember. It's never made sense to me, but I swear this town loves the drama of it all. They moved the company here before I was even born, you'd think they'd let bygones be bygones by now, but who I am to tell them how to live their lives—bitterness and all.

I slap Marcus's shoulder and point her way. He raises his eyebrows at me, and I let out a sharp laugh. Looks like he'll be getting lucky tonight too.

Natalie catches my attention from across the room. I can't help but stare as I take her in from this distance. I've honestly never really even looked at her. We've had this unspoken understanding to steer clear of each other over the years, where we would never even acknowledge that the other person existed. Why haven't I ever noticed how damn cute she is?

She really is though.

Checking out the way her tight jeans hug her ass perfectly makes my dick come to life again for a reason other than the girl who's currently trying way too hard to attract it.

Natalie has on a tank top that sits just above her waistline, and her boobs—my fucking God, does she have amazing tits! How have I never noticed them?

HOW WE HATED

I'm lost in thought, wondering what they would feel like against me, when Trish acknowledges the bulge in my pants getting bigger and thinks she's to thank for it.

She leans down and whispers, "I'm down to leave early to really get this party started if you want."

She reaches down and rubs her hand across my jeans, and I have to close my eyes at the sensations that run through me just to get ahold of myself.

After I inhale a deep breath, I grab her ass. "Patience. We have all night."

I give her a quick kiss on the cheek, which seems to settle the issue, as she goes back to talking to her friend who's sitting next to us.

I look back and lock eyes with Natalie, but just as fast as we do, she looks away, acting like it never happened.

That's when I remember who I'm actually looking at. I've never noticed her body because I never cared to notice her, and I still don't.

Pushing her completely out of my thoughts, I turn my attention back to Trish and the people we're sitting with.

As the night progresses, the beer is flowing, and right along with it, my *I don't give a fuck* attitude is coming out. Trish pretty much hasn't left my lap all night, but I haven't minded, especially with the rubdown she's been giving me on and off this entire time. With the way she's teasing me, Lord knows, by the time we actually get alone, I'm going to need to come right away. I hope she's just as turned on when we get to that point.

The party is thinning out, and there's just a handful of us still sitting in the hangout room when someone yells out, "Let's play Never Have I Ever."

"Oh, I'm down," Trish says, waggling her ass in my lap for the hundredth time tonight.

We go around the room with about fifteen of us playing along. Some questions make us laugh, and some are just lame, but that's the nature of the game, I guess.

When it's Natalie's turn, I'm shocked when she says something as bold as, "I've never slept with anyone who's playing this game right now."

Trish eyes me playfully, and we clink bottles before each taking a drink. I look around to see who else is taking a drink and am shocked when I see Eli take a swig. That dog. He's so quiet that he even keeps that shit to himself. Looking around the room, I'm dying to know with who, but I know he'll never tell me, so I shrug and move on. It's kind of shocking just how many people take a drink, so I guess there's no real way to tell anyway.

We play a few more rounds before even more people take off, and it's just my crew of Marcus, Maya, Ben, and Eli, along with Trish, Natalie, Susie, and Ashley hanging out.

Trish leans in to kiss me, and I let her for a second before I pull back and tell her I'm going to go get another drink. I'm all for hooking up tonight, but I'm not a huge PDA kind of guy. Our time will come. She huffs as she gets off my lap and lets me head out of the room to where the beer is kept.

After I close the fridge, I turn and see Natalie coming out of the bathroom.

"Nice of you to finally make an appearance at one of Ben's parties," I state as I crack open the beer.

HOW WE HATED

"I'm surprised you even noticed with Trish hanging all over you all night," she bites back.

"Oh, I noticed," I say, then instantly question what I'm doing. I don't flirt with Natalie. I try to save myself by adding, "Jealous much?"

She lets out a harsh laugh and shakes her head. "Get over yourself."

As I watch her walk back to the room, glued to the way her ass looks in those jeans, all I can think about is getting under her, and that's a huge fucking problem.

I don't care how banging her body is, everything else about her is rotten to the core.

When I walk back out to where everyone is and look at Trish, who's eyeing me like she wants to get out of here, I'm suddenly very tired and, honestly, kind of bored with the idea of being with her again.

Blaming it on the beer, I walk up to Ben, who has a half-asleep Maya curled on his lap. "Hey, I'm going to crash here tonight. Is that cool?"

"Yeah, you know where everything is." He motions to Maya. "We'll probably crash out here anyway."

We slap hands, and I head back to his house without saying a word to anyone else.

Trish texts me:

Where did you go?

I respond with:

Sorry not tonight.

Then, I shut off my phone knowing she'll whine about me leaving, and I walk my sleepy ass to Ben's house to crash for the night.

I wake up the next morning and head back to the barn. I'm not surprised when I enter and see Ben and Maya wrapped around each other, fast asleep. Any other person who entered this barn and saw them like this would think they definitely fucked last night, but I know sleeping like this is all they ever do.

I slap Ben's foot, making him jolt awake. "Get up."

"No," he whines and holds on to Maya tighter.

Her eyes flutter open, and she gives me a small smile. "Morning, Dalt." Only she's allowed to call me by that nickname.

"Morning. You guys want help cleaning this place up?" I ask.

"Not if it means I have to get up," Ben says.

"Then, you're on your own." I laugh.

"Maya will help me." He nuzzles into her neck.

I watch as Maya's eyes flutter shut. Shaking my head at them, I head out to my truck to go home, where I'm sure no one even noticed I was gone all night.

Sundays are spent being lazy at Ben's place and I'm so ready to do just that.

When I arrive, Maya and Ben are already cuddled up watching a football game making me laugh. "Have you guys moved at all since I left yesterday morning?"

Maya grins from ear to ear. "Not really."

HOW WE HATED

"We showered and ate, that's all that really needed to be done anyway," Ben replies.

"Showered? Together?" I tease, pointing between the two of them in question.

"Shut up," Ben says throwing a pillow at me.

I take my spot and lie down as Marcus, Ashley and Eli arrive around the same time.

"Well, Ashley, good to see you," I point out rather loudly, making a point that they must have finally hooked up.

She turns bright red, and Marcus closes his eyes with a chuckle as he comes to slap my hand hello. "Way to be subtle, bro."

Ben and I both laugh. "You know we have to give you shit. Your flirting ass was taking way too long," Ben says.

"Yeah, well"—Marcus grabs her and brings her closer with a quick kiss—"she'll be hanging out with us more often now.

"Yay! More girls." Maya slides her legs up under her where she's lying with Ben on the couch. "Take a seat."

Ashley and Marcus sit on the end of the couch as Eli takes his normal spot on the chair beside us all.

"And you, Eli? How's that phone?" I ask.

He sighs and puts it away. "Sup," he says as his greeting.

Ben and I eye each other knowing whoever he's seeing must be someone good because he's never kept it this tight lipped before.

After a while, I get up and grab the guitar sitting in the corner of the room. I've played for years and it's not uncommon for me to play while we're all hanging out like this.

"Are you working on anything new?" Maya asks.

"Yeah, there's a few that I've been playing around with, but one is really sticking with me right now that I heard on the way here and I want to learn it." I pull it up on YouTube to play for them. "Have you heard the song 'Pretty Little Poison' by Warren Zeiders?"

"Fuck yeah," Ben says. "That song's fire. *Kiss on her lips just like cyanide,*" he sings out the lyrics making even Maya raise her eyes at him. He's normally not one to sing out loud like that.

I nod feeling the same way. As the song plays, I strum along with it trying to figure out the chords.

Ben is right, this song is fire and it's hitting different after the way Natalie caught my eye last night. She's poison that's for sure, and I need to cut that shit out of my mind real quick.

CHAPTER 11

Dalton

It's a pretty shitty feeling having to start my Monday morning off with Natalie. As if Mondays weren't hard enough, knowing I'll have to work with her today just puts me in a foul mood. All weekend, I couldn't get the way her ass looked out of my head, which just pissed me off more. I should *never* have looked at her like that.

I enter the class and head straight to my desk, plopping down with a big thud and pulling my hat even lower than it already was, hoping to catch just a few seconds of shut-eye before the class actually starts.

"Morning, everyone," Mrs. Anderson says after the bell rings. "I'm in a giving mood so though it was supposed to be done today, I will let you interview one another in class one more time if you haven't finished. If you've already completed your interviews, you can start working on the written portion of the assignment to hopefully complete it during class time. For those of

HOW WE HATED

you who haven't finished your interviews"—she literally stares at Natalie and me—"you will have to work on the written portion tonight as your homework. So, go ahead. Either head outside if you need to talk to each other or please stay at your desk and get to writing."

Everyone pulls out their laptops and gets their notes out from the interviews they did last week. Natalie and I are the only people to get up and head outside.

I throw my notebook on the table we sat at last week before sliding my feet in so I'm facing her.

"Do you think we can actually finish this without you walking away again?" I ask.

Natalie doesn't even look up at me. "Whatever. Just give me five things you like to do, and we'll be done with it."

She sits with her pen in hand and notebook open, waiting for me to talk.

When I don't say anything, she finally looks up at me.

I raise my eyebrows slightly, saying, "It's an interview. You're supposed to ask me questions."

She inhales a deep breath, looks down at her book, and begins. "What's your middle name?"

"Delmont," I state matter-of-factly.

"Delmont?" she asks in a tone that shows she thinks I'm lying.

I give her a closed-mouth grin as I nod. "Yes, Delmont. It's my dad's middle name and my grandfather's middle name. You know, family traditions and all."

"What other family traditions do you guys have?"

"Do you really want to know about my family?"

She puts her pen down and tilts her head to the side.

"This is how interviews work. I ask a simple question that hopefully leads to better, more intriguing things. What can I say? It's worked. I'm intrigued."

"Besides my dad making me go to Stanford because it's a family tradition," I say, mocking his tone. "He's the only one out of our family who went there, so it's hardly a tradition."

"Why don't you want to go?"

I look around, wondering if I should actually tell her, then decide, *Fuck it.* "Though you might think my entire family is all wrapped up in the tech world, I'm not."

Her eyes open wide at my confession. Everyone just assumes I'm a techie, like my father, but I couldn't care less about that world.

She shakes her head and holds out her hand to me. "I'm not buying it. Give me your phone."

I laugh, knowing she'll see just how un-techie I actually am. I don't give a shit about all of the apps and games my friends play, and, no, I don't have them downloaded on my phone. Yes, I have Instagram and Twitter, but only for my football posts—to build who I am as a player for colleges—but besides those, I only have Snap to keep in touch with my friends and my music apps.

I unlock the screen and hand it to her, staring directly at her as she takes it all in. I watch as she swipes once because those are the only two pages I have on my phone, and the first page only has a few apps because my screen is a picture of my truck, and I don't want stupid app icons blocking it.

HOW WE HATED

"Of course you have TimeLand on here," she smugly says, trying to throw it in my face.

The company first started out as a desktop gaming system, and with the invention of smartphones, their sales went through the roof due to the ease of just hitting a button to download the free game. Well, free with a side of a thousand different options to buy to make the game better. That's where they make all their money.

She goes to hand it back to me, but I don't accept it.

"Open the app."

Yes, I have the app on my phone, but, no, I don't play it. It actually keeps track of how many days you've played and logged in and blah, blah, blah. Most people show that shit like a badge of honor. I don't.

She opens it, and right there on the screen, it says in big bold letters, *Welcome back! It's been 489 days since you last logged in.*

Her eyes meet mine, and I grin.

"Do you believe me now?"

"Fine." She hands the phone back to me, and I take it this time. "So, you're not a tech guy. You don't want to go to Stanford. Where do you want to go then?"

"Michigan," I state clearly because, to me, there's not a doubt in my head.

"Why?"

I chuckle under my breath. "I'm guessing you don't follow college football."

She raises her eyebrows slightly as she shakes her head. "Sure don't."

"Well, their football team is always ranked high. And I like that it's similar weather to what we're used to. Plus, my grandpa went there."

"So, that could still be following your family tradition."

"I like to think so. If only my dad did too."

"What does your grandpa say?"

I bite my inner lip, trying not to have the emotions come up that always do when I speak about him. "He passed four years ago."

She looks down, shy all of a sudden. "I'm sorry to hear that. Were you two close?"

I sigh and nod. "I was his bud." I laugh at the memory. "At least, that's what he called me." I pause and think about how much I should say. "My dad works all the time, so I kind of felt like my grandfather was more of a dad to me than my dad. He's the one who would throw the ball with me and really taught me the game of football. My dad was always more into computers, where my grandpa actually played for Michigan so football was our connection."

A silence lingers between us, and I decide that's enough about me for the moment, so I move on to her. "What's your middle name?"

"Marie," she responds, kind of annoyed.

"Why did you say it like that?" I ask with a bit of a laugh.

She shrugs. "It's just the most common middle name in the world. I wish I had something more original."

I laugh out loud. "Delmont is definitely not common, but I can't say I love the name."

She smiles. "Yeah, not a fan either, but it has meaning."

I nod. "My dad actually did something right there, I guess." I pause and think what kind of interview

HOW WE HATED

question I can ask her that might spark something interesting. "What is your dream job?"

She doesn't hesitate when she responds, "Running the ranch."

"Seriously? Out of everything in the world, that's what you would want to do?"

She nods. "Yes. My dream is to get the ranch back to the way it was before TimeLand took over this town."

I place my hands down on the table and lift myself slightly to stare into her eyes from a higher point to make myself very clear as I level with her, frustrated that it always comes back to that between us. "What do changes in your ranch have to do with TimeLand being here?"

"You really don't get it, do you?"

I tilt my head to the side, trying not to come off as an ass, but feeling annoyed that she would even bring it up. "Enlighten me."

"Before TimeLand moved here, we employed most of this town and the neighboring towns. With that many employees, we were able to run the ranch at twice the size that it is now before the fire ruined the other half. Can you imagine how much more we were able to produce with two thousand acres running at maximum turnaround?"

I squint my eyebrows. "Huh?"

"If you can't find employees to work for you, you can't run the business you want to run. As my Pops says, 'You're only as good as your employees,' and we can't find enough to run it like we used to."

"There are people all over, looking for jobs. That's not TimeLand's fault."

"What's easier? Working behind a desk all day or working in a field, doing physical labor?" She raises her eyebrows in question, and I get her point, so I don't say anything and let her continue. "Our town is still relatively small, and people realized they could actually make more money at TimeLand than with us and work half as hard. At the time, TimeLand was desperate for employees and willing to train anyone to help them when the app game was created."

"Okay, fine, but what does that have to do with not being able to find employees? There are still plenty of people who would move here for work."

"When TimeLand first came here, they brought some employees with them, which also brought money. Places to live were swooped up, and more were built, but supply and demand. Houses got more expensive, especially when places like your mansion and others like it started to pop up. Leighton River got to be a pretty expensive place to live in a very short amount of time, which means wages needed to go up to support a livelihood here. It was no big deal for most people because they charged more for their services, but we can't. We still sell to the very small towns across this state that don't have a huge corporate living situation dotting their once-beautiful hills."

"So, you really think it is all TimeLand's fault that your ranch wasn't able to keep up their two thousand acres?"

"I don't think. I know." She drops her head and says with a sigh, "Then add in the fire…"

I have no idea what she's talking about with the fire

but that has nothing to do with TimeLand so I tilt my head in question. "Is this why your family hates us?"

"Ding, ding, ding! He can be taught!" she mimics Genie from *Aladdin* by acting like she's swinging a wand at me.

"That's not our fault though. It's not like our parents moved back here on purpose, just to bring down your family business. Call it collateral damage, not intentional."

"Did you really just say the fact that my family's ranch is dying by the second is collateral damage?" She gets so mad, so fast that I swear it looks like a vein is about to pop on her forehead.

I hold my hands out to her. "I'm just saying it's not our fault. Things change. People and industries change. They didn't move the company here just to ruin your family's ranch."

"Oh, yeah? Why don't you ask your father just how much animosity he had toward my Pops in high school? Then, I think you might start to understand."

She gets up from where we're sitting and takes off, once again leaving me alone on this picnic bench with a paper to write and still knowing very little about her, but I'm starting to understand her anger. Justified or not.

CHAPTER 12

Dalton

After practice, I head home and get ready for my nightly run. With my earbuds in, I start out the back gate of our property and go down the same path I run on a daily basis.

When I look out, I notice something that I've never really paid attention to before, but until now, I guess I never really cared what it was. Straight ahead, across the river, I see the back side of the Spencer Ranch, but what I see is definitely not being used anymore.

Barns that look like they've seen better days stand empty with nothing growing around them, and every fence seems to have been either broken or knocked over completely and left there to rot.

How could I have never noticed what's been right in front of me this entire time?

I continue on my run until I see Natalie across the river, standing next to a horse.

HOW WE HATED

I duck behind a tree so she doesn't see me, but now, I can see just how visible I've been to her. Yet here I am, kicking myself for never once noticing anything around these hills that I run on every day.

I watch as she brushes the horse with one hand while her other hand rests on the horse's nose. It's obvious the horse loves her by the way it nudges its head into her palm, almost like it's thanking her for brushing it.

I'm completely mesmerized how she's caring for something so large, yet she does it so calmly. The way her hand slides down its back, like she's petting a small dog and not a large, wild animal three times her size, surprises me.

I've never been around any animals besides Maya's little shih tzu–poodle, Ming. She's cute and all, but she's still just a dog. There's something different in the way Natalie is looking at this horse. I can tell she cares for it very deeply. The thought kind of blows my mind a little.

Do I care about anything in my life that deeply?

I close my eyes and shake my head of whatever thoughts seem to be entering and how foreign they feel to me and get back to focusing on my run.

Once I'm back at my place and I've eaten and showered, I realize that paper is due tomorrow, and the only thing I know to write about Natalie is that her middle name is Marie, she loves horses, and she hates me.

I laugh at the idea of putting that last thought in the paper, but think against it, knowing the teacher probably wouldn't like it much if I did.

I don't have a choice, so I pick up the phone and text Natalie.

LAUREN RUNOW

Paper is due tomorrow. Give me something I can write about.

Nah. You can get an F for all I care.

You can't be serious.

If you paid just the tiniest bit of attention to the world around you and weren't so self-centered, then you could figure out enough about me to write about. I was able to find what I needed about you, and my paper's done.

I think about all the things I want to say back, but decide on throwing my phone against my bed in anger instead. My face heats up with frustration as I try to figure out ways I can finish this paper.

Maya pops into my head, and I pick up the phone, pressing her name and waiting for it to FaceTime her.

"Hey, Dalt," she says as Ben comes into focus.

"What's up, guys? I need your help."

I watch as Ben checks his phone in question.

"Did I miss your call?"

"No, I knew Maya would be able to help me more with this one. I didn't even realize you'd be there."

"When is he not here?" Maya teases as she pushes him off her lap and sits up on the couch she's on.

I'll never understand the two of them, so I just stopped trying to figure them out years ago.

"What do you know about Natalie?"

HOW WE HATED

"Spencer?" she asks with a scrunched face.

"Besides that she's a raging bitch?" Ben says before I can answer, making me chuckle a bit.

"Yeah. Remember we're doing this project together? Well, we should be, but she won't help me, so I'm stuck trying to figure things out about her on my own."

"See, my point exactly." Ben snaps his fingers, proud that he was proven right.

"Maya, please help. You know everyone at school. What can I write about? All she gave me is, she loves horses and wants to run her ranch when she graduates."

"That's a given with her dedication to FFA at school," Maya responds.

"Dedication? What, besides raising her animals?" I ask, confused.

"She's the FFA president. Has been for the last three years."

"I didn't even realize FFA had a president," I state truthfully.

She laughs. "Yes, they have a president. She runs that whole thing. I heard someone talking about how they didn't know what they were going to do without her next year."

I scribble some notes on my paper, then look back at them on the phone. "Anything else?"

She squints her face. "She played clarinet in the fifth grade …" She's obviously just as clueless about her as I am, and her expression says so.

"Everyone played clarinet in the fifth grade," I say with a sigh.

"No," Ben says. "I played trumpet."

"Ugh, that thing was so annoying." Maya shakes her head at the memory.

"You loved me practicing on the phone with you," he responds.

"That's a big fat no!" She laughs. "That thing hurt my ears."

"Your ears? Do you remember what a clarinet sounds like?" he taunts back.

"Okay, back to me. Hello? I have a paper to write." I'm starting to panic slightly with the lack of information we all know about her.

"Sorry, Dalt. Maybe check the yearbook. I'm sure you'll find some info on her in there."

I hop up to where I keep my yearbooks on my shelf in my room. "Good idea. Thanks!"

"Have fun writing your paper as I go back to taking a nap on Maya's lap," Ben calls out right before I hang up.

Opening the yearbook, I flip to the back, which has an index of what pages people are on. I learn that she's not only in FFA, but she also had a role in the school play and is on our student council. I figure I have enough to write what I need and close the yearbook to get started on my paper.

Wednesday morning, I walk into class, feeling like I just want to go back to bed after the horrible night's sleep I had, when I'm greeted by Mrs. Anderson.

HOW WE HATED

"Dalton, I'd like to speak to you and Natalie after class, please."

I force a nod and a tight smile. "Sure thing."

I was proud of what I came up with for the assignment to turn in yesterday with the little info I'd had, and I still turned it in on time, but obviously, Mrs. Anderson doesn't agree.

I take my seat and watch as Natalie enters the room and is greeted with the same lovely message. I wait for her to at least glance my way, but she ignores the fact that I'm sitting right in her line of sight as she heads toward her desk. She doesn't spare me one glance all throughout the class.

Once the bell rings, I gather my things and step up to Mrs. Anderson's desk, waiting for Natalie to do the same.

Before Mrs. Anderson says anything, she hands us each what looks like our papers, which is weird because we turned them in electronically. When I look down at it, I notice it's not my paper; it's hers.

"What's this?" I hold it up in question.

"These are your papers, written about each other. I want you to read it and see what you think."

I shrug and turn to leave, but am stopped short.

"Then, I want you to do the assignment again."

I close my eyes in frustration and take a deep breath. "What was wrong with it?"

"Let me guess. You got most of that information from the yearbook?" Mrs. Anderson says, and I try to hide my reaction. "It's pretty obvious. And, Natalie, yours is a little better, which tells me he gave you more information about himself than you gave him about yourself, but it still wasn't enough. The point of the paper was to learn about who the other person is on the inside. Not what they show everyone here on school campus. You can have until Friday to turn in a new draft, but I will not give you any more class time, so you two have to figure out another time to work together."

I glance at Natalie, and she still hasn't given me the time of day. She just nods her head to Mrs. Anderson and turns to leave without saying a word.

How can she be so mute all the time?

I put up my hands to my sides in disbelief to show Mrs. Anderson what I have to deal with, and she just shrugs one shoulder.

"This project is more about working with different personalities than just writing the paper. You'll figure it out."

She walks away from me, leaving me more irritated than ever that I have to work on this bullshit.

I exit the class and head straight to the couches, where I plop down and drop my head back against the headrest, crumpling the paper in my hands.

"Bad day?" Maya asks, placing her hand on my knee.

I turn my head toward her but keep it lying back. "Let's just say your yearbook idea didn't work, and I have to rewrite the paper."

"Ouch. Sorry." Her expression matches her words.

I sit up and run my fingers down my face. "How can I learn something about Natalie if she won't even talk to me?"

"You're going to have to make her. Show her this feud between our parents is just that—between our parents—and it has nothing to do with us," she says.

HOW WE HATED

"Yeah ... I tried that, and it pissed her off even more when I said her ranch failing was collateral damage to an ever-changing world," I respond.

"You didn't!" She smacks my leg.

I hold up my hands in defense. "I'm just stating the truth. Not my fault it sucks."

"Truth about what?" Ben says as he lifts Maya up, then places her back down on his lap, taking the spot where she was sitting.

"This whole feud between the ranch and TimeLand," I reply. "Mrs. Anderson is making us redo the paper because we didn't dig deep enough."

Ben blows me off. "That's drama none of us need."

"Yeah, except it's messing with my English grade right now." I unfold it and show him the big red *0* across the paper.

"Shitty," is all he says.

Maya places her hand back on my knee. "You're going to have to force her to talk to you, and you need to figure out how to do it without insulting her. That's your only option—unless you want to keep that zero." She jumps off Ben's lap and smiles big. "*Adios, amigos!*"

She leaves with a bounce in her step that I know Ben watches for a few seconds too long for someone claiming he doesn't have those kinds of feelings for her.

I smack his chest. "You're such an asshole when it comes to her. Just admit it already."

He rolls his eyes and stands to head in the opposite direction of her, ignoring what I just said.

CHAPTER 13

Dalton

After practice, I head to the FFA area in search of Natalie. Maya's right. The only way I'm going to get this paper done is if I make her talk to me.

As I turn the corner, I spot her working.

"We need to talk," I state as my hello as I approach her.

"No, we don't."

I grab the shovel she reaches for before she can grab it herself.

"Give me the shovel." She holds her hand out to me.

"Give me something I can write in my paper." I raise my eyebrows at her.

She drops her hand and takes a big inhale. "Fine." She thinks for a second, then looks back to me. "I took a class last year that taught me how to give a hand massage."

HOW WE HATED

I raise my eyebrows at her in question. "A hand massage?"

She forcefully grabs the shovel from me. "Yes. A hand massage. My dad had to have surgery on his hand, and the therapist said it would help, so I learned how to do it so I could massage his hand three times a day to help his healing. And guess what. It helped a ton. So, that's something no one really knows that you can put in this stupid paper."

"What kind of surgery did he have?"

She starts shoveling, and when my foot suddenly gets doused in dirt, she doesn't bother looking up as she talks. "He injured it while working at the ranch. They thought for a second that he might not be able to grip anything ever again. Obviously, that would be devastating to someone who works with their hands." She pauses and gives me an incredulous expression. "And I don't mean by typing away on a computer. I mean actual work."

I grab the shovel from her. "Stop saying stupid shit like that. I'm not my dad."

"Yet you've never really worked a day in your life."

"Am I supposed to feel sorry that I haven't? Most people would call me lucky."

"Lucky until something happens and you realize you don't have the life skills to live off the land. What would you do if you had to survive without your phone and DoorDash?"

"Funny since I never order DoorDash. Dinner is always ready when I get home."

"Ah, yes, I've heard about the chef who cooks for your family. Must be nice."

"Don't be jealous. It's not a good look."

"Neither is a man who doesn't know how to provide."

My lips tilt in a slight grin. "Oh, I provide just fine."

She hits my shoulder as she walks by me. "Get over yourself."

I follow after her. "I need more about you."

She stops short, and I have to do the same quickly so I don't smack into her.

"I'll make you a deal. On your little run tonight, come across the creek and let me test my theory on you. I'll tell you all about me as I watch you try to fix the fence. I bet you won't be able to do it, and I'll write my paper on the fact that you're hardly a man."

I look straight into her eyes. "I'll prove you so wrong, and then I'll just make up shit about you for this paper, and *anything* I write, you have to tell the teacher it's the truth. Then, I'll give you things you can write about me."

"You got yourself a deal."

She turns and heads back to the workshop as I go in the opposite direction toward my truck, conversation over.

I'm startled as I turn the corner into the living room and see my mom sitting there, reading a magazine. She's never home, just hanging out.

"Oh, hey, Mom. Do you know where Dad keeps a hammer?"

HOW WE HATED

She looks up at me with her eyes pinched. "A hammer? Why?"

I figured if I'm going to fix a fence, I should show up prepared, but I'm definitely not telling my mom that. "I just need one to hang something in my room. Where would it be?"

She shakes her head. "You can look in the cabinet in the garage, but I'd be shocked if there's one in there. We normally have Steve do that kind of stuff when needed, but he's gone for the day."

Steve is the guy who takes care of our property, which, until now, I never thought was that odd. All of my friends have guys who work on their houses, so why should I have thought differently?

I head to the garage, and my mom was right. There's nothing in here that even comes close to resembling any type of tool.

I close the garage and head out for my run without any way to fix this fence. I hope Natalie has the tools that will be needed, or I'm fucked.

When I arrive at the river, I look for a place to cross, seeing a few rocks I can jump on to do so. As I do, I see her waiting there for me. I press pause on the music playing in my ears and remove the earbuds, sticking them in my pocket.

"You came," she says with her arms crossed, looking pissed off.

"Don't look so happy."

"I'm not. Follow me so we can get this over with, and then I can turn in the paper I've already written, talking about your failures."

"Ye of little faith."

She rolls her eyes and walks me to where a fence looks like it hasn't been touched in twenty years. She turns to me, then asks, "Where are your tools?"

I open my arms to the sides. "It's not like I have my own customized tool set. This isn't something I do every day."

"Figures." She grabs a toolbox she had sitting where I couldn't see it.

"Aw, you do care," I taunt.

"Just fix the fence."

She walks to her horse and leaves me there to figure out what the hell I'm going to do. I'd be lying if I said she didn't nail a flaw of mine, but I'll be damned if I let her know about it. I always played with Legos when I was younger. I'm sure this is no different.

After I assess the situation and see how the rest of the fence was built, I get to work. Even though I have no clue what I'm actually doing, I hide that fact the best I can and stick my AirPods back into my ears and hum "Straight and Narrow" by Sam Barber as I work.

Only a few minutes go by before I figure out how the fence should come together, and I grab some nails that she brought. Holding the nail with one hand, I swing the hammer with my other hand, missing slightly and pounding my thumb instead. Playing off that it doesn't hurt is probably the hardest thing I've ever done in my life, but there is no way I'll let her know what just happened. I'll never give her that kind of satisfaction.

With a steady breath, I hold the nail again, and this time, I don't miss as I pound the head in at an angle to get the board next to it. With one board up, I step back to examine my work, proud of what I've done so far.

HOW WE HATED

I quickly get back to work, knowing I have about ten more of those to go before I'm done.

The more I work, the more I realize just how much fun this actually is. Rewarding too. I get three more boards up, and the fence is really starting to take shape. I place my hand on the last board I nailed in and give it a good tug to make sure it's secure. To my surprise, it's stiff and not going anywhere.

I've never been so proud of myself. I came here, not having a clue what to do, but I'd say I did a pretty fucking good job.

Removing my AirPods, I head to where she's been sitting with her horse with a grin on my face. "Boy, are you going to regret making that deal with me."

"Oh, really?" She tilts her head like she doesn't believe me.

"Go check it out yourself." I nod my head in that direction and then turn to walk back, not waiting for her.

She's a few steps behind me, and it takes all my willpower to not turn around and gloat about what I accomplished. I know my silence is killing her, but my work speaks loud and clear.

Not only did I fix the fence, but I also made it ten times better than it was originally, and there's no way she can deny it.

Even though she won't look my way, she doesn't have to. I won our little bet, and I can't wait to make up shit about her to turn in to our teacher.

I stifle a laugh as I put the tools I used away. She just sits there, fuming, with her arms crossed, staring at the amazing fence I fixed.

"I'll get back to my run now. For your paper, you already know about my middle name and how I like to run on my property. You can add that I do in fact cook sometimes, and not every meal is made by our personal chef—my specialties are lasagna and chicken sliders. I can also sing a mean George Michael song, but don't ever ask me to show you. Have fun writing your paper."

I start my run back across the creek and to my property, never looking back, but feeling more confident than I ever have in my life.

CHAPTER 14

Dalton

Whoever thought writing a paper could be so much fun? Everything I've ever written for school had to be factual with citations and research, yet for this paper, I got to make stuff up, and I had more fun than I should have.

At first, I thought I shouldn't get too in depth with lies, but then I thought what kind of stuff would she make up about me if I couldn't fix that fence? So, I thought, *Fuck it*. If I had to write this paper about her, I might as well make myself laugh at the same time. I did keep some things true though with her hand massage and wanting to run the farm someday so the teacher wouldn't suspect too much that it was mostly lies.

When I enter the classroom, she's already sitting at her desk, trying her hardest not to notice that I just entered, but she can't hide from me. I hope she's nervous about the stuff that I wrote because she should be.

HOW WE HATED

I hand it to Mrs. Anderson with a big smile on my face. "Thank you for giving me this opportunity to learn such personal things about Natalie. She really opened up to me, and I was able to write the paper exactly how you wanted."

Mrs. Anderson grabs it from me with a suspicious look before she turns her sight to Natalie. "Do you have your paper to turn in as well?"

With a huff, Natalie reaches into her bag, grabs a paper, and walks it up to Mrs. Anderson, obviously without the same giddyup in her step as I have.

"Did Dalton share with you as much as you shared with him?" Mrs. Anderson asks.

"I gave her a ton of stuff to write about," I respond for her.

Mrs. Anderson turns to her for clarification. Natalie just nods, then turns back around and walks to her desk, sitting down with defeat written all over her face. I'd say this is the best morning I've had in a while.

I walk past her chair to my desk in the back row, but can't help myself when I stop and say, "Thanks again for all your help. Sharing all those intimate details really made for a great piece."

The way her eyebrows pinch together, and her face turns beet red makes me want to bust out laughing, but I compose myself and walk to my desk, taking a seat, feeling like I'll be riding high for the rest of the day.

Class goes pretty smoothly, and Mrs. Anderson even gives us time to finish our homework, which is always fine by me. The less work to do after practice, the better.

The bell rings, and we all start to exit the room when

I hear Mrs. Anderson say, "Natalie and Dalton, I'd like to talk to you for a second."

She slides my paper across the desk and looks to Natalie. "Natalie, do you know what he wrote in his paper?"

Natalie nods her head while continuing to hold it up high. "I do."

Knowing she's gonna keep her end of the bargain puts a small smile on my face.

"So, you really told him that you peed your pants in class and dropped a water bottle on your lap to pretend it didn't happen?"

She shrugs, her expression completely straight, like she expected Mrs. Anderson to ask that. "You told me to get personal, and we didn't want to have to write the papers again, so I got as personal as I could possibly think of."

Damn … I understand accepting what I wrote because she'd lost the bet, but seeing that she's willing to lie to the teacher and admit everything I wrote in the paper is true kind of makes me look at her differently.

Mrs. Anderson inhales a deep breath as she places the paper back down on her desk. "Okay then, you both can go."

Natalie turns and leaves without giving me a second glance.

"Thanks, Mrs. Anderson. Have a good rest of your day." Yes, I might be gloating, but winning a bet has never felt so good.

When I exit the classroom, Natalie is nowhere to be found, so I head to the couches to relax before my next class.

HOW WE HATED

"How was English?" Maya asks as she plops down next to me.

Ben swoops in and picks her up and places her back on his lap before I can answer.

"It actually went better than I'd thought," I respond. "I made a bet with Natalie about fixing her fence, and I won, so I got to make up shit about her for the paper I had to write. I wrote some pretty crazy nonsense, and when Mrs. Anderson questioned her, she owned up to every bit of it."

"Sounds like an easy A. At least that's done," Ben says as he wraps his hand in between Maya's thighs.

Maya doesn't even notice he's rubbing her leg when she asks, "What kind of bet involves fixing a fence?"

"She thought I couldn't do it. But guess what? I did," I brag boastfully.

"Serves her right for doubting you couldn't do it," Ben states.

"You fixed a fence?" Maya asks, shocked.

"Don't sound so shocked," I defend.

"No, that's pretty cool. I'm just impressed, is all. I can't believe she held up her side of the bet with Mrs. Anderson."

"Yeah, I was a little surprised too," I state.

"Hey. A bet's a bet. Maybe she is more human than we thought," Ben says as he grips Maya's hips and lifts her off his lap. "I've got to head out. See you guys later."

Ben leaves as Maya takes her spot back.

"So, it wasn't too bad, having to work with Natalie, was it?"

I raise my shoulders, then drop them down. "Up

until fixing the fence, it absolutely sucked, but winning that bet felt pretty good."

She smiles sweetly. "I bet it did." She jumps to her feet. "Well, Spanish awaits. *Adios!*"

"*Adios*," I say as I stand as well and head to my second period class.

Natalie is already sitting at her desk, so after I take my seat, I lean forward.

"That was pretty cool that you owned up to your part of the bet. Can't say I'm not a little surprised."

She doesn't bother turning around to face me, just says over her shoulder, "I lost the bet. What else was I to do?"

I don't say anything in response and instead lean back in my seat with a slight grin on my face. Winning always feels good, but this win is especially yummy.

Monday morning, I'm sitting in English class, trying my hardest to stay awake after the intense workout I had this morning and not getting to eat afterward since I was running late to class.

I'm staring at the clock, counting down the minutes to get to my locker, where I have some food, when Mrs. Anderson announces our second partner project.

"Now that you've gotten to know all of the special and unique things your partner can do, it's your turn to try one of them for yourself."

"What?" I say out loud rather than to myself as I sit up, thinking I didn't hear her right.

HOW WE HATED

"Your next project is to try something they like to do that you've never done, and then write a paper about your experience and if you liked it as much as they did."

I drop my head back in frustration, and when I sit back up, I see Natalie sitting with her head down on her arms that are folded on her desk.

Nice to see she's as happy about this as I am.

"Since I've read all of your papers, I know that most of these things cannot be done in school, so I'm giving you three weeks to work on this project. Within that time, you should be able to get together and then write your paper."

The bell rings, and Natalie grabs her stuff in a huff, leaving the classroom before anyone else.

I exit the room and head to the couches, where Maya is already hanging out.

"What happened with Natalie? She stormed out of that classroom and almost knocked me over."

I plop down and slap my hands on my knees. "For the second part of our partner project we have to actually get together and try something the other person loves to do."

"Ouch," she says with a sigh, then remembers. "Wait. You made up your paper. What did you write that she loves to do?"

I shake my head. "That part I wrote was true. Believe me, I would have made up something way better if I had known this would be the next part. I only made shit up about the more personal stories we were supposed to share. For her hobby part, I wrote about her horse."

"That should be fun. I've always wanted to ride a horse. I guess I shouldn't be surprised she has one."

I laugh at that thought. She's probably the only person I know in Leighton River who has one. I've never even considered riding a horse. Why would I? It's not like my parents were ever into animals of any kind, especially barn animals. They're more of the Mercedes and Porsche types for their transportation.

Eli walks up and sits in his same place, typing out something on his phone.

I kick his leg. "Who are you always texting? Every time I see you, you're off in your own world—more than usual, I mean."

Maya perks up and faces him. "You know, he's right. I do see you texting on that a lot. And since we're all here, we know you aren't texting one of us. So, who are you texting?"

His raised eyebrows are his only response.

"Well?" I ask.

He hits Send, then places the phone in his pocket. "Don't worry about it."

Ben walks up and slaps his shoulder. "Yeah, he's got new pussy. God forbid we know who though."

He picks up Maya, sits down and places her on his lap.

She slaps his chest. "Don't be so crude."

He shrugs. "Just stating facts. It's Eli. You know that's all it will be."

Maya looks at Eli, saddened, knowing Ben is right. He hooks up with girls—we never hear about who they actually are—then moves on just as fast as it started. I've gotten used to it, and you would think girls wouldn't give it up, knowing this is how he is, but he still gets the play. It's like the girls think it's a game and they'll be the ones to change him. I can tell you right now that they won't.

"Well, I must get to Econ. See ya," I state as I stand and walk away.

When I enter, Natalie is going through her bag, no doubt trying to avoid eye contact with me. I give her the satisfaction, and then once I'm sitting, I lean forward.

"Your house or mine?" I taunt, trying to make a joke about our situation.

To my surprise, she turns to face me. "I don't even know what you wrote, so I figured it didn't matter anyway."

"Sorry, babe. I actually did that part truthfully and wrote about your horse."

"First, don't ever call me *babe* again. Second, you're not riding my horse."

"Fine, grab another one of your horses, and I'll ride that one. I'm sure you have plenty."

She rolls her eyes and shakes her head. "Just write about the first time you rode. She won't know the difference." She turns to face forward before I can respond.

I lean forward again and get right up next to her. "Problem is, I've never ridden. So, looks like you get to be my riding instructor for the day."

She faces me again.

"You're kidding me, right?"

I sit back in my chair and kick my legs out so they are more invading her space than sitting in mine. "Nope. You'll have to show me if I can write a truthful paper."

She rubs the side of her eyes as she closes them, obviously not happy about what she's hearing.

Am I an asshole to admit that seeing her so unhappy is actually making my day?

Just to rub more salt in her wound, I get up close to her again, making her flinch when she realizes I'm in her space. "What did you write about me that you have to do?"

She shakes her head and looks up, saying something under her breath that I can't understand.

"What was that?" I ask in too chipper of a voice, which I know eats away at her.

"I wrote about you running," she says.

I laugh out loud as the bell rings. "Well, at least you didn't say football. Looks like I have a new running partner tonight. Meet you at the same time?"

Natalie huffs and turns to face forward as Miss Hernandez begins the class. It's obvious Natalie's day is ruined, yet I feel like mine just picked up immensely.

CHAPTER 15

Natalie

I have a pounding headache that won't go away, but I know it's not from anything other than the stress this day has caused. Learning in first period that I was going to have to spend more time with Dalton pushed me over the edge of an already-shitty morning.

Getting up early to help my father is normally the highlight of my day, but when we have to do a job that's suited for ten people and we only have four, things tend to get out of hand quickly. Getting all of the hogs back to where they needed to be proved how outmatched we were, and let's just say the scoreboard is Hogs 1, Farmers 0.

George, our ranch hand, finally had to go create another portable fence around a bigger area because there was just no way we were going to win.

I had just enough time to shower and rush off to

HOW WE HATED

school with my hair still wet, only to find out I'd have to work with Dalton again. After learning that, I officially just wanted to go back to bed and start the day new tomorrow.

No such luck though.

With school finally out, I'm heading toward my brother's truck when I get a text from Dalton.

Don't forget to meet me tonight.

I roll my eyes and don't bother responding as I drop my head back in frustration.

"Who was that text from to cause that much of a reaction?" Thomas asks as he bumps into my side, almost knocking me over.

If there's one person who hates Dalton more than I do, it's my brother. I think he takes on hating the TimeLand crew as his family duty, and any chance he has to prove his point, he does.

I'm not in the mood to listen to him bitch about them or say I need to tell the teacher to fuck off again. If he were in my shoes, he'd take a zero instead of working with Dalton, no doubt.

So, instead, I say, "Just realized I have to do a project tonight that I really don't want to do."

He heads to his side of the truck. "Sucks to be you."

"Gee, thanks." I hop in once he unlocks the door.

"Church Bells" by Carrie Underwood comes on, and I imagine being able to slip something in Dalton's whiskey that no one will ever find, like the song suggests.

I know I'm being ridiculous, but that's what he does to me. He brings out this side that I only have with him.

I can tolerate Eli, Ben, and Maya, but there's always been something about Dalton that makes me not even able to stand the sight of him.

Now, I can't seem to get away from him.

Once we're home, I get some of my homework out of the way before I start my daily chores around the farm and head out to see Brandy. I know Dalton thinks we'll be doing his hobby first, but there's no way I'm running after the day I've had, so he'll just have to do my hobby today.

As I walk through the barn doors, a calmness washes over me. This is my true home. Being with Brandy always soothes my soul, no matter what problems arose during the day.

"Hey, girl," I say as I run my fingers down her mane. "You ready to go for a walk?"

She rubs her nose into my hand, like she always does.

I place my head against hers and whisper, "It's good to see you too."

I walk to the next stall, where Jasper—another one of our horses—is housed. He's the feistiest horse we have and seeing him puts a slight smile on my face. If Dalton hasn't ridden a horse before, then Jasper will be perfect for him.

I pat his side. "Come on, Jasper. Let's get you ready to ride."

When Brandy huffs next to me, I shout out, "Don't worry. You're coming too."

After I have them both saddled up, I hop up onto Brandy and hold Jasper's reins as we head out of the stalls.

HOW WE HATED

Thankfully, all the ranch hands have left for the day, so I don't have to explain to anyone where I'm going with the second horse.

As we turn the corner to where we can cross the river to Dalton's property, I see him already standing there with a scowl on his face.

"You're late," he growls as I approach.

I stop Brandy and hop off of her. "Get over it. I'm here."

He motions his head toward Jasper. "Why the second horse?"

"I've had a shit day, and I don't want to run, so if you want to work on this project, we're doing my hobby tonight."

He crosses his arms over his chest. "You think you can just demand that?"

I nod with a smile. "Yes, I can, and I just did. Now, get on."

I throw him the reins. He catches them but doesn't move.

Paying him no attention, I put my foot in the stirrup and hop back onto Brandy with ease. When I see him still standing there, I open my eyes wide in question. "Are you coming?"

I stare at him as he approaches the horse with his hand out, like he's afraid of him. As he touches him ever so slightly, he jolts back, as if he just touched an electric fence and got shocked.

Laughing, I say, "He won't bite you."

Dalton pays me no attention as he examines the saddle and how he might get on.

"Are you joking right now?"

He turns to me in question. "What?"

"You've seriously never ridden a horse?"

He glares at me but doesn't respond.

"Have you ever even been around a horse?"

"Does it look like I've ever been around a horse?" he deadpans. "Give me a break. I'm trying to figure this thing out before I fling my body over it."

"This *thing* is a horse. And you don't just *fling* your body over him."

Dalton puts his foot in the stirrup and places his hands on either side of the saddle, preparing to hoist himself up.

"Be careful. If you do it wrong, he'll buck you off, and you don't want to break an arm or leg if that happens."

He pauses, and I see the worry cross his face, making me instantly bust out in a fit of giggles.

"I'm kidding," I say once I catch my breath.

"That's not funny. I have a lot riding on my body being in tip-top shape. I can't go breaking something over a stupid assignment."

I kick my leg slightly, motioning for Brandy to head closer to Jasper, where I hop off.

"Here." I motion for him to move to the side so he can see what I'm about to do. "You place your foot here, your hands here and here, and lift yourself up in one swift movement." I demonstrate getting on Jasper, then hop off and step aside for Dalton to try.

He does as I said and practices his push-off a few times before he takes the final plunge and hoists himself up all the way.

When he lands less than gracefully on Jasper's back and literally holds on to his neck for dear life, I can't

HOW WE HATED

help but laugh out loud when Jasper begins to jump from side to side.

"Make him stop!" Dalton cries out, making me laugh even harder. "Natalie!"

I try to inhale a deep breath before I place my hand on Jasper's side. "It's okay, Jasper. He's not going to hurt you."

Jasper calms down long enough for Dalton to adjust his position and sit up like he should.

"You good now?" I ask.

Dalton doesn't respond, just takes in everything around him and underneath him with this look of fear that he's obviously trying to hide but doing a horrible job.

I shake my head as I hop up onto Brandy and kick my legs to start her forward.

Jasper is quick on our heels, and within seconds, we're in a fast trot down the riverside.

"You good back there?" I ask over my shoulder as the wind blows my hair backward.

When he doesn't respond, I kick my legs again to signal to go faster.

Jasper keeps in line until I hear Dalton say, "Slow ... down," all choppy and bouncy, like the ride is literally shaking the words out of his body.

"What? Too fast for you?" I go a little faster.

"I. Can't. Hold. On," he bounces out again.

I decide he's had enough torture and slow down to a walking pace. When Jasper comes beside me, I see Dalton's literal white knuckles gripping the reins so tight that I think he's lost all blood in them.

"You can breathe now," I tease.

He closes his eyes and inhales, acting like he seriously forgot that breathing is something he needs to do to survive.

I give him a break and decide to walk slowly for a little while, letting him get accustomed to the horse in silence.

Every time I glance to the side, he's fidgeting with something and looking just about as comfortable as a person would if he were sitting on a porcupine.

"Why do you look like that?" I finally ask.

"Like what?"

"So … I don't know … afraid?"

"Maybe because I am, okay? This thing has a lot of power, which you showed me right off the bat with no warning—fuck you very much for that—so, yeah, I'm just a little freaked out over here."

"He won't hurt you."

"Yeah, but he can buck me off with one simple movement." He repositions himself, looking even more uncomfortable.

I sigh and give him some advice. "Come on. You're too rigid." I stop Brandy, and Jasper stops as well so we're side by side. "Take a deep breath in and let it out slowly."

Surprisingly, Dalton does as he is told.

I watch as his shoulders loosen a little, and he looks slightly more comfortable. I hop off of Brandy and walk to Jasper.

"Here, give me your hand." I hold my hand out to him.

He hesitates for a second, then does as I asked. I take his hand and place it on the neck of Jasper, running

HOW WE HATED

it down to the side. When I get to as far as his arm can reach from his position, I lift it, bring it back to the top, and repeat the same movements.

Our fingers intertwine as I continue the motion a few more times. When I look up to Dalton, he's staring at me, not Jasper, which catches me off guard.

I instantly remove my hand and walk back to Brandy and hop back on, doing the same thing to Brandy that we were just doing to Jasper.

"You have to become one with the horse. They have to trust you just as much as you have to trust them."

Dalton rubs his lips together as he continues to pet Jasper. With every movement, I can visibly see his body relax. When he takes a deep breath in, I know he's more comfortable being here now.

"You ready to walk some more?" I ask.

He nods. "Just walk though."

I laugh. "Fine. Just walk."

I pat Brandy, and she starts off in a slow walk down the riverside some more.

"I didn't realize your property came back this far," Dalton says.

"Yep. All the way to Eli's place."

"Seriously? That's far from here."

I laugh out loud. "Yeah, two thousand acres is a lot of land."

"How come I didn't know it was that big?"

"Used to be, remember?" I glare at him, then look forward again. "Now, it's a lot of empty land."

He doesn't say anything in response, so we continue in silence for a few minutes.

"You doing better now?" I ask.

He nods and looks around like he's lost in thought as he takes into account everything around him, then turns to me. "Yeah. This is better. It's kind of peaceful."

I take in a long inhale and let it out with a happy sigh. "It sure is. I love it out here."

"I can see why."

I look toward him. "Thanks for the embarrassing story you told Mrs. Anderson."

He lets out a sharp laugh, making me roll my eyes. "Thanks for going along with it."

I shrug my shoulders. "A bet is a bet. That's what I get for thinking you couldn't fix that fence."

"Still surprised I did it, huh?"

"Yeah. Even more now after seeing you try to ride a horse."

"Hey, if you had started out at this speed, then I would have done just fine."

"But where's the fun in that? I had to get you back for that made-up paper somehow." I click my legs against Brandy. "Let's go, girl."

Brandy takes off in a trot, and Jasper is quick to try to outrun her.

"Not this time," Dalton says from behind me. "Yeehaw," he calls out as he kicks his legs and starts to pass me.

I laugh so hard that I almost lose my balance. "Did you just say '*yeehaw*'?"

Determination crosses his expression as he buckles down and grips the reins harder, hitting Jasper again. "Go, go, go." After he passes me, he calls out over his shoulder, "Is that better?"

I'm still cracking up when I respond, "Anything is better than yeehaw."

HOW WE HATED

We ride like that for a few more seconds until he gives in and pulls on the reins to slow Jasper down to a walk again.

"See, I can do this, too, just fine. Ye of little faith," he states proudly as he sits up straight, looking way more comfortable on Jasper now.

"What is up with the word *ye* with you?"

"Yee, yee," he says with a cocky grin, copying the words of Granger Smith. His smile fades, and he gets more serious. "What is wrong with yeehaw? That's what cowboys always say."

"In 1820 maybe. No one says that now."

"Then, we should bring it back. Tell everyone all the cool cowboys are saying it."

I laugh for a completely different reason than just a few minutes ago. I went from laughing at him to him making me laugh. It's a weird feeling, but I decide not to focus on it and just play along. "Cool cowboys? How many cool cowboys do you know?"

He holds his hands out to his sides. "One. Me."

"You ride a horse for all of five minutes, and you're suddenly a cowboy?"

"Yep. All of our teachers have always said we can be anything we want to be, and right now, I want to be a cowboy."

The way he's being so playful is making me smile even though that's never something I want to do when I'm forced to be with him. It's obvious he's kidding, but the way it comes off him so freely is kind of refreshing.

I shake my head. "You're ridiculous."

"So what? Life is too serious sometimes. It's nice to be out here without a care in the world." He looks me in the eye. "I can tell why you like this so much."

His stare catches me off guard, and I lean down to adjust something on Brandy for no other reason but to break our eye contact.

"Okay, let's head back before it gets too dark," I suggest.

Dalton raises his hand back to where we came from. "Lead the way, cowgirl."

"No. Don't ever call me that again."

"Okay then, little lady. I'll just mosey along behind you as you lead us back to the prairie," he says in a slow, old-fashioned Southern accent.

"Oh God, please no," I plead, but I can't stop the laughter caused by his actions. "That's way worse."

His lips tilt to the side in a grin that makes him suddenly way too attractive to look at, so I take the reins and turn Brandy, feeling the need to get us back to his property line as soon as possible. Our riding lesson needs to be over—now.

CHAPTER 16

Dalton

I arrive at school a few minutes early, so I go sit on one of the couches and chill before the first bell rings.

"Hey, Dalt." Maya sits right next to me and places her hand on my knee like she always does. "You ready for the big game tomorrow night?"

"You know it."

I open my hand and rub on the rope burn I got the other night, hoping it heals a little more by then. I felt it a few times at practice, and it wasn't the best of sensations.

She grabs my hand and turns it toward her. "What happened to your palm?"

"It's nothing. I got rope burn."

"From what?"

"Riding a horse," I say nonchalantly.

"Oh, yeah. With Natalie. I can't believe her dad allowed you on their property, let alone on his horse."

HOW WE HATED

"He probably didn't know."

Her expression goes from shocked to flabbergasted. "You were on his property, and he didn't know? Are you crazy? I wouldn't put it past that man to shoot you for trespassing."

I blow the notion off. "It was no big deal. Our properties butt up against one another, so she met me there, and we rode down the riverbank."

She raises her shoulders and squishes her lips as she mimics my words. "*Oh, it was nothing. Just out riding horses with my family's sworn enemy's daughter. That's all.*"

"It was nothing."

She eyes me and tilts her head to the side. "How come I don't get the vibe that you hated every second of it?"

I shrug. "It was fun. I'd never ridden a horse."

"Okay then ..." The warning bell rings, and she stands up. "Off to class I go. Bye!"

She walks off with a hop in her step, like she always does. Feeling good for a change, I copy her enthusiasm, only to feel a small twinge from a muscle I didn't know I had. It doesn't hurt, but it's a reminder that I was on a horse for the first time and definitely using muscles I never have before.

As I turn the corner to enter the classroom, Natalie is the first person I see. Her eyes meet mine for a brief moment, and when she's quick to look away, a weird feeling races through me that I try to ignore.

I purposely kick her backpack as I walk by. When she doesn't yell at me for doing so, a little bit of disappointment runs through me.

Class drags on, and I'm glad to get up when the bell rings. When I enter my second period class, Natalie is already in her seat, so I sit down and lean forward.

"Tonight, we run."

"If you say *at midnight* and finish it off with a *yeehaw*, I will backhand you," she responds.

I laugh out loud, causing people to look our way. The expressions on a few of our classmates' faces when they see us talking make me want to laugh even more.

Yes, it is possible for me to talk to someone I've hated for years.

"No. Not at midnight. Same time. Make sure you wear running shoes."

She turns in her seat just to make sure I see the look of *no shit* she's giving me. When Miss Hernandez begins her lesson, I motion with my pointer finger for her to turn around to face the front again.

Her eyes narrow before she huffs and moves to face the front.

Why does seeing her annoyed with me make me so fucking happy?

I head out for my run, excited to see just how bad I can get back at Natalie after her little stunt last night. I know running doesn't have the same fear she was trying to instill in me, but giving her a good ass-kicking will give me the same satisfaction I'm sure she got.

To my surprise, when I arrive, she's on my side of the river, wearing cutoff jean shorts and a tight tank top

HOW WE HATED

that shows off curves that should definitely not look as tempting as they do.

"Look who's on time," I say as my hello.

"And look who's late." She doesn't even try to hide her frustration with me.

"You do realize we never set an actual time, right?"

"Yes, which means I got here a half hour ago, thinking you'd be here."

"Well, whose fault is that? If you wanted a specific time, then you should have said so. Now, let's go." I smack her ass as I run past her.

"Don't you dare touch me like that again," she bites back.

"Don't get your panties in a bunch. I'm a football player, and you're training with me. It's what I do to all the guys. Now, keep up. Oh, and jean shorts? Not the smartest outfit choice."

I hear her huff behind me as I pick up my pace and run along the riverbank, just like we did on the horses, but on the opposite side.

Instead of turning around to check on her, I slow down and allow her to catch up with me, only so I can run behind her. Then, I cross to the other side of her, then run ahead of her and cross over again.

"You can stop now," she bites out in irritation.

"Why? I think it's fun. I'm literally running circles around you."

She doesn't miss a beat with her steps. "Ha-ha. Very funny. You have no idea. I can keep up with you just fine."

"Oh, really?"

"Yep. Try me."

She puffs out her chest, and I don't know whether to be offended or turned on. I've never met a girl who challenges me like this.

"Okay then." I run faster, and instead of heading straight, I take a turn up a path that leads back up to my property.

When I glance over my shoulder, she's right on my heels, so I pick up the pace a little more.

Her labored breathing rings in my ears, so I shout over my shoulder, "You tired yet?"

"Nope," she says between breaths. "Just getting started."

I decide to test her even more by heading up an even steeper path that has more challenging terrain, making each step a little more difficult than the previous one.

We run like this for a few minutes, and even I'm starting to get winded, but no matter what I do, she's right there behind me.

I hear some commotion behind me, and then she squeals, so I stop and turn to see what happened.

She's bent down, reaching for her ankle.

Oh shit.

I take the few steps back to where she is. "Are you okay?" I lean down to examine where she's rubbing.

"Got ya!" she yells as she takes off running, leaving me in the dust.

Because I'm taller, it doesn't take long for me to reach her, and when I grab her waist, picking her up to stop her, she screams in surprise, only making me laugh so hard that I have to put her down so I can catch my breath.

"You suck. That wasn't nice," I say as I take long inhales and exhales.

HOW WE HATED

She takes a few seconds to catch her breath, acting like she's about to hyperventilate. "Neither was taking me on a run that's kicking even your ass."

I lean down and put my hands on my knees. "I ain't gonna lie; I'm surprised you could keep up."

She lets out a sharp laugh. "Me too. My desire to not be beat by you kicked into overdrive."

I press my lips together and nod slowly as I stretch my arms up. "Competitive nature. I can dig that."

"Good." She's still having trouble breathing. "Can we walk back then?" she says with the most pleading expression I've ever seen.

I chuckle under my breath. "Yeah, that's fine." I lead the way, and instead of having her walk behind me, I walk on the side of the path to make room for her to walk beside me. "How come you don't play sports if you're so competitive?"

"I do barrel racing in the summer with Brandy."

"No shit?"

She laughs. "Why does that surprise you?"

I shrug. "I don't know. I didn't know people around here did that."

"Do you really just live in your TimeLand bubble?"

I turn to her as we continue to walk. "Now, what does that mean?"

"You do realize we live in Montana, right? Horses are kind of our state motto." She sighs. "At least everywhere but in Leighton River."

"I guess I just never knew people here rode like that."

"There's more to our area than TimeLand and football."

I turn around to face her and walk backward as I ask, "Why do you always throw TimeLand in my face?"

"I don't throw it in your face. I just state facts, and your facts are that you only pay attention to football and things that involve TimeLand. There's a whole world you know nothing about."

I flip around and continue to walk forward. "Not true. I …" I pause, not sure what to say.

"I'm waiting."

"I go wakeboarding and paddleboarding up at the lake."

"Okay, but what about fishing? Have you ever fished at the lake?"

I pause, and when she turns to face me, I finally answer, "I used to. With my grandpa." My mood turns somber every time I think of him, and right now is no different.

"How come you don't go anymore?"

I sigh. "My dad was never into it. I guess I just didn't have anyone to take me after Grandpa passed, and I honestly haven't thought much about it since I was able to drive myself. It wouldn't feel right without him."

"I'm sorry."

I don't respond as I inhale a deep breath. I hate that the mood has changed so much, just like my life has since he passed. Every time I think about him, I take that feeling deep in my soul, push it down, pretend like it's not there, and do what I always do. Compete.

"Race ya!" I slap her arm, then head off down the path in a full-blown sprint until we get to the bottom.

She never gives up, but by the way she's gasping for air, I can tell she wishes she did.

HOW WE HATED

I give her a few minutes to catch her breath as I stretch my legs.

"I. Hate. You. You. Know. That. Right?" she says as she breathes heavily.

"Nah, you don't. You love the competition." I start to make my way back to my house. "I play tomorrow, but I'll meet you back here on Monday, and I'll give you a rematch."

I don't wait for her to respond. If she truly has that competitive nature that I think she has, then she won't miss the opportunity for a rematch, and honestly, I'm up for it too.

CHAPTER 17

Natalie

After school the next day, Susie turns and falls against the locker next to mine with a huff.

"That bad?" I ask.

She lets out a long sigh. "Just wish there were more options of who to date here in Leighton River. Now that Ashley's with Marcus, I'm always the third wheel." She keeps her head against the lockers but turns her gaze to me. "Are you going with us to the game tonight? Pleeease," she begs.

"Yeah, I'll go," I answer with no hesitation at all.

She stands up straight and narrows her eyes. "Really? I thought I was going to have to get down on my knees to get you to go."

I close my locker and lean my side against it so I'm facing her. "It's not that big of a deal."

"What's not that big of a deal?" Ashley asks as she walks over to us, holding hands with Marcus.

HOW WE HATED

"She's going to the game tonight," Susie states.

"Really?" Ashley jumps for joy.

"Of course she's going," Marcus pipes in. "The entire town will be there. We're ready to shut this game down tonight. With me, Ben, Dalton, and Eli"—he rubs his chest with a cocky grin—"we're unstoppable."

"You talking about me over here?" Dalton says as he approaches behind Marcus.

Marcus turns, and they slap hands. "I was just telling them it's going to be on tonight."

"It's going to be good competition for sure," Dalton replies. "Natalie knows what that's all about." He gives me his own cocky grin, then hits Marcus's shoulder. "You comin'?"

"Yeah, one sec." Marcus turns to Ashley and places his finger under her chin. "I'll be looking for you in the stands tonight."

"I'll be the one wearing your number," Ashley says, all dreamy-eyed before they kiss.

It's moments like this when I used to roll my eyes, but something feels different now, and when I glance at Dalton, I swear I catch him looking at me, but he turns suddenly, trying to play it off like he wasn't.

They finally break away from their kiss and say their goodbyes as Marcus leaves to join Dalton, who's already a few steps ahead of him.

Susie practically jumps on me, catching me completely off guard. "Okay, what was that?"

"What was what?" I ask, confused.

"Dalton. He was totally looking at you when they were kissing. And that comment? Natalie knows all about what?"

I try to blow her off even though the fact that she noticed it, too, does weird things to my insides. "No, he wasn't."

"Um, yes, he totally was." She nudges me with her arm. "Maybe he's seeing another side of you with this project you guys have been doing."

"Believe me, he hates that side just as much as he hates the other side he already knew." I step forward to end this conversation and head home for the day.

"Well, I saw what I saw," she singsongs, swaying the books she's carrying against her chest side to side.

Ashley, Susie, and I all arrive at the game together—them wearing all the Leighton High gear, and, yes, I even allowed them to paint our school colors of blue and yellow on my face in cute little paw prints to represent our mascot the Wild Cats.

We find some seats in the student section just as the team is busting through the big paper that the cheerleaders painted for them. The crowd roars to life as every player races onto the field.

Fire bursts into the air from flame machines as loud music blares around us, hyping up the boys and the stands.

Once everyone takes their place in a line across the field, we hear the announcer say, "Please rise for our national anthem."

We do so as I search for two of my FFA members, who will be riding their horses through the field, carrying

HOW WE HATED

the American flag. As they appear, the crowd cheers, and I scream right along with them, loving the way they look, racing across the field with the flag flowing in the wind behind them. At the end of the song, every player raises their helmets as applause erupts once more.

The players go through their warm-up routine as the opening ceremony festivities are cleaned up.

Before kickoff, I look out onto the field and see Dalton standing on the sideline, looking even bigger in his football uniform with the number 81 written across his back.

"There's Marcus." Ashley points to where he is on the field. "Number 24."

From this distance, the difference between him and Dalton is almost comical, as I've never realized Marcus was that much smaller than him, but I guess that's what makes him so fast. Everyone has their role on the football field—and in life.

Ashley screams out, "Go, Marcus!"

He must have heard her because both Marcus and Dalton turn at the same time, and Marcus spots Ashley waving like a lunatic right away. She blows him a kiss, and he blows one back.

My eyes meet with Dalton's just as the announcer comes over the loudspeaker again. "Leighton River High is glad you decided to spend your night with us. Now, let's stand for the kickoff as we take on our rival school, Mason Creek!"

Everyone cheers as some of the players run out to get in position for the kickoff.

The game is a battle, back and forth, but for the first time ever, I'm actually really into it and I feel bad I haven't really supported my brother before this.

With ten seconds left in the game, Eli throws the ball to Dalton, and I literally grab Susie's arm in anticipation. When he catches it and stiff-arms the opponent, running it in for a touchdown to take the lead, I lose my freaking mind, jumping up and screaming at the top of my lungs with the rest of the crowd.

They kick the extra point, and Mason Creek gets the ball back with seconds to spare. They try for a Hail Mary play, but don't come anywhere near being able to make a touchdown as the time expires, and everyone jumps to their feet again, cheering on our hometown boys.

As we all come back to our senses and start gathering our things to leave the stadium, Susie nudges me with her shoulder. "Since when do you like watching football? I swear I thought you were going to dig your nails into my arm for a second there at the end."

I laugh and shrug. "I guess I never realized just how intense it could get."

She tilts her head to the side. "That wouldn't have anything to do with a certain player on the field, would it?"

"Please. You know I'm never going there."

She grins as she grabs her water bottle and purse, and we all make our way down to the field, where everyone gets to hang out with the players after the game.

I go straight to my brother. "Great job tonight."

He nods his head. "Thanks for coming." A friend of his calls out his name. He acknowledges them then turns back to me. "See you at home."

I nod then head back to my friends who are trying to find Marcus as the crowd starts to thin out.

HOW WE HATED

Once we spot him, Ashley takes us straight to her new boyfriend, who, of course, is standing there with Ben, Eli, and Dalton. She runs up and jumps into his arms, and he spins her around.

They're off in their own little world, leaving the rest of us standing in an awkward silence for a few seconds until Maya joins us and jumps on Ben's back, who catches her with ease, like they've done it a thousand times before.

"Are we all going to Ben's?" she asks the group, but looks right at Susie and me, almost to make sure we know we're invited too.

She's always been that way, trying to include everyone even though I know she hates me, just like the rest of the TimeLand crew. It's something that actually annoyed me before, but right now, I'm not too bothered by it.

I look to Ashley, who's still wrapped up with Marcus, then to Susie and shrug. "You want to go?"

Susie laughs. "Normally, I'm the one begging you to go out, and now, you're asking me if I want to go?"

I chuckle to myself, realizing she's right, then meet eyes with Dalton, who's looking at me intensely. I pause for a minute too long, then look back to Maya. "Yeah, we'll go."

Maya jumps down off of Ben's back. "Great." She smacks Ben's arm. "Now, hurry up and go shower so we can get going."

Ben flings his sweaty head on her as she pushes him away. "Gross!"

The guys all head to the locker room while Ashley, Susie, and I walk toward our car.

"Maya"—Ashley turns back around to where Maya is picking up her bag with no one else around her—"do you want to just ride with us, so you don't have to wait?"

I guess I've never really thought about Maya and who she hangs out with. I know she has friends—shoot, she has the entire cheerleading crew—but I realize now that I've only ever seen her really hang out with the TimeLand guys.

She mulls it over in her head, then shrugs. "Sure. I'll just text Ben and let him know."

I lean in to whisper to Ashley, "Are she and Ben a thing?"

She chuckles under her breath in response. "I wondered the exact same thing until I saw Ben hooking up with someone else the other night, so I'm going to guess that's a no."

"Okay then."

Maya joins us, and we continue to walk back to Ashley's car.

"Thanks for letting me tag along," Maya says once we're all in.

"Anytime," Ashley responds. "Where should we go while we wait on the guys to get there?"

"Oh, don't worry about that," Maya says. "That place is my second home. We can go there and hang out until they come."

Ashley looks at me sitting in the front seat, repeating my same confused stance as before. "Okay then."

I shrug in agreement as she puts the car in reverse and heads out of the parking lot.

Leighton River still has that small-town vibe as you drive through the streets until you get to the outskirts

HOW WE HATED

of town, where it feels like you've entered a different dimension of reality.

Old oak trees that the city was built around turn into perfectly designed landscaped parkways with flowers and trees evenly spaced on each side, proving that nature didn't grow them and they were planted this way. LED streetlights change the feel from the old-school yellow glow to this clear blue hue. From this parkway, side roads branch off, leading to the mansions sitting on the side of the hills.

I don't come back here often, as it saddens me to see just how different our town has become.

Ashley turns onto one road that leads us up the hill even more until we see Ben's house sitting there like a luxurious painting instead of a real home. We drive around to the back, where the barn is.

"Let me go say hi to Ben's parents, and then I'll be back out." Maya opens the door and climbs out.

I watch as she heads up the long walkway that leads to the back end of their house. Ben's mom opens the door and greets her before she even gets to knock. Their interaction seems very warm and welcoming as they hug and chat for a few minutes before she walks back to us, motioning for us to join her as she heads towards the barn.

We all hop out of the car and follow her. Watching her little frame manhandle the large door makes me chuckle to myself. She's a feisty one, and it shows in the way she throws the thing open with all her might.

"Come on in." She motions before walking in herself and turning on the lights.

I slowly make my way in. Being here with no one

else gives me weird vibes. A month ago, I would have avoided this place like the plague, and here I am, walking in for the second time this school year only now before anyone else is even here.

Maya opens the fridge. "Do you guys want anything?"

"I'll take a water if there's one in there," I respond. Ashley and Susie agree.

She brings one back for each of us. I crack the lid and take a drink, then sit down on the couch, feeling more out of place than I've ever felt in my entire life.

"So, Ashley," Maya starts, "you and Marcus are getting pretty cozy."

Of course, Ashley beams with excitement. "He's so amazing."

"Yeah, I've always thought he was pretty cool," Maya responds. "What about you two? Are you guys seeing anyone?"

"Well, Natalie here—" Susie says, and I instantly choke on the water I'm drinking as true fear of what she's about to say races through my veins. "You okay?" She pats me on the back.

"Yeah," I barely get out. "Just went down the wrong pipe."

To my dismay, she starts talking again, and my heart pounds so hard until I hear her say, "Natalie and I are sick of the boys in this town."

A sense of relief washes over me. After her few comments about Dalton today, I would have been mortified if she'd even mentioned his name, especially because there is nothing going on between us.

HOW WE HATED

Maya falls back against the seat cushion, her body language proving she agrees. "Don't I hear that."

"But what about you and Ben?" I ask, surprising even myself that I went there.

She sighs. "He's my bud. It's not like that. Our moms were best friends, so we've been connected at the hip since we were born. We literally have pictures of us together as newborns. I feel like he's put this label on me though that screams to anyone, *She's not available.*" She looks off in space as she takes another drink. "Whatever. Just like you said, it's not like there's anyone else I'm pining over."

Just then, the guys enter the barn, seemingly larger than life as the four of them walk in a straight line, shoulder to shoulder, like the defensive line on a football team.

"Who's ready to party?" Ben yells out.

The sound of car tires along the gravel road catches my attention as lights sweeping across the barn shine brightly in my eyes.

Once a few more guys from the team trickle in, Ben heads to the stereo system and flips a button that blasts music all around us. "For the Glory" by All Good Things begins with their drawn-out techno-like beats.

Ben climbs on a chair, pounding on his chest as he yells out the lyrics, "*Better back down, you're in my domain. Got the whole crowd screaming out our name!*"

All the guys join in on singing the song about being champions and doing it all for the glory.

Watching them all bounce around, acting like fools as they celebrate their win, makes me laugh so hard, and by the end of the song, my cheeks hurt from smiling so big.

Ben screams out one more time once the song is over, then jumps down and heads to the fridge to get a drink.

I'm lost in the theatrics of it all, so I don't even notice Dalton is standing above me until he says, "You know that's my seat, right?"

I jump at the sound of his voice and feel my face flush when I look into his eyes. It takes me a second to remember that I do have a voice—or to even breathe—before I say, "You think I care?"

He lets out a surprised laugh, then picks me up, swinging me around until I'm sitting on his lap and he's sitting where I just was. His hand rests on my thigh, and I instantly jump up from the feeling of his touch.

"How dare you!" I yell.

He laughs as he holds his hands out to his sides. "I told you this was my spot."

Remembering him doing the same thing to Trish last time I was here fills me with disgust. She might have liked sitting on his lap, but not me.

"Ugh," I say as I roll my eyes and find a seat on the other couch, next to Susie.

When I look up, I see Trish staring at us, and I know she just saw all of that go down.

Don't worry, sweetheart; he's all yours.

The night goes on, and I'd be lying if I said I wasn't having a good time. Thankfully, Dalton has kept to his side of the party, sitting on the couch, while I've walked around and enjoyed the company of my fellow classmates.

HOW WE HATED

Wanting to get some lip balm from my purse, I head out to Ashley's car, where I left it. After grabbing it, I shut the door and am startled when I see Dalton sitting in the dark on the side of the carport that we're parked next to.

"You scared me." I place my hand on my chest to calm my breathing.

"Sorry," he responds nonchalantly. "I didn't mean to."

"What are you doing out here?" I ask as I approach him.

He holds the beer bottle in his hand and points it up to the sky. "Looking at the stars."

"By yourself?"

"Yeah. What's wrong with that? I just wanted some quiet for a second."

"Oh. Okay." I turn to head back to the party.

"Join me," he says, stopping me in my tracks.

"I thought you wanted to be alone."

"I said quiet. Not alone." He scooches over on the curb where he's sitting and pats his hand down, like he's giving me instructions to sit right there.

I don't know why, but I follow those instructions and sit next to him.

"Want a drink?" He offers me a sip of his beer.

"Nah, I'm good."

He leans back as he turns to the side to look at me. "You really are a good girl, aren't you?"

"If by good girl, you mean that I don't party or slut my way around school, then, yeah, I guess I am."

"Slut your way around school?" he questions my phrase.

I shrug. "That's the definition of a good girl, right?"

He raises and drops his shoulders quickly in agreement, nodding his head as he takes a sip of his beer, holding it with the tips of his fingers.

His feet are drawn in while he rests his arms on his knees and dangles the bottle between his legs. His massive frame is so different than mine as I sit, cross-legged with my knees inches off the ground, next to him on the curb.

"Good catch tonight," I say.

He glances my way. "Thanks. I didn't know you came to the games."

"Not all of them. But I went tonight."

"And what did you think?"

"It was fun. You guys played well."

"Dalton," Ben yells from the door of the barn where he can't see us. "Stop looking at the fucking stars, you weirdo, and get your ass back in here. We're about to start a game."

Dalton closes his eyes with a slight chuckle as he finishes his beer, then looks at me. "He knows me too well." He stands to his feet and looks down to where he's offering his hand to me. "You coming?"

I stare at his hand for a brief moment, then grab it and stand up myself. "Yeah, I'll be right there. I'm going to go get something from Ashley's car." I point to where I already was, hoping he doesn't realize I'm lying through my teeth.

"Cool." He nods his head and heads back inside while I walk to the car to do absolutely nothing but buy me time so people don't get the wrong idea when they see us walk back inside together.

CHAPTER 18

Natalie

Today, I had zero interaction with Dalton. Not in first period and definitely not in second period, where he sits directly behind me. It was like we were back to our same selves, completely ignoring the fact that the other person even existed.

I should be happy about that, but it doesn't explain why I'm sitting here at the end of my property, waiting for him to go for a run.

All day, I kept telling myself that I wasn't going to show up. He'd said nothing of it since Thursday night. He didn't mention it at the party when we were outside, and he hadn't reminded me today at school, yet here I am, waiting on him.

It makes no sense, even to me, but a part of me had to see if he would show up.

And I don't mean just for his run because he does that every night anyway.

HOW WE HATED

I mean, if he actually wanted me to run with him.

I can't get out of my head the question of, *Why? Why would he tell me to meet him here to run again?* I was horrible at it. He kicked my butt. But here I am, waiting like a fool, in capri workout pants that caught my eye when us girls went to the shopping center over the weekend.

Ashley and Susie both know I don't work out, and thankfully, they didn't ask why I suddenly wanted to invest in a pair of thirty-dollar pants that were only meant to do just that.

Without Dalton in sight, I hop off of Brandy and tie her to the fence that he fixed.

When I turn back around, my chest tightens at the sight of Dalton heading down the hill, across the river, and straight for me.

No words are said as he hands me one of his earbuds.

I pinch my eyebrows together in question as I take it from him.

"Running is better with music," he responds even though I didn't actually ask a question. He turns to leave and starts running away from me as he says over his shoulder, "Nice pants, by the way."

The fact that he noticed my pants fills me with excitement, then instantly pisses me off.

What the hell am I doing here? Why am I going to run with my sworn enemy? I need to leave.

He notices I'm not following him, so he stops and turns to face me. "You coming?"

Even though everything in my body is telling me I need to turn around and go back home, my feet move toward him instead of away, and before I know it, I'm standing by his side, putting his earbud in my ear, where I hear hard rock music blasting through it.

His nod is the only reaction I get from him before he turns back around and starts up the hill with me right behind him.

He takes it easier tonight with a good tempo and not the sprint that he had last time. We run up and down the hill through paths that I didn't even know existed, all while more rock music plays between the two of us, louder than I would want in just one ear.

When we get to a steep portion of a hill, I silently say a curse inside, thinking I might die if he takes me up there, and I want to hug him when he stops at the base.

I take a few seconds to catch my breath. Sweat drips down my forehead so I lift my shirt to wipe it dry. When our eyes meet, something electric bounces between the two of us, and I instantly drop my shirt, covering my stomach and I'm sure part of my sports bra too.

To change the mood, I go for my same old snarky type of comment. "I'm not going up that."

He nods. "Yes, you are. But don't worry. We'll walk it. I want to show you something."

He doesn't wait for my response and starts heading up the steep hill. Of course, I follow right behind him.

You would think walking up the hill would be easier than the running we were just doing, but it's absolutely not. My legs are burning, and my chest is tight as I force myself to look down, focusing on taking one step in front of the other while listening to the music playing through one ear to get me through it.

"You good?" he asks over his shoulder.

HOW WE HATED

"Yeah." I surprise even myself that I was able to get the word out. Thank God it's only one syllable.

I want so badly to stop. I need to stop to breathe, I need to give the fire in my legs a break, but I don't. I don't know why I refuse to let Dalton see me weak in any way, but he triggers a fire so deep inside me that I didn't even know it was there. When I'm with him like this, I push harder than I ever have before.

He takes off like a bat out of hell in front of me, and my insides instantly die at the thought of having to chase after him. Looking up, I'm filled with absolute relief when I see we're almost at the top and he just sprinted the last few feet up.

It takes everything in my soul to lift my legs higher and faster, but I do it, and in five seconds, I'm standing at the top of the hill, feeling like I'm going to die.

"Look around," I hear him say, but right now, all I can focus on is not having a panic attack as I suck in air that seemingly can't get in my body fast enough.

"I—" I hold up a finger while I'm bent over with my hands on my knees, trying to breathe. "Need—" I breathe some more.

To my dismay, I collapse on the ground with my arms open in a spread-eagle format before covering my face with one arm and trying to breathe more steadily.

Embarrassment washes over me, and I wait for the belittlement I'm sure is coming until I feel movement next to me.

When I turn my head, I see Dalton lying next to me in the same position. I watch as his chest bounces up and down while he tries to catch his breath as well.

"I swear these last two runs have pushed me more than my coach does," he says through heavy breaths.

I let out a hard laugh. "You mean you don't normally run like this?"

He matches my same laugh at his reaction. "No. These are normally my cooldowns after practice."

I flip to my side and slap his chest. "You jerk," I say more playfully than really meaning it.

He grabs my hand, holding it on his chest as he laughs harder. I feel his heart beating so fast. Tie that with the pure easiness of his laugh, and a feeling of comfort washes over me, calming my breath.

"I wanted to break you, but damn, girl, you don't quit."

When I realize he's still keeping my hand on his chest, a sensation of panic races through me, and I pull it away, sitting up fast and propping my knees up to rest my arms on them.

It's now that I take in where we are for the first time. "Wow," I say in honest amazement.

He lifts up and sits the same way I am. "Yeah. The view up here is amazing."

From here, you can see all of Leighton River and beyond. The sun is just starting to move down the sky, giving off pink, purple, and orange hues that mix in with the clouds floating above us.

We sit like this with silence between the two of us but music still blasting through our ears.

"Barbie Girl" by Aqua comes on, and I turn to him in question. "Is this really on your playlist?"

He starts laughing so hard that he falls backward and lands on his back while I sit and stare at him in

HOW WE HATED

confusion as the song talks about undressing the girl everywhere.

"The guys and I used to mess around to this song in the dugout during Little League," he finally gets out once he can talk.

"And you still listen to it?"

He sits up with the cheesiest grin on his face. "Let's just say it's nostalgic."

I close my eyes and shake my head ever so slightly. "Whatever you say."

He nudges my arm. "What? You don't have those songs that are ridiculous but bring back fun memories?"

"Of course I do, but I always thought that was more of a girl thing."

"Guys can't have funny songs too? Does that make us less manly or something?"

I nod. "Or something," I kid, causing him to nudge me again. "Hey, at least it's not 'I'm Too Sexy.' I would have died if I'd heard that."

He huffs out a laugh. "What is that?"

I slap my head with my palm. "Oh no. I'm going to create a monster with that one."

He takes out his phone and pulls up the YouTube app. "Who sings it?"

"I have no clue. It's crazy old."

I sit and watch as he types *I'm too sexy* in the search bar. Dalton turns the screen so I can see the first video that popped up is by Right Said Fred.

Just by the quality of the video and how old it looks, I inhale and close my eyes, not wanting to hear the crazy song right now, but knowing he'll never drop it, so I agree, "That has to be it."

He clicks on it, and the song starts right away without any ads. I chuckle to myself over that fact. Of course the tech guy has the paid YouTube subscription that I've always thought was a waste of money.

The familiar voice talking about being too sexy streams through my ear, making me instantly drop my head to my chest in giggles.

Dalton starts to dance next to me. "Hell yeah. I'm digging this one."

It's my turn to nudge him. "Oh no. Please stop. You and dancing do not mix."

He hops to his feet faster than I ever knew someone his build could do and starts shaking his butt to the music. I try to hide my enjoyment, but when he sticks his hands on his knees and starts to twerk, I bust out in laughter.

His expression lights up at my reaction, and he stops as he laughs at himself and looks back to his phone. "Okay, this song gets a little repetitive."

"You think?" I joke.

"But I saw this one on the list after it."

A dance beat plays through the AirPod, talking about, "*I work out.*" I glance up at him in question.

"Just wait." He grins.

When the song talks about being sexy and knowing it, I roll my eyes and drop my head back. "Oh jeez."

He holds out the phone to me so I can see the screen. "Don't you think I could pull this off?"

I look at it and feel like my eyes could pop out of my head at the sight of a guy in a Speedo bathing suit, slinging his junk back and forth.

HOW WE HATED

Dalton pulls the phone away from me and motions like he's going to strip his shorts and show me himself.

"No. Stop. Please don't." I cover my eyes while trying to hide my giggles.

"I'm just kidding."

I peek through my fingers to see him searching on his phone. "Let's play something a little more *our age* of music."

"What was that?"

"It's called 'Sexy and I Know It' by LMFAO."

"Dirt Road Anthem" by Jason Aldean begins slow with the guitar strings, and I instantly know the song and start singing quietly when the lyrics come on.

"Yeah, this is better for right now." He holds out his hand to me. "Come on. Let's head back."

I moan at the thought of moving as I raise my hand to meet his and he lifts me to my feet.

"Don't worry. We can walk back down."

I don't complain one bit as we slowly make our way down the hill, listening to some of my favorite songs all the way.

When we get to the river that separates our property, I remove the AirPod and hand it back to him. "That playlist was more my style," I say about the country tunes we just listened to.

"Yeah, that's my chill playlist. It's good for a cooldown after a workout."

"You have quite an eclectic taste in music."

"I like a little bit of everything. My grandpa taught me how to play guitar, so I like this type of music because I can play it on my acoustic."

My eyes widen in shock. "You know how to play the guitar?"

He grins almost proudly. "Sure do."

"How come you didn't tell me during our interview? I could have written about it."

He leans in slightly with his eyebrows raised. "Because you wouldn't ask me any questions."

I roll my eyes and blow him off. "You mean, this whole time, I could have had you show me how to play guitar instead of going on these crazy runs?"

"Yep." He pops his P like he means, *Your loss.*

"I still want to hear you play," I say without thinking it through first and instantly regret it.

What the hell am I doing? I've hated this guy for years. Have I forgotten that? Why am I even standing here with him right now?

"I'll bring it tomorrow. After our run, I'll play you some songs."

I cross my arms over my chest and lean back slightly. "Our run? What makes you think I'm going to continue to do this?"

He starts to make his way back up the hill to his house, but then he turns back to me and points to what I'm wearing. "When you bought those pants, I knew you were hooked. If you'd had those already, you would have worn them the first day. See you tomorrow."

I watch as he places the AirPod in his ear and runs up the hill, leaving me standing here, frustrated because I know he's right.

CHAPTER 19

Natalie

Why?

Why is it that all I can think about is our run tonight?

This isn't me. I normally think about Brandy or what needs to be done for FFA, but here I am, sitting in sixth period—which is my favorite class, by the way—just waiting for my day to be over.

It all makes no sense!

But it's my truth.

Every step I've taken this morning I've taken in agony. My legs are so sore; I didn't even know this kind of feeling could live within me. I dig my thumb into my thigh, where I feel a crazy knot that seems to just be getting worse, but it still doesn't make me want to not go tonight.

I don't like to run. I've never liked running. I would do everything in my power to not have to run the mile in PE, yet here I am, running for fun. Who does that?

HOW WE HATED

Dalton.

That's who.

This morning, in English, as he walked past my desk, he brushed my arm with his finger.

It was the simplest of touches and something I thought I was mistaken by, but when I looked up in question, his smooth reply of, "Morning," sent chills down my spine.

Then, in Econ, he tapped my shoulder and asked, "You won't flake on me tonight, will you?"

This rush of excitement raced through me so fast that I couldn't respond. Instead, I just shook my head as the bell rang, starting the class.

I've never been so thankful to turn around and pay attention to the teacher since I could just feel my face getting redder by the second and I didn't want him to see.

After class is over, I head out to my locker, where Ashley and Susie meet me.

"Finally, the day is over," Susie says as she falls back on the bank of lockers.

"Tough day?" I ask at her overdramatics.

"The worst." She stands up quickly, like the best idea just popped into her head. "Let's go to Fosters tonight. You know they do that milkshake deal on Tuesdays, and I could really go for a chocolate milkshake."

Marcus walks up behind Ashley, wrapping his arms around her waist.

"Sorry," Ashley says as she rests her head on Marcus's chest. "Marcus and I have plans after his practice."

"Boo." Susie motions to Ashley dismissively, then turns to me. "You'll go with me."

I bite the inside of my lip, trying to think of an excuse for why I can't go. "Sorry. I have to help my dad tonight."

One thing about owning the ranch is, none of my friends truly understand what all goes on there, so I could tell them a long list of chores, and they would believe any one on any given day. Thankfully, she doesn't pry about what I have to help him with tonight.

"You all suck." She stands up straight and holds her head high. "I'll just get milkshakes by myself."

"Ask Dalton to go with you," Marcus speaks up, making my head turn to him so fast that I think it causes whiplash. "He's addicted to those damn milkshakes."

"Hmm. Then, maybe I will."

"No," I blurt out and instantly want to slap myself for it. "We have the project we have to work on."

"Damn. How many times have you guys had to work on that?" Ashley asks.

I glance at Susie, and she's eyeing me suspiciously, so I look back at Ashley. "Hopefully, this is the last one."

"But what about your dad?" Susie asks, raising her eyebrows knowingly.

"We're just working over the phone. Thank God we don't have to meet in person again." I hope I answered that smoothly.

Marcus and Ashley are suddenly off in their own world, not even paying attention to my response, but Susie heard me loud and clear, and I don't think she's buying my lie one bit.

HOW WE HATED

I stare at the clock until it's time to go.

I went and bought a few more pairs of workout pants before I came home from school. Now that I've felt the difference firsthand between running in jean shorts or soft, formfitting leggings, I will never run in anything else but those.

When I arrive, I'm surprised to see Dalton already there standing next to a chair and a blanket set up, making me stop in my tracks.

What the hell is he doing?

He notices me from across the river and motions for me to cross to his side.

"What is all of this?" I ask when I get closer, hoping he doesn't hear how nervous I am all of a sudden.

He holds up his guitar. "I told you I would bring my guitar today."

"So ..." I pause and look around. "No running?"

He lets out a soft chuckle. "Nah. I figured your legs must be killing you. It's good to take a break. I also brought stuff to help you roll out."

"Roll out?" I ask, almost afraid to know what that means.

"Don't worry. It feels good most of the time and will help with the soreness."

I look down at his setup, impressed with all he brought. "Snacks too?"

A few bottles of Gatorade, bananas, and wrapped bars of some kind are sitting on the blanket haphazardly, like they were thrown down.

He shrugs like it's no big deal. "This is always what I eat after practice. Just brought some to share."

He sits on the chair, and I instantly give him sass. "What? You get a chair, and I don't?"

He quickly sits up. "You can have it."

I hold my hands out, palms facing him, waving them from side to side. "I'm kidding. The ground is fine."

"I only brought the chair so I could play. It's hard, playing on the floor."

"Makes sense." I grab a banana and peel it open.

Our eyes meet as I take a bite. A weird electricity flies through the air between us, making me turn my head to the side, pretending to see what kind of bars he brought. That's when I see the bag open with things inside that I've never seen before.

"What are those?"

He leans down and grabs a circular black pipe-looking thing that has little bumps all over it and is about five inches wide. Holding it up for me to see, he says, "This is how you roll out."

I raise my eyebrows in question. "Come again?"

He drops from the chair to his knees so he's right next to me. "Here. Lie down on your stomach."

"Excuse me?"

He laughs softly. "Trust me."

Two weeks ago, if Dalton Wick had told me to trust him, I would have slapped him in his face and ran as fast as possible away from him, not knowing what kind of stunt he would pull. So, how did I get to the point where I actually do trust him?

I cautiously lie on my stomach, keeping my eyes glued on him.

Okay, maybe I don't trust him as much as I thought I did.

"Now, take this"—he holds up the tube—"and roll it on your legs while your elbows are holding yourself up."

HOW WE HATED

He demonstrates where to roll it while still sitting on his knees, facing me.

He hands it to me, and I lift my body to place it under my quads. He gets even closer, and I swear my chest tightens so much that I have to pause to make sure I'm still breathing.

What is wrong with me?

"Now, use your arms to move your body up and down so you're rolling your leg on the roller."

"They got real creative with the name of this thing," I joke, trying to change whatever emotion I can't understand that is racing through my body.

He laughs out loud, which only makes the feelings inside me more intense with the sound of his deep baritone.

"Nope. No fancy name. But it gets the job done."

I follow his instructions and instantly feel a pain that hurts but weirdly feels good at the same time.

"Now, move your body around side to side and up and down until you feel spots that need to be rolled out."

I do as he said and squeal when I get to a spot that's exactly what he was talking about. "Oh God." I bite down. "Why does it hurt so good?"

He drops to his butt in laughter. "I love that. So true. It hurts so good." He pauses as he watches me roll up and down on this torture device. "Once you feel like you got that leg, just switch it to the other side. Then roll to your back and get your calves and hamstrings too."

I do everything he mentioned and experience the intense pain I just felt all over again on the opposite side.

Once I feel I've gotten both sides good, I move to

my back and roll my calves and hamstrings, which surprisingly hurt just as bad as my quads.

As I painfully roll over every tight muscle in my body, Dalton sits in silence, staring off at the land around us. He looks so peaceful as I sit here, causing extreme pain to myself.

After I feel like I've gotten everything good enough or I can't stand the torture anymore—those seem to go hand and hand right now—I grab the roller and sit back up, handing it to him.

"Do I want to know what else is in that bag?"

"Probably not, but you'll love me for it tomorrow when you aren't as sore. The second and third days are always the worst."

My eyes open wide. "How can it get any worse than it already is?"

He grins a devilish grin. "Oh, just wait. Maybe I won't help you now so you can experience the pain for yourself."

I throw my hands toward him. "Gimme!"

He hands me a device that literally has Rollerblade wheels on either side and opens up just enough to get my leg through. I'm intrigued just as much as I'm terrified.

"Now that you've broken up the first layer, this sucker will get in there and really get those knots. Here, sit here."

We both get up, and I sit on the chair while he kneels next to me.

When he places his hand on my leg, my eyes instantly meet his. We stare at each other for a breath too long, but for the life of me, I can't look away.

HOW WE HATED

"Whatever you do, don't kick me."

I laugh out loud. "Then, don't do something that would make me want to kick you."

"Just like you said, 'It hurts so good.' Just trust me and don't forget to breathe."

He opens the device wide and slides it onto my leg. The damn thing is so tight that I'm afraid it's going to squeeze my leg to death, if such a thing could ever happen.

"Ready?" he asks, looking straight into my eyes.

I nod, and he starts to roll this new torture device slowly up my leg. Without thinking, I instantly jolt out my arms to grab his shoulders; the tank top he's wearing allows my fingers to dig into his bare skin.

"Oh my God."

He chuckles under his breath. "Breathe."

I keep my hands on him as he rolls it up and down my leg. When he gets to a spot that hurts, I squeeze him harder, and when he moves on to where I don't have knots, I loosen my grip. He does this up and down both legs, going side to side for a few minutes, before he pops the device off my leg and sits back on his heels.

The distance between us makes me lose my grip on him, and I drop my hands to my lap.

"How's that feel?" he asks.

"Horrible and amazing at the same time."

He laughs with a smile. "Yep, that pretty much sums it up."

When I see the marks I just left on his shoulder, I gulp in a ton of air and cover my mouth in embarrassment. "I'm so sorry."

He checks out my work, then blows them off. "All

good. Not the first time a girl has dug her nails into my back."

In shock at what he just said, I push him farther away from me.

He laughs. "I'm kidding."

I stand up and bring my foot to my butt to stretch out my quads more.

He stands as well. "Just continue to move and stretch the next few days, and it won't be so bad."

I walk around our little area he set up to get the feeling back in my legs while he gets up to grab his guitar before sitting back in the chair.

With my back to him, I raise my arms in the sky, leaning from side to side to stretch out my body. It's rare that I see this view of our ranch. How massive it is, how empty it is, and, really, how sad it's become.

I wonder what was going through his head as he stared off into space the same way I am now. Does he even know the damage his family has caused?

Feelings of guilt wash over me. I shouldn't be here with him. My dad would be so upset, hurt even, knowing I'm even giving Dalton a second of my time.

Him strumming on the guitar breaks my rabbit-hole thoughts I was going down, and I turn to face him.

His eyes are closed as he plays a tune I've heard before, but can't put my finger on. He looks so intense about what he's doing, but at the same time very peaceful, like this is special to him.

The more I watch, the more I'm entranced by him, by his presence, by his grace, and I slowly move closer to him.

I need to leave.

HOW WE HATED

"So, um ... if we're not going to run, I need to go get some chores done."

He drops the guitar and instantly stands up, almost knocking me over. I didn't even realize I had gotten that close to him until he's gripping me for balance and mere inches from my face.

We stare at each other like this. Neither of us blinking. Me having to bend my neck to meet his height and him looking straight down at me like he's about to devour me.

His eyes dart from my eyes to my lips.

I suddenly can't breathe. I don't know if it's fear, excitement, curiosity or what, but I'm so lost in his eyes that I feel like time has slowed down indefinitely and it's just him and I right now.

He licks his lips, and I instantly know what emotions I'm feeling.

It's fear.

Fear of what we're doing.

Fear of knowing it's wrong.

Fear of not wanting to stop it.

I sense him moving even closer, and I instantly bolt back.

"I've got to go," I state firmly, keeping my eyes locked with his for a moment longer, then turning and racing back to my side of the river.

No matter how much it kills me, I don't dare glance back at him as I untie Brandy, hop on, and ride back to my house, where I'm safe from these feelings for Dalton Wick.

CHAPTER 20

Natalie

When I got home last night, I already had a text from him. My heart pounded like crazy as I stared at his name, not wanting to open it up, but dying to know what he had to say.

Finally getting the nerve, I swiped his name and saw all he texted was:

Take an Epsom salt bath. That will help too.

I threw my phone on my bed and went to take a shower, hoping to rid my mind of anything that might lead to me thinking about Dalton.

It didn't work. I tossed and turned all night long and had to drag my butt to school this morning.

Thankfully, first period has us break up into groups with the people we're sitting next to, so I am able to

HOW WE HATED

avoid him, but as I walk into second period, my stomach turns with emotions I'm not ready to face, knowing he'll be right behind me.

He's not there as I enter so I sit down and busy myself with my backpack that I placed down on the opposite side of the row he'll walk through so my back will be facing him as he arrives.

I feel his presence around me as he slides into the desk behind me. I keep my composure, searching really hard for nothing at all.

The bell rings, and our teacher gets the class's attention, so I stop what I'm doing and face forward, forcing myself to breathe but having a hard time doing so, knowing he is behind me.

Miss Hernandez starts her lecture by writing something on the board, so I move my phone that's sitting on my notebook to the side and open it to a clean piece of paper to take notes.

I nearly jump out of my seat when I hear the familiar buzz of an incoming message on my phone.

Everyone I know is in school, and my parents never text me, so worry races through me as I wonder if something is wrong with them. Frantic, I pick it up and am blasted with a different set of emotions when I see Dalton's name on the screen.

He's literally texting me while he's sitting behind me. There's no way I can ignore it. He's physically watching me as I stare at his name, not swiping to see what he said.

When the phone goes off again with another text, causing me to twitch, I decide to swipe it open.

Why did you leave so fast?

I'll keep texting until you answer.

I close my eyes, not wanting him to see my reaction, but knowing it's almost impossible with him right behind me. When I don't respond, he texts again.

I wanted to kiss you.

I try my hardest not to move a centimeter, in fear that he'll notice the way I can barely breathe at the sight of his words.

I can see the goose bumps on your arm.

You wanted to kiss me too.

I can't take it anymore. I drop my phone face down with a huff, keeping my hand over it as I force myself to take a deep breath. The commotion I caused makes everyone, including Miss Hernandez, look my way.
"Everything okay, Natalie?" she asks.
"Uh-huh." I nod, not able to say anything else.
She sighs and gets back to her lesson as I hear Dalton chuckle under his breath behind me.
He doesn't say anything for the rest of class. As soon as the bell rings, I stand up and race to the restroom, hiding in there until third period starts.
Lunch comes around, and I say a silent curse when I remember that Ashley is dating Marcus. This never

HOW WE HATED

really was an issue until today, when it gives Dalton an excuse to come sit with us.

"What's up, my man?" Marcus says as they slap hands.

"Mind if I join you guys?" Dalton asks, sliding into the bench seat and not waiting for a response.

I want to scream out, *Yes, I mind. You can't sit here*, but I know that would only bring more attention to us, especially because I'm on the opposite end of where he just sat.

Susie nudges me with her leg, but I try to blow it off as I dig into my lunch bag to remind myself of what I brought.

Yes, we've hated each other for years, but we could stand being around each other in some situations. We've learned this silent way of ignoring the fact that the other exists, only now, there's no way for me to ignore the seemingly grown man who's sitting at the end of the table, causing my hunger to disappear in a matter of seconds.

It's like he's taunting me now.

He couldn't have sat farther away from me, especially when the space directly in front of me was open.

So, if he is here for me, why didn't he sit there?

"Earth to Natalie," Susie says, taking me from my trance.

I turn my head to face her and instantly lock eyes with Dalton. Just seeing his lips lift ever so slightly to the side in a knowing grin frustrates the hell out of me.

"Yeah," I say, forcing myself to give Susie my full attention.

She's talking, but I hear nothing as I see Dalton out

of the corner of my eye. Frustrated, I stand up and walk to the other side of the table so I'm facing her, making it impossible to see Dalton.

In my head, my movement was graceful, silent, but the way the entire table is looking at me proves it was anything but.

Okay, I might have gotten up with a huff while Susie was mid-sentence, and I might have slammed my hand down on the table as I stepped my foot in, followed by the other.

I close my eyes in embarrassment.

Why does he do this to me?

"You okay?" Ashley asks, who's now sitting directly next to me.

"Yeah, I just didn't want to sit, turned like that." I give my attention back to Susie. "Sorry, you were saying?"

Again, I don't fully take in what she's talking about because my brain is trying to focus more on Dalton's voice and the conversation he and Marcus are having.

"Yeah." I nod to Susie, feeling like I need to engage with her so I'm not too obvious.

She closes her eyes and shakes her head, her eyes roaming to Dalton and then back to me.

I must have done something wrong because she stops our conversation altogether.

Seemingly to torture me more, she asks Dalton a question. "So, Dalton, you've never joined us for lunch before. What's new?"

My eyes widen as I watch Susie try to hide her laugh.

"Not much. Ashley has hijacked my friend here. Figured if I wanted to hang out with him, I needed to be over here."

HOW WE HATED

She shrugs. "Good reason."

It's my turn to nudge her, but my nudge comes off more as a kick under the table. Instead of saying *ow* or making a big deal that I hurt her, she laughs—hard.

"What's so funny?" Ashley asks.

"Oh, nothing." Susie stares at me, causing me to get even more frustrated.

I'm alone in the FFA area after school, trying to clean up … or busying myself so I don't think of Dalton—no difference really.

I hum to the sounds of "Tennessee Orange" by Megan Moroney that starts to play through my AirPods, and it hits me so hard.

The entire song is about going against your family's wishes for a guy.

Talk about perfect timing for this one.

Yes, the song is about cheering for Tennessee football instead of Georgia, but I feel like it's talking about my own situation here. People in the South take their college football seriously—obviously, if there's an entire song that starts off with, "*Don't ya tell daddy, he'll blow a fuse.*"

Ain't that the truth?

If my dad even knew that I was hanging out with Dalton, I don't know what he'd do. I'm afraid to find out.

I can't find out.

That's why I need to just stop whatever is going

on and go back to my life before him, before this little project we were forced to work on.

I close my eyes and sing, "*But I'm wearing Tennessee orange for him,*" feeling it deep in my soul.

"You'd wear it for me, wouldn't you?" I hear behind me and almost completely jump out of my shoes.

I turn to see Dalton standing a few feet behind me, staring at me intensely. He's dressed in his football pads and carrying his helmet.

He slowly steps closer to me. "Would you go against your father's wishes and wear Tennessee orange if I played there?"

"What are you doing here?"

"You didn't answer the question."

He's right next to me now, towering over me. I have to tilt my head up just to be able to see him.

"No, I wouldn't," I state, hoping I sound as secure as I'm trying to play off.

"Liar."

"You didn't answer my question." I change the subject and turn it back on him.

He raises his eyebrows like he didn't know I'd asked one, so I say it again. "What are you doing here?"

"I told Coach I had to get something out of my truck." He places his hand on my hair, moving down slowly to remove the AirPod I have in my ear.

I try to act unfazed by his presence, his touch.

"Your truck isn't back here anymore."

"I know."

He doesn't elaborate as we stare in silence, only inches away from each other.

My heart pounds and breathing has become

HOW WE HATED

something I'm not sure I can do anymore. My eyes are burning, but I'm afraid if I do anything—even something as little as blinking—this last wall between us will burst down, and we'll do something we can't come back from.

"I will kiss you at some point," he states matter-of-factly making my stomach flip on its side with fear and anticipation.

"No, you won't," I respond in barely above a whisper.

He parts his lips, coming even closer to me.

I should push him away.

I want to push him away.

But I don't.

I stand there like a complete idiot, allowing him to control the situation.

"I will," he whispers, placing the AirPod in my hand. Then, he backs up and walks away, leaving me standing there with my head tilted back, my lips parted, and my heart pounding.

I close my eyes and take a deep breath.

"I might have to look into Tennessee football now just to prove my point," he shouts over his shoulder.

"Ugh!" I yell out and stomp my feet in frustration now that I've been broken from the Wick spell.

What is wrong with me?

CHAPTER 21

Natalie

It takes everything in my power to not head to the river to meet Dalton tonight. I keep telling myself that he never said to, so why should I? I'm lying on my bed, convinced I did the right thing until I get a text.

Why aren't you here?

> **Why would you assume I would be?**
> **We never said we would meet tonight.**

My stomach turns as I watch the three little bubbles dance on my screen, waiting for his reply.

We need to talk.

> **About what?**

HOW WE HATED

You know what. Come down here.

I stare at his text, then put the phone face down on my bed.

Of course, I know what he means, but seeing it in writing makes it feel even more real. He's right though. Something is happening between us. I need to put a stop to it before it goes any further.

My phone dings again, and I panic when I read the text.

I can come there if you think that's better.

I jump off my bed, my heart feeling like a teen is beating on it in the drumline. He most definitely cannot come here.

I'm on my way.

I exit my room and go down the hall to where my mom is working on a quilting project.

"Mom, I'm going for a ride," I say, leaning in the door.

"Okay, sweetie." She glances up at me and pauses. "Everything okay? You look a little flush."

I internally roll my eyes at the way my own body continues to betray me.

"Yeah. I just got a little frustrated with my schoolwork. I'll be fine when I get back."

She smiles, and I head out of the house and toward the barn, feeling good that I technically didn't lie to her.

This all started because of my schoolwork, and I intend to end it now.

I ride out to the river and am startled when I see Dalton on my side of the property, working on the fence again.

"What are you doing?" I ask as I hop off of Brandy.

"You left me here, waiting, so I thought I would straighten the rest of the boards as much as I could without tools."

He walks toward me, and I take a guarded step back.

"Just stay there." I hold up my palm to face him.

He doesn't listen. "Why?"

"You know why."

"No, I don't. Tell me."

I take a few more steps back. "You know this can't happen, so just stop it now."

"Stop what?" He's wearing the smuggest expression as he steps within a few feet of me.

"Dalton."

"Natalie."

The way he says my name sends chills throughout my entire body.

Why does my name sound so different when it comes from his lips?

Lips I've despised for years.

Lips I thought were disgusting when other girls would say how cute he was.

Lips that I can't stop thinking about now.

"This will never work," I whisper, not able to raise my voice any louder.

He's so close that I place my hand on his chest

HOW WE HATED

and feel the way his heart is pounding out of control, matching my own.

He's just as nervous as I am. The cocky, arrogant Dalton Wick is having the same reaction to me as I am to him.

How is this possible?

This isn't us.

We shouldn't be standing here like this.

"What will never work?"

He's going to make me say it. He's going to make me admit that I do have feelings for him. That I do want him to kiss me right now.

I blink and look up, meeting his eyes and his molten stare. "Us."

He doesn't budge or show any emotion to what I just said.

"We can't do this," I barely get the words out, my breathing is so labored.

"I thought you were competitive."

His words confuse my already discombobulated thoughts. It takes a minute for it to compute in my brain. Squinting my eyes and shaking my head, I ask, "What?"

He brings his hands up to my arms, griping me, not tightly but firmly enough that I feel his emotions coming from his fingertips directly to my soul.

"Fight for us," he says with so much determination I almost lose it all together.

I feel like I'm the football player and coach just gave the most inspiring speech to get us pumped for what's to come, yet it was only three little words that came out of his mouth.

My eyes bounce back and forth, like a tennis match of indecisiveness, as I stare into his gaze.

His tongue slowly moves across his mouth with confidence, like he's a trained soldier preparing for battle, making my entire body go weak.

I close my eyes and take a deep breath, forcing myself to clear my mind and remember my family, my parents, and how wrong this is.

"I can't." I open my eyes and am locked with his. "We can't," is what I say, but my body is once again betraying me. Though those words just came out of my mouth, my body is screaming, *Yes.*

With so much determination, he says, "Watch me," and his lips crash into mine.

Electricity shoots from my lips to my toes as I raise my arms to wrap around his neck, afraid that if I don't, I might fall to the ground.

The stability he gives me as he brings his arms around my waist and lifts me slightly to meet his height only fuels our fire more as our tongues move around each other in a seductive dance for the first time.

I pull him closer to me as I run my fingers through his hair.

My chest is so tight that I feel like I can't breathe, yet the only air I need is him.

A gunshot rings out through the air, causing my entire body to stiffen in a fear I've never felt before.

My dad.

I jump away from Dalton and search around us for any sign of somebody who saw that.

Dalton holds out his hand. "It's okay. It was probably just someone hunting."

HOW WE HATED

Panic washes over me as all the blood seemingly leaves my body. I wrap my arms around myself, hating the feeling of cold that's covering me now that his warmth is gone.

I shake my head. "No. No. No," I repeat, not sure if I'm saying it out loud or only in my mind.

My eyes meet him again. He's so gentle, holding out his hand to me in a caring way, which only causes my internal struggle more.

"I told you, we can't do this." I storm past him to Brandy and put my leg in the strap.

He stops me before I can get on by putting his hands on my waist and pressing his body into my back.

"Don't fight this," he whispers into my ear.

I gulp in air and close my eyes, leaning back into him. His touch is soothing the worry within me, but then I snap back to reality and remember that it's his touch that is causing this pain.

I grab for the reins and push him off of me so I can jump up.

"We just can't," I bite out, my voice cracking from the tears that are forming.

I kick my heels into Brandy and turn the reins to point her back to my house.

Where I belong.

No matter how much I try to stop myself, I look back, only to see Dalton standing there in shock as I ride away with uncontrollable tears racing down my face.

CHAPTER 22

Dalton

Fuck!

I stand here in shock as I watch Natalie race away from what was no doubt the most amazing kiss ever.

I know she's scared. Hell, I am too. I've never felt this way about a girl. I don't understand why she's fighting this so much.

It's obvious there's something between us. That kiss more than proved it.

I know our families have history, but that's their problem, not ours. There's no reason why that should stop us from being together.

I turn in frustration, cross the riverbed, and head straight up the hill for my run. If there was ever a day that I needed an ass-kicking, it's right now.

I run until my legs burn and I can barely catch my breath.

HOW WE HATED

Stopping on top of the hill, I drop to the ground, pain radiating through my entire body. Trying to calm my breath, all I can think about is that kiss, which is making my heart pound for another reason.

The sun begins to set so I drag my ass off the ground and slowly make my way back to my house.

"Have a good run?" Mom asks as I enter the house.

"No," I bite out.

She stares at me for a beat, then raises her eyebrows, feigning interest in my life, which is rare. "Want to talk about it?"

I grab one of the premade protein drinks out of the fridge and slam it shut. "No. I'm going to go take a shower."

She doesn't say anything else, which doesn't surprise me. She barely asks questions or engages in my life. As her youngest child who's about to graduate, I sometimes think she has senioritis more than I do.

I step in the shower when it's still freezing cold, letting what feels like icy shards of water pound on my sore body. Closing my eyes, I relish in the feeling of the water slowly getting warmer, wondering what Natalie is doing right now.

After I finish my shower, I dry off, get dressed, and plop down on my bed with my phone in my hand, ready to figure out what is going on.

Why are you fighting this?

Bubbles instantly appear and disappear a few times, but I don't send another text. I wait for her reply. I've had enough with the games between us.

You know why.

No. I don't. Tell me.

Our families will never approve.

Fuck our families. This is our lives not theirs.

Easy for you to say. I care about what my father thinks. Don't you care what your father thinks?

No. He's never cared about me a day in his life.

I'm sorry to hear that.

It's the truth.

We just need to stop.

You obviously want this.

There's a pause in our conversation, and I would kill to know what's going through her head right now. When she doesn't respond, I text back.

I fight for what I want and I want you.

I don't wait for a reply. I said what I needed to say. There's no way this is over. It's just getting started.

HOW WE HATED

The next day, I head to our classroom early so I'm standing at the door before she arrives. As she walks up, I watch the way her breath catches when she sees me. That's all the confirmation I need.

She tries to enter the classroom, but I block her way. Keeping her head down, she tries again to step beside me. Being this big of a guy has its advantages, as there's no way she can go by me. She has no other option but to look up at me.

I feel the hesitation falling off of her as she slowly meets my eyes and her shoulders fall. She's sad, and that breaks my heart, but it fuels me even more.

No one should stand between us.

No one.

I lean down so only she can hear me. "You're about to find out just how competitive I truly can be," I whisper to her.

Her breath hitches, and she blinks a few times, but doesn't respond.

I see other classmates heading our way, so I move, letting her enter the room and following in behind her.

When class is over, she exits faster than anyone would if the building were on fire. Internally, I just laugh. She thinks she can get away now, but she must have forgotten that I sit behind her in the next class. I'll let her have this win, so without a care in the world, I make my way out of the class to the couches.

"What's that smug expression you're wearing this morning?" Maya asks as she sits next to me.

I grin and look at her out of the side of my eye. "Just having a good morning so far."

She raises her eyebrows in surprise. "Anything in particular?"

I wink but keep my mouth shut as Ben lifts her before putting her on his lap.

"What are you guys talking about?" Ben asks.

"Dalton here is having a good morning, and it makes me wonder why—or rather, who is causing this good morning," Maya says with a grin.

Ben narrows his eyes, then questions, "What girl are you fucking now?"

Maya slaps his chest. "Don't be so nasty."

He grabs her ass and legs. "It's not nasty. It's amazing."

She blows him off, then looks at me like she's expecting an answer.

I don't reply, so Ben takes that as his cue.

"Ah, he's not fucking her yet. So, the question is, who are you trying to fuck?"

Maya slaps his chest again, but this time, he grabs her hand and keeps it on his heart.

I raise my eyebrows in confirmation, and Maya squeals.

"Oh, let me guess who!" She looks around, searching for the culprit.

"And just like that, I'm out." I slap my palms on my knees and stand up. "You two have fun."

"I'm going to find out who!" Maya yells.

I chuckle to myself without turning around and head to my second period class, anxious to go play with Natalie more.

HOW WE HATED

Natalie

I sit in the restroom stall until the last bell rings. It will be the first tardy I've ever gotten, but I don't care right now. My plan is to slip into class late and pray to God Dalton leaves me alone.

I close my eyes, inhale a deep breath, and exit the stall, heading straight for my second period class.

"You're late, Miss Spencer," Miss Hernandez says.

"Sorry," I mumble as I head to my desk, keeping my head down so I don't make eye contact with Dalton.

I slide into my desk and release the air I was holding, glad I made it in without seeing him.

Miss Hernandez turns to the board to write something, and chills instantly run down my entire body when I feel Dalton lean forward and whisper, "Did you really think you could hide all day in the bathroom?"

I sit there, still as can be, trying to act unaffected from him being so close.

Trying being the operative word.

"Meet me tonight."

"No," I force out in a whisper.

"Then, I'll knock on your front door and ask your dad for his permission to date his daughter."

I totally forget where I am and turn to face him so fast that I knock my notebook on the ground. "No!"

His smug expression makes me want to slap him silly.

"Excuse me, Miss Spencer?" Miss Hernandez asks, bringing me back to reality.

I face her, embarrassed. "Sorry, Dalton kept kicking my chair," I lie.

"Dalton, keep your hands and feet to yourself," Miss Hernandez replies, then goes back to writing something on the board.

"I'll keep my feet to myself, but there's no telling what my hands will want to do," Dalton whispers before he leans back in his chair, his long legs stretched out to the side of my chair, like he doesn't have a care in the world.

When his leg brushes against mine, goose bumps race over my skin so fast that I have to reposition my seating, almost afraid of what else his touch will do to me.

I close my eyes in frustration, but not because of his words. I'm frustrated at the way my body reacted to the idea of his hands doing things they shouldn't—to me.

I stare at my phone the entire afternoon. Even though I keep telling myself I won't go meet him, I keep checking my phone to see if it's time to go yet.

I'm so screwed.

Focusing on my homework is impossible, though I try my hardest to push every thought of Dalton out of my head and stay on the task at hand.

That is, until I see the clock, and without a second

HOW WE HATED

thought, I jump off my bed and head straight for the door.

I'm royally screwed.

No one is in the kitchen or living room, so I sneak out the back door, only to swing the door open with too much force—directly into my mom, who's walking back into the house.

"Oh. Sorry." I stumble to get my bearings.

"You okay, sweetheart?" Mom says as she moves my hair off my face to see me better.

"Yeah. I, um ... I was just frustrated with my homework again. I need to get out and go for a ride to clear my head."

She smiles sweetly, making me feel bad for lying to her. "That's not like you. What class is giving you so much trouble?"

I open my arms and hug her, silently apologizing for having lied so much lately—something I've never done before. "I'll figure it out," I say.

"Okay. Let me know if you need help when you get back."

I turn and close my eyes, taking a deep breath. *I'm a terrible daughter.*

I don't say anything else because I can't bring myself to actually speak.

What am I doing?

My entire life, I've been told how horrible TimeLand is, and the extensive damage Mike Wick, Dalton's dad, caused to our ranch. Yet here I am, lying to my mom to go see Dalton.

With every step I take, I keep telling myself to turn around, but as I throw my leg over Brandy, I learn firsthand just how much stronger my heart is than my brain. As I kick my legs against her to get her to go faster, I feel like I'm crossing a line that I know I'll never come back from.

Yet I go anyway.

When I arrive, Dalton is already there, standing like an armed guard with his legs wide, arms folded across his chest, and a stern expression I can see from hundreds of yards away.

I ride Brandy to him and dismount her, holding on to her reins. He doesn't move an inch, and neither of us says a word as I step closer to him.

When I'm two feet away, he nods his head ever so slightly, breaking his statue-like stance. "You came."

I nod, inhaling a shaky breath.

"You know what this means?" he asks, his face not changing one bit.

I nod again, but don't dare speak it into existence, still afraid if I say the words out loud, I might crumble.

He unfolds his arms and steps toward me with a small grin. "Good," is all he says right before he wraps his hand around the back of my head and brings me to him, crashing his lips into mine.

Electricity shoots down my spine and through all my limbs. I fall limp in his arms, allowing him to take full control of me, of us, and the situation we've found ourselves in.

I have no idea how this is going to work, but I'll be damned now if I do anything to stop it. I'm helpless in his arms, yet there's nowhere else I'd rather be.

CHAPTER 23

Natalie

I stayed with Dalton until it got dark last night. I don't know why, but I felt like once I left there, everything would be different. I'm not going to lie; the thought still terrifies me.

Now that I'm walking into school, I have no clue what to expect.

Yes, we want to be together, but that doesn't change anything about my dad not approving. Because he will not.

Last night, I wanted to live in our little bubble and ignore that fact. I'm glad neither one of us ruined the vibe we had going by bringing it up, but today, we have to face it head-on.

I walk into first period, seeing he's not there yet. Sitting at my desk, I gather my things from my bag and am startled when I feel someone brush their hand

HOW WE HATED

down my arm. Instantly, I sit up and see that Dalton just walked by. Though he's acting like he did nothing, my body knows it was him by the chills still rushing through me.

Once he sits down, I turn to ask the person behind me if they have a pen I can borrow, just so I can see him. As they search for a pen, my eyes meet his, and my heart sings when his lips tilt into a small smile.

After class, I head to the hallway, where Susie is standing.

"Morning," I say.

Susie eyes me suspiciously. "Morning. Aren't you chipper today?"

I shrug, meaning to say something, only to have my thoughts erased when Dalton exits the classroom, and I'm suddenly speechless.

He walks by me, closer than he probably should. His hand brushes against mine for a brief second before he's gone.

It was so quick that I even question if it really happened—that is, until I see Susie's expression.

With her eyebrows raised, she steps closer to me and whispers, "Did that really just happen?"

I jerk my hand up, pretending I was playing with my hair the entire time and she saw nothing. "What just happened?"

"Ha!" She holds her hands up in defeat. "You know exactly what I'm talking about, but if you're pretending it didn't happen, I will too. Lord knows you should definitely keep whatever is going on between you two to yourself."

Her words make my stomach turn.

She's so right, but I can't help it.

She notices the way I'm stuck in thought while biting my lip and places her hand on my shoulder. "Hey. I couldn't give two shits if you guys are into each other. I have nothing to do with either of your families. I don't even really know why you guys hate each other so much. Just be careful, okay? I don't want to see you get hurt by him or your dad because that's the only way this can really go. You know that, right?"

I close my eyes and nod.

"I don't blame you. He's hot. I get it. Have fun while it lasts, but just know, it can't last, so don't get in too deep, okay?"

I nod again, and she gives me a hug.

"Off to second period I go. Be good," she singsongs. "Or don't. Just don't get caught."

She laughs as I turn to drop my back and head against the lockers, knowing I'm so screwed, yet I won't do anything to stop it.

When I walk into second period, Dalton is already sitting at his desk, eyeing me as I make my way through the classroom and sit directly in front of him.

He leans forward. "You smell so good. Funny how it used to piss me off when you walked in, and now, I'm so turned on that I hope I don't get called to the board."

I laugh out loud, then cover my mouth, pretending that I'm coughing and praying no one is paying enough attention to care. They aren't.

I cannot focus for anything during the entire class with him behind me, no matter how hard I try. Playing footsie takes on a different meaning throughout the class when his long legs keep invading my space. I used

HOW WE HATED

to kick them away, but now, I crave the touch of them against my feet.

How could we make a one-eighty like this?

The thought makes me laugh as the bell rings. Dalton stands up first and runs his fingers along my bare shoulder as he walks by. I take a second to gather myself before leaving, suddenly bummed, knowing I probably won't see him for the rest of the day.

At lunch, I sit with Susie and Ashley.

"Where's Marcus?" I ask Ashley.

Susie lets out a harsh laugh, and I want to slap my forehead for how obvious I must be.

Thankfully, Ashley doesn't catch on. "They have a meeting for tonight's game. You guys are coming, right?"

"I'm in, but we might have to drag Natalie out of her house, kicking and screaming, to go with us. You know she hates going to watch the guys play football," Susie says, trying her hardest to be serious but knowing I want to smack her.

Ashley turns to beg me, "Oh, please come. It was so much fun last week."

"Yes, please come for us and no one else, not even your brother who will be on the field as well," Susie teases.

I fake a sigh. "Fine, I'll go."

Ashley squeals her excitement before turning back to her lunch.

"I'll bring eye black to put numbers on our faces. I know Ashley will be wearing number twenty-four. What about you, Natalie? What number shall we put on your face?" Susie jokes some more, making me want to kick her.

"We can just put *LRH*," I state clearly, asking her with my eyes to stop.

She hides her laugh. "Okay, and some paws too."

"That's fine."

We eat our lunch and continue to chat, but my eyes are glued to the locker room door that's off the quad at our school. If they are having a team meeting, then the meeting must be in there.

When the doors open, I freeze as I watch all the guys pile out, looking pumped for the game tonight.

Marcus heads straight for our table, and I've never been so happy that he and Ashley are dating because it gives Dalton an excuse to walk here too.

"Hey, baby," Marcus says to Ashley as he slides in next to her.

When they kiss, I instantly look at Dalton. Seeing him stare at me with this deep lust I've never seen before on anybody makes my heart pound out of control.

I hate that he's keeping his distance from me, but, on the other hand, I'm glad he is. We might have been all over each other last night, but nothing has been discussed on how we would handle us being an us, especially with my brother at this same school. For now, we will continue to pretend we still hate each other, like we have since we were little.

The warning bell rings, and Dalton says goodbye to Marcus before raising his eyebrows the tiniest bit to me and walking off.

Ashley heads off to class with Marcus while Susie

HOW WE HATED

practically jumps on me, squealing with excitement, "Please tell me you've kissed him."

I drop my chin with laughter, not able to hide my huge smile.

"Oh my God, you have!" She slaps my arm. "I can't believe you. It's like you're a whole new person."

I sag my shoulders. "I know. I don't know what he's doing to me, but I can't stop it."

"Um, no. Please don't stop anything. He's Dalton freaking Wick. Do I need to remind you how many girls would die to be in your shoes right now?"

"But would they really? My shoes in particular?" I tilt my head in question, hoping she gets my drift.

She blows me off. "Whatever. Screw your parents. Or rather, please screw him and then tell me all about it."

Now, it's my turn to slap her arm playfully. "Slow your roll. Last week, he was still my sworn enemy."

"And now, he's your secret lover," she drawls out her words with a little shimmy to her hips.

I laugh at her antics, but also at the fact that I can't believe it myself.

Dalton Wick and I are secret lovers.

How the hell did this even happen?

CHAPTER 24

Natalie

"I'm so glad you're coming tonight!" Ashley says as I hop in her back seat.

Susie turns to me with a sly grin on her face, but thankfully doesn't say anything. I feel bad for not telling Ashley, but I need to figure out what's really going on before we tell the world. There are a lot of other things that we have at stake here that other people don't have to deal with.

Ashley drives away as a rush of excitement races through me. I know I won't actually get to talk to Dalton until after the game, but knowing I'm going to go see him play is doing weird things to my insides that I'm not used to.

I hop out of the car after we get to the school, and Susie stops me before I can walk toward the entrance.

"First, we need to decorate your face."

HOW WE HATED

I hold my chin up high and to the side so she can get a good view of the area she's going to decorate.

"Number ... eighty ... one ..." she says slowly as she draws on my face.

"Susie!" I stop her, and she breaks out laughing.

"What's so funny?" Ashley asks.

"I told Natalie I was drawing a dick on her face, and she believed me," Susie responds, making me narrow my eyes at her. "Chill. It's just a paw print."

Once she's finished, we head to the gate with our prepaid tickets up and ready to scan on our phones.

Entering the gates suddenly feels very different. In the past, when I came to a football game, it was because I had been basically forced to by either my friends or my parents to support my brother. Now, I get the level of thrill other people feel, and it makes me a little sad I've waited until my senior year to get to this point.

We grab some sodas, then head toward the stands to sit in the student section with just a few minutes to spare before the kickoff.

"Um, I think someone is looking for you." Susie nudges me, and when I look out onto the field, I see Dalton turned to face us, scanning the crowd.

"Woo! Go, Dalton!" Susie yells at the top of her lungs as she waves her hands in the air.

I grab her, but not in time because Dalton stares right at us, a huge smile growing across his face.

Seeming satisfied that he found us—or me rather—he turns to face the field and slides his helmet over his head.

"Oh, this is so much fun," Susie says, grabbing me to show her joy.

When Trish, who's sitting in front of us, turns and eyes me questioningly, I realize just how bad this really could be if people were to find out.

The game starts off with a bang when Dalton catches a long pass and runs in for a touchdown.

Everyone hollers, but I honestly feel like I'm the loudest with how excited that one play made me.

I've turned into a madwoman who is jumping up and down, screaming, "Go! Run!" at the top of my lungs.

I have no clue who I am becoming, but I'm loving how happy it's making me so far.

The game ends with us winning, and everyone rushes the field to congratulate the players. I look for my parents first, so we can all congratulate Thomas together on the win.

My dad looks so proud as he hugs Thomas. "Great job tonight, son."

"Thanks." He turns to me. "Look at you, coming to all the games so far."

"Yeah, sorry I never came before. These have been really fun," I admit.

Dad puts his arm around me. "We're sure glad your friends finally convinced you to come too. These are the days you're going to miss."

Guilt washes over me and I've never wanted to get away from my family as much as I do right now. That thought depresses me even more, but I push it aside and take a deep breath.

"I'm going to go hang with Ashley and Susie. See you guys later."

I give my dad and mom a hug, then slap my brother's shoulder pads. "Good job tonight."

HOW WE HATED

I run to where everyone is standing trying to wash my body from the worry that my family just caused.

Ashley and Marcus are all over each other, so the rest of us ignore them and talk about the game.

"What did you guys think of my boy here kicking ass tonight?" Ben asks as he pounds on Dalton's shoulder pad.

"You should have seen Natalie losing her mind up there," Susie says. "Definitely a first for her to act that way while cheering over a football game."

"Hey, there were some great plays," I say, trying to defend myself and not make it so obvious.

"There sure were." Maya jumps into our conversation with her same enthusiasm as always.

Ben picks up Maya and has her step onto his knee, and she swings around in a move that throws her onto his shoulders so she's sitting, straddling his head. It looked so smooth and seamless; I can't believe she was able to get up there so easily.

"To the showers!" Maya points to the locker rooms, like she's guiding a group into battle on the back of a horse.

"Oh, I'll throw you in the shower all right." Ben holds on to her legs as he starts running, then stops as they both laugh.

The group begins to follow them, but before I turn to do so, I'm stuck, staring at Dalton, wanting nothing more than to wrap my arms around him and kiss him like he kissed me last night, but knowing there's no way in hell I could.

He raises his eyebrows ever so slightly before giving me a shy grin and heading off to join his friends.

I don't even notice Susie right beside me until she's pulling on my arm.

"Girl, this shit is fire! God, why can't I be you? That look was intense!"

"Um, yeah. Care to explain something?" Ashley butts in as she approaches us. "Even I saw that."

I close my eyes in horror, not sure if I want anyone else to know.

"They totally kissed!" Susie whisper-blurts out.

I instantly freak out and check around us to make sure no one else heard what she said.

"No. Fucking. Way," Ashley states, just as shocked as I was when it happened.

"Yep." Susie pops the P sound to state her fact. "Those two got something going on."

"Like what?" Ashley's eyes open up wide.

I wave my arms in front of me, like I'm trying to shoo away bugs—or rather, this conversation. "Not out here!" I say sternly but try to keep my voice down.

Ashley wraps her arm around mine and starts walking us back to her car. "Then, to the car we go! I can't believe we drove all the way here and you didn't tell me!"

Once we're in the car, Ashley wastes no time and doesn't even bother cranking the engine before she turns to me. "Spill it."

I close my eyes and let out a deep breath. "I honestly don't even know how it happened. It just did."

Ashley looks at Susie, who is sitting in the front passenger seat next to her. "Oh, yeah. No biggie. Just you kissing your lifelong sworn enemy. I mean, that's not a big deal or anything." She fakes nonchalance.

HOW WE HATED

I slap her shoulder. "Stop. Believe me, I know it's a big deal." I sit back in my seat with a sigh, dropping my head back as well. "This can't happen."

"Oh, but it's already happening." Susie laughs.

"So, fill me in. Like, he just stopped you after you were done with your assignment and kissed you?" Ashley asks.

"Not exactly ..."

They both raise their eyebrows like they're waiting for me, making me chuckle to myself as I decide to really fill them in.

"I've been meeting him at night to run."

Both of their faces scrunch into balls of confusion.

"You've been ... I'm sorry ... running with Dalton Wick? How? Where?" Ashley asks, her tone proving just how unbelievable—or rather, crazy—this all sounds.

I sigh. "It was part of our project. I had to show him horseback riding, and he showed me running."

"And you kept going after the project part was over?" Susie asks slowly.

I cover my face with my hands. "Yes."

"And you liked running with him?" Ashley asks.

I slowly run my hands down my face, exasperated. "Every minute sucked because he absolutely kicked my ass, but then, yeah, I did like it." I pause and take a deep breath. "Turned out, he liked running with me too. Said I pushed him to go harder, be more competitive."

They both laugh.

"Well, he hit you on the head with that one," Susie states, almost like saying *duh*.

"You mean, he hit the nail on the head?" I ask, laughing.

She blows me off. "You know what I meant."

I lift my shoulders up and down quickly. "That was pretty much it. We had a moment, he kissed me, and then I freaked out and ran."

"You ran?" they ask in unison.

"Yeah, I ran. This cannot happen between us, remember? If my dad finds out …" I shiver at the thought.

"He won't find out. We'll make sure of it!" Ashley tries to be promising.

"So, was this last night, and this morning was the first time he saw you since you ran?"

I cover my face again and shake my head.

"There's more?" Susie asks, excitement dripping from her as she bounces in her seat, grabbing my hands and forcing them away from my face.

"I tried to get him to drop it, but he wouldn't. He can be pretty persistent."

"Oh jeez, how did you handle one of the hottest guys in school not wanting to leave you alone?" Susie teases, and I slap her shoulder playfully.

"I kept telling myself I wasn't going to go see him and I was going to stop whatever was happening between us, but there I was last night, riding Brandy out to see him."

"Then, what happened?" Susie asks, on the edge of her seat.

"Once I got there, he asked if I knew what me being there meant." I watch as both of their eyes get big with anticipation. "When I nodded … he kissed me." I drop my head back against the seat again with a sigh. "God, did he kiss me."

HOW WE HATED

"O-M-G," Susie squeals. "What that means is, you're his girlfriend."

I raise my arms up, then drop them by my sides. "But how?"

Ashley turns in her seat and starts the car. "I don't know, but it looks like you'll be hanging out with me at Ben's place a lot more." She laughs.

I lean forward in the car so I'm closer to them, making sure they know how serious this is. "You can't tell anyone! Please! I need to figure this out first before anyone else knows."

"Girl, we got you. Our lips are sealed," Ashley says.

"As long as your lips are sealed on his and you tell us everything." Susie laughs as she turns to face forward and buckle her seat belt.

"To Ben's we go!" Ashley says.

"To Ben's we go," I whisper under my breath, wishing it were seriously that easy.

CHAPTER 25

Natalie

We stop to get ice cream as we wait for the guys to shower and get to Ben's. By the time we arrive, the place is flooded with people everywhere.

I'm not sure if it's the dairy from the ice cream or my nerves of knowing Dalton is in there somewhere that causes my stomach to turn in a not-so-fun way as we exit Ashley's car.

Susie wraps her arm through mine as she guides me to the barn. "There's nothing to be afraid of. He likes you. This is a good thing."

"It's not him I'm afraid of … it's my dad," I respond.

"Well, your dad isn't here, and there's no way your brother would ever be caught dead here, so you're good to go for the night. Try not to worry and try to actually have some fun."

I inhale and take a deep breath just before we enter the barn.

HOW WE HATED

The lights are dimmed, so it takes a moment for my eyes to focus as I see everyone around us.

Ashley grabs my other hand and makes a beeline for the couches in the back, knowing that's exactly where Marcus will be. I'm not sure whether to be embarrassed that she's dragging me there or excited because I know Dalton will be there too. Right now, I'm a little bit of both, which causes my stomach to tie in even more knots.

When we get there, my eyes instantly lock on Dalton, who's sitting there, looking out into the crowd. His eyes soften, and a small grin graces his gorgeous face, almost like he was searching for me and now that he's found me, he can stop his quest.

He mouths, *Hi*.

I mouth, *Hi*, back as I stand on the far end of the couches.

He doesn't motion for me to come join him, and I must say it's a bit of a relief that he doesn't.

We haven't spoken about keeping us a secret for now, and I'm glad he realizes that we need to. If there's one thing any small town loves, it's gossip, and it spreads through our school like wildfire. Everyone knows our families hate each other, so it would be top news if they found out there was something going on between us.

Oh God, not if—when *they find out.*

My stomach turns some more, and I close my eyes, willing myself to not feel the way I do for him. When I open my eyes, all I see is him with a worried expression covering his beautiful face.

I try to ignore the battle in my head as I engage in meaningless conversation with my fellow classmates about the game and homecoming, which is still a month away.

Every once in a while, I'll sneak a peek toward Dalton, who is still facing me and hasn't moved an inch since I got here.

"Are you going to the dance?" Lisa, a girl in my math class, asks.

I shrug. "Not sure yet."

"How about all of us go as a group?" Ashley speaks up, grabbing Marcus so he knows she means him too. "It will be fun, and then no one has to worry about not having dates."

Her eyes meet mine, and I know she's saying this for me since there's no way in hell I could go with Dalton.

"That'd be cool." Marcus nods his approval.

"Yeah, you could get Ben and Dalton and some other guys on the team to go, too, right?" Ashley asks.

"For sure."

"You guys in?" Ashley asks the rest of our little circle.

They all nod, and I smile at Ashley, mouthing, *Thank you.*

She blows me a kiss just as my phone dings in my pocket. I grab it, and when I see Dalton's name across my screen, I realize, first, I need to change his name to something else so people don't see, and, second, that when I look up, he's not sitting there anymore.

I swipe the phone to read what he sent.

Come outside to where we sat last time you were here.

HOW WE HATED

I type a quick:

OK.

I put my phone back in my pocket, then touch Susie on the shoulder as I get up. "I'll be right back."

She looks to where Dalton was sitting, then gives me a cheesy grin. "I want details."

I laugh, then turn to head out of the barn to the place where we sat last time.

It's dark in that corner of the yard, and I don't see him until he grabs me and swings me around before he lifts me up to his level and kisses me softly. Our tongues dance together in a hungry swirl that leaves me breathless when he places me back on my feet.

"Hi," he says before kissing me one more time.

"Hi, yourself." I stare into his eyes, melting at the sight of them.

He holds me close to him. "I've wanted to do that since you walked in the door."

"Well, I'm glad you didn't," I tease.

He looks deflated, letting go of me and sitting down on the curb.

"Hey." I nudge him as I sit down too. "What just happened?"

He stares off ahead of him. "I know we didn't really discuss things, but I figured, today, at school, you wanted to keep things low, so I did until we could really talk about it."

"And?"

"And now, we're here. Hiding. Away from everyone."

I sigh. "Yep. This is us. Hiding."

"Is this how it's going to be?"

I nod emphatically. "Yes. I told you we couldn't do this."

He takes my hand and plays with my fingers. "But we are."

I rub my lips together in thought, a million things going through my head.

"I like you, Natalie. I like the way you push me. I think you and I would be good together."

"That's the problem," I state a little too firmly.

His eyebrows pinch together. "Problem?"

I look into his eyes. "I think that way too. But the only way I can see this working is if we hide. No one can find out."

He tilts his head to the side, pinching his eyebrows more. "No one?"

I laugh. "Okay, maybe a few trusted people. I already told Ashley and Susie."

This brightens his mood a little. "Oh, you did? What did you tell them?"

"That I kept fighting it."

"You could have fought harder," he taunts. "I was having fun wearing you down."

I slap his shoulder with my other hand, and he grabs it, bringing both of my hands together with his.

"Ashley's already helping our cause out." I smile.

"Oh, she is, huh?"

God, he looks so handsome when he's being playful with me.

"She just set up a group of us to all go to the homecoming dance together so no one has to worry about dates. This way, we can still go together at least."

HOW WE HATED

He stares off ahead of him as he nods his head slowly, letting everything sink in. "So, we're keeping this a secret?"

"We don't have a choice. But, hey"—I put my finger under his chin, turning him to face me—"sneaking around could be fun." I lean in and surprise even myself when I kiss him.

I've never felt so bold, so brave in my life. I've never kissed a boy first. I've always let them kiss me, yet here I am, kissing Dalton Wick—the most popular guy in school, my family's sworn enemy, and now my secret boyfriend.

Lord help me.

CHAPTER 26

Dalton

I've had the best few weeks of my life. Who knew sneaking around would be so much fun? If I'm not trying to steal kisses from Natalie in the restroom at school, I'm staying with her until late at night at the back of our properties.

She's had to push our meeting time back so she doesn't miss dinner with her family. At first, I thought it was crazy, but then realized it would give me time to still get my run in, then shower and meet up with her later, so it's worked out pretty well.

Now that it's Sunday, I've convinced her to go driving with me just to go do something different.

I head out of my house to pick her up from school. She needed to do some stuff with the FFA, so her parents won't question anything, thinking she's still there.

When I pull into the back of the school, there's not

HOW WE HATED

a person in sight as she runs to my truck and hops in, sliding over to give me a kiss, then keeping her spot right next to me on the bench seat.

I never thought having an old truck like this would benefit me in this way, but there is something to be said about having a girl being able to sit so close to you while driving. That's not possible in new trucks.

I laugh to myself before I sing, *"Rollin' on thirty-fives. Pretty girl by my side,"* from the Luke Bryan song "That's My Kind of Night."

She giggles—which is the cutest sound ever—as I wrap my arm around the back of her and lean it on the seat. It's ridiculous how happy this girl makes me.

"Where are we headed?" she asks as she puts on her lap belt.

"Thought we would just cruise and see where this takes us."

"Sounds good to me."

She places her hand on my knee as I put the truck in gear, then wrap my arm around her again as we drive away from the center of town to the back country roads to see where the road will take us.

"With a Woman You Love" by Justin Moore plays on the radio, and I look at her and smile, the song making more sense now.

These last few weeks, I've only wanted to be with her. I've dated other girls, but no one hit me as hard as her.

I turn onto a country road that leads to a creek, where I find a place to park.

"I brought us some dinner. Thought we could have a picnic," I say when she turns to me in question.

"You did not." She laughs with amazement.

I lean back, acting offended. "Why do you sound so surprised?"

She reaches up to kiss me. "I'm not. That's sweet. What did you bring?"

I open the truck door, and she climbs out on my side as well.

Reaching in the back, I grab a bag I placed there, as well as a blanket, then take her hand to lead her to a flat place to set up. "You'll see."

We walk for just a few feet, where I set down the bag and lay out the blanket for her.

We climb on top, and I open the bag to pull out the sandwiches I made. Handing one to her, I say, "Okay, don't get too excited. It's just a turkey sandwich, but I did make it myself."

"That's so sweet," she responds as she takes it from me.

I get the rest of the stuff I packed in my bag. "I also got us some grapes, chips, and waters."

She smiles as she takes a grape from me and pops it into her mouth. "It's perfect."

We eat our sandwiches in each other's arms, just relaxing in the amazing temperature of the season.

Once the sun has fully set, a cool breeze sets in, so I hop up to get a sweatshirt from my truck for Natalie to wear, but get another idea as well.

Turning on my KC lights, I spin the ignition just enough to get the radio to come on and connect my phone to play one of my favorite songs—something that reminds me of her when it talks about a girl coming from a happy family and the only bad she's ever done was to see the good in the boy.

HOW WE HATED

Somehow, I feel like this fits us right now.

"Sun to Me" by Zach Bryan plays as I walk to her, placing my hand out, inviting her to dance with me.

Shyly, she grabs my hand and stands up. I pull her into me, and we dance in the lights from my truck to a soulful love song.

I pull back to look her in the eyes, amazed at what she's done to me in such a short amount of time. When I kiss her, I know I'm completely done for this girl.

Our kiss intensifies and all I can think about is thank God we're standing because if we were lying down, I know I'd take this much further but not here, not like this.

When I slow down our intensity and move back slightly, I know she feels the same way by the way she grips me tighter like she doesn't want me to stop.

It takes everything in my power to pull away from her completely and kiss her forehead just as the song ends. We both inhale, bringing us back to reality of where we are and sit back down, letting the music continue around us, enjoying these last few minutes we have together.

With her wrapped in my arms, I look down at my phone when I see a text come through from Maya.

Where are you?

I laugh as I text back.

None of your business ;-)

I will find out who she is. You know that, right?

Yeah, but this is fun for now.

She sends back an emoji that's sticking out its tongue, making me chuckle to myself.

"Who was that?" Natalie asks.

"Maya." I set the phone to the side. "She knows I'm seeing someone and hates that I won't tell her who."

I feel Natalie get stiff in my arms.

I hold her tighter. "I won't tell her if you don't want me to."

She sighs. "It's just that they're part of TimeLand."

"And so am I, yet …"

I lean down, turn her head to face me, and kiss her lips. She melts into my touch and whines ever so slightly as I pull away.

"No one cares about our parents' feud. They'll get a kick out of hearing we're together."

She sits up, brings her knees to her chest, and bows her head.

I sit up and rub her back. "What did I say?"

"No one else cares because it didn't affect you guys the way it did us, my family."

I grab her shoulders and bring her back to me, lying down so she's resting on my chest. "That's their problem. We shouldn't let it be ours."

I hear her take a big breath, but she doesn't respond as we watch the sun set. I hate my father for making her feel this way, but what's done is done. We need to be able to live our lives without our parents' feelings on the matter.

HOW WE HATED

The next morning, we walk out of English class with her in front of me, acting like I'm not right behind her. When she turns right, I take a second too long, watching her leave, and am startled when I feel someone slap my stomach.

Instantly, I jump into fight mode until I see Maya standing there with a cheesy grin.

"Oh, I need details," she says, laughing in shock.

I walk past her, trying to blow her off. "Details about what?"

We head toward the couches, where I plop down and sling my bag onto the floor.

She sits down right next to me and gets in my face with her eyes wide open as she whispers, "Natalie?"

I close my eyes with a chuckle and shake my head.

She slaps my chest again. "OMG. Don't lie. I figured it could only be her since you guys were working on that project, but I thought, *No way.*"

I open my eyes and look into hers, not saying a word, but raising my eyebrows to confirm she's right.

"Seriously?" She bounces in her seat. "Talk about loving the game of cat and mouse. What? You could have any girl at this school, and you just had to get the one girl you couldn't?"

I laugh out loud. "You know it didn't go down like that."

Ben walks up and grabs Maya like he always does and places her down on his lap. "Went down like what?"

"Nothing." Maya looks off to the side, like she's five and she has a secret that she won't tell anyone.

"What, that Natalie and Dalton are fucking?" Ben says nonchalantly.

My head spins almost as fast as Maya's as we both stare at him.

"You knew?" Maya asks.

"We're not fucking," I clarify at the same time.

He looks at me. "Sorry, bro, I just figured you would have by now."

"How did you know?" Maya asks, and I squint my eyes at him, wondering the same thing.

He responds, so blasé, "Come on. It was obvious. He's always liked the chase. She's the ultimate prize."

"You know it's not like that," I defend myself.

"Uh-huh. Keep telling yourself that. Just don't let her dad find out," Ben states.

I throw up my arms in frustration. "Why should we care? She's so worried about that."

Ben raises his eyebrows at me. "Then, obviously, you don't know the whole story."

"What story? That they moved the company here? Obviously, I know how we ended up back here and not in California."

Ben shakes his head. "Nope. There's a reason your dad wanted back here so bad, and it has everything to do with beef between him and Randy Spencer. My dad told me a few years ago. That shit was fucked up. They all tried to act like they moved it here for other reasons but it's not true. Mine and Maya's dads went along with it because they wanted our moms back. They've kept

HOW WE HATED

these secrets because moving here for love was a way better story than vindictive shit."

Maya looks just as confused as I am. "What are you talking about?"

Ben holds his hands up in defense. "I was told to keep it quiet. It's not like it matters now anyway."

I roll my eyes. Of course my dad would hold some kind of grudge. "Obviously it matters to Natalie. To her dad." I sigh and shake my head. "Why would he move an entire company here to piss off one person?"

He lowers his head to me, looking out through his eyelashes. "Do you remember what your dad is like?"

I drop my head back on the couch, knowing all too well exactly what my dad is like. "So, what happened? What am I truly up against?"

He shakes his head. "That I don't know. My dad didn't go that into details. I just know he came back here to ruin Randy's life. Unfortunately, he's pretty much succeeded. So, yeah, her dad might have a problem with any of us, but especially you."

I grit my teeth. *Yet another way my dad is screwing up my life.*

CHAPTER 27

Dalton

I wake up Sunday morning, still stiff from Friday night's game. It was a tough one, and I took an ass-kicking for sure, but we poked out a win, so all the licks I took were worth it. Wanting to just chill for the day, I text Natalie.

> **Meet me on the corner of West and Main Street.**

Her text bubbles appear instantly on the screen, and it's ridiculous how happy that makes me.

How am I going to get there? I can't just ask my mom or brother for a ride saying just drop me off on the corner.

> **Call Ashley or Susie.**

HOW WE HATED

I wait for her bubbles, but they never flash on the screen, and I hope she's texting them instead.

Ashley will come get me. Meet you there at 10?

See you then.

I hop out of bed, invigorated for the day all of a sudden.

When I exit my room and head down the hall, my dad is the first person I see in the kitchen.

"Morning," I say.

"Morning." He doesn't even bother looking up from his iPad that he's reading on. No surprise there.

I grab some juice from the fridge and pour a glass, setting it down on the counter before I take a sip.

"You're going to put that away, right?" he asks.

"Yeah. I've had it out for two seconds. I just wanted a sip first," I respond.

"No problem with putting it away, then taking a sip." He still hasn't looked up at me. He's just talking while staring at his screen.

I inhale a deep breath as I turn to put the juice away. I've learned there's no reason to even talk to him when he's like this. It will only make it worse. So, I grab a banana and head back to my room, not wanting to be in his presence anymore.

Once I'm ready to head out, I get my truck keys and walk to the front door.

My mom is sitting in the living room, so I shout out, "I'll be back."

She doesn't say a word, just raises her hand and waves me away. There's no question as to where I'm going or who I'll be with. Not even a spoken word goodbye. This isn't something new, but knowing how Natalie has to lie to her parents to see me and how my parents couldn't care less just rubs me wrong.

As I walk to my truck, annoyance from my family kicks in even more, and only the crank of my engine and roar of the country music blaring through my speakers help calm those thoughts.

"Cowgirls" by Morgan Wallen comes on and I blast it feeling like it's talking about my cowgirl in particular.

I head to the corner of West and Main and smile when I see Natalie hop out of Ashley's car and open the door to my truck.

I guess my thoughts were off. Seeing her makes me happier than the music does.

I lean over to kiss her. She stiffens instantly as she looks around to check if anyone can see us.

I pull back and put the truck in drive. "Are you that afraid of being seen with me?" I ask out of frustration with my family more than her, but really, it's this entire situation.

Her expression says it all—she is.

I drive to the lake by Mason Creek and park facing the water away from where everyone is setting up for a day in the water.

"Is this private enough?" I don't hide my disdain.

She reaches for my hand. "You have to understand how upset my dad would be."

In the moment, I can't hold back, so I turn to her and say, "Then, why are we doing this? We can't hide forever."

HOW WE HATED

She looks forward, closes her eyes, and takes a deep breath. "I know. I'll figure it out." She takes off her seat belt and slides across the seat so she's right next to me. "I want to be with you though."

She kisses my lips, and I'm a sucker for her touch, so I kiss her back. My frustration softens, but not enough to make me fully content. I just hate that she puts so much emphasis on her family.

"Please," she whispers when she sees I'm holding back some. "Please just be with me right now."

I look into her eyes, loving what I'm seeing, then realize, "Is this what you're feeling?" She looks at me confused so I continue, "I want to be with you, out in the open, for everyone to know, and it makes me so mad we can't."

Her mouth turns slightly down in a frown as she closes her eyes and drops her head to her chest. I place my finger under her chin and bring her line of sight back to me.

"But I can't stop this. I don't want to be anywhere but with you."

Her eyes don't lie. The way she looks at me with so much love, hurt, desire and her true soul pouring out all of her emotions directly into my heart is all I need to know.

I place my palm on her cheek. "We'll figure this out."

She grabs my hand, holding it to her face, and nods.

I lean in to kiss her feeling like we just brought our relationship to an even higher level and wanting to solidify it with a kiss so deep and true it makes me want to rip my heart out and give it to only her.

I nudge her ever so slightly back and she goes

willingly. We scoot as one until she's on her back with me towering over her across the bench seat of my truck.

Running my hand down the side of her neck, along her arms and then at the bottom of her shirt sends visible chills throughout her body. I know she wants this as bad as I do, and I can hardly contain myself for what she does to me.

I slide my hand up her shirt, feeling her soft skin against my rough hands. Moving around to her back, I grip her firmly, bringing her even closer to me, but I still can't get enough. I hope she can tell what she's doing to me because, fuck, I've never been so turned on and it's only for her.

"Dalton," she says my name in a plea and it damn near kills me just by the sound because I've never heard something so beautiful in my entire life.

"I'm here, baby. I'm not going anywhere," I whisper never meaning my words more than I do right now.

Just as I grip her breast, feeling like I might lose myself all together, a kid screams out, "Mom, can we play over here?"

We both freeze, reality washing over us like a cold bucket of ice water thrown on us when we realize just how public of a place we are in and it's not even eleven in the morning.

I drop my head on her shoulder as she laughs.

"Maybe we should," I grit out with my head buried in her hair, not wanting to finish that statement.

She laughs as she places her hands on my back. "Yeah, maybe we should."

Neither one of us want to actually say the word *stop* but we both know we need to.

HOW WE HATED

Begrudgingly, I sit up and move back to my seat while she slides up herself. When we glance out the windshield, we see a mom staring back at us with an expression of disapproval written all over her face.

"Yeah, let's go," I chuckle under my breath and crank the engine.

Maybe parking along the lake on a Sunday morning wasn't the best idea.

CHAPTER 28

Natalie

Another week has gone by with Dalton and me living our secret lives. Every night, we spend time together at the back of our properties, and every Sunday, we've been hanging out, so I'm not surprised when I get a text from him, asking to do something, but I am surprised when he asks me to go to Ben's with him.

Come on. Ashley and Marcus will be there,
too, so no having to lie to your parents.

Do they know about us?

Yes. Ben figured it out two weeks ago.
And look, they've kept it a secret.

Hearing they've known for a while does make me feel better about going. If they made it through this long

HOW WE HATED

at school and said nothing, then maybe I should trust them too.

Okay, I'll call Ashley.

He texts back a smiley emoji, making me laugh as I press Ashley's name to give her a call.

"So, he talked you into it?" is all she says as she answers the phone.

"How did you know?" I ask, surprised.

"That's how he knew I'd be going. I told him he should just make you come. Not everyone thinks it's as big of a deal as you're making it. It will be just fine."

I sigh, terrified to make us so public, but hoping she's right. "Okay, come pick me up. I'll go with you."

"Yay! I'll be there shortly."

I hang up and text Dalton.

See you soon.

Can't wait.

Ashley and I pull up to Ben's place, and I hop out of the car with a knot in my stomach when I see Dalton's truck parked out front. Something about walking through that door will make everything about Dalton and me official. I've been able to compartmentalize my thoughts and feelings on this, keeping him tucked away as this little secret, but after I walk through that door, I can't pretend anymore.

Dalton must have been watching for us because he's out the door and greeting me by the car before I can even take a step toward the barn.

"Hey," he says as he leans in to kiss me.

"Hey to you too," Ashley yells over the car, making him laugh.

"Thanks for bringing my girl," he replies, sending chills down my spine.

That's the first time he's called me his girl. Actually, it's the first time I've heard it said out loud like that. I have to close my eyes to let it all sink in.

Yes, this is happening. No, I don't know how my dad will react, and, no, I don't want it to stop. I'm a horrible daughter.

He takes me by my hand and walks me into the barn.

"Yay!" Maya yells out and rushes toward me. "So glad you guys are finally going public with this."

I smile nervously. "Yeah, it's kind of crazy"—I grin his way—"but good."

"It will be just fine. We've let our parents' feud get between us for too long. I want to get to know you better."

Maya has never been mean to me per se, but we've always kept our distance from each other because we were told to. Maybe Dalton is right—that's our parents' issue, not ours. Obviously, they all feel that way. Maybe I can too.

We head to the couches in the back, where everyone else is already hanging out, and sit down. Maya sits on

HOW WE HATED

Ben's lap, and Ashley and Marcus are already cuddled on the love seat. Eli is seemingly off in his own world on his phone as I sit down next to Dalton, and he wraps his arm around the couch behind me.

Sitting here feels as normal as ever, so I settle in and cuddle into Dalton's side as we hang out and chat about nothing in particular.

At some point, Maya gets up and grabs the guitar to bring it to Dalton. "Natalie, have you ever heard Dalton play?"

I smile as I remember the first time we hung out when things felt different between us. He played then, but I didn't really hear what he was doing because I was so in shock about the moment and what was happening.

"He's only played for me a little bit," I respond.

She hands it to him. "I want to hear the Taco Bell song."

I chuckle under my breath. "Taco Bell song?" I ask, thinking she can't be serious.

He sits up to grab the guitar from Maya. "It's 'February 28, 2016.'"

"Still confused. Is that a song title?" I laugh a little harder.

"It's the funniest song with an addictive melody that makes me laugh," Maya says.

"It's about a night out, hence the name. It must have all happened on February 28, 2016, so that's why he called it that," Dalton explains.

He sits up and gets in position and starts to strum the chords. When he sings the lyrics, my eyes open up wide. Knowing he played the guitar was one thing, but hearing him sing is completely another.

His voice is deep, soulful, and calming. The trifecta of all of those combined has me in a trance as he sings, "*La-la-la-la, let's pull over.*"

I smile in awe at Maya, not believing what I'm hearing.

Maya joins in, "*Who is sober enough to take me to Taco Bell?*"

I drop my head in laughter. The song is seriously about turning the music up, having to stop because they have to pee, and being sober enough to drive to Taco Bell, but it's all sang in a soothing tone.

When it ends with him talking about needing a taco, I laugh out loud. "Is that a real song?"

He grins. "Yes, it's by Koe Wetzel. You've never heard of him?"

I shake my head, then remember him playing Zach Bryan when we danced earlier, which has a very similar vibe to it, so I ask, "You like these slower, more soulful artists, don't you?"

He leans in to kiss me. "Guilty."

"Weren't you working on another one?" Maya asks. "Did you get it down yet?"

He nods slowly. "Yeah, finally learned that one." He turns to me. "Want to hear another one?"

"Absolutely!" I say as genuinely as possible. Even though the song was as silly as could be, I still loved hearing his voice.

"This one isn't as funny. More serious, but it's one of my favorites." He looks down at his guitar and strums a few chords before belting out lyrics that touch me deep in my soul—about a guy asking for advice from his dad.

HOW WE HATED

He sings, "*Keep your nose on the grindstone and out of the pills.*"

The song goes on to plead how he's trying, but just can't catch a break, and the father keeps on with his fatherly advice—how if you keep your nose on the grindstone and out of the pills, then you'll get what you're working so hard for.

When he finishes, I'm speechless.

Maya and Ashley clap, so I join in with them.

"That's some cool shit," Marcus says as he gives Dalton knuckles, and Ben agrees too.

Even Eli yells out, "Fuck yeah. Love that one."

Dalton nods his thanks.

"What's the name of it?" Marcus asks.

" 'Nose on the Grindstone' by Tyler Childers," Dalton responds.

He puts the guitar down, and I curl into his side.

"That was really good. How come you didn't tell me you sang?"

He chuckles to himself. "How many times did I tell you that you had to ask me questions?"

I slap his chest playfully, and he grabs my hand to keep it there.

There's so much about this guy that I never saw before. I guess I just never wanted to see it before. I'm glad I am now though.

CHAPTER 29

Natalie

"You look beautiful, sweetheart," Mom says with tears in her eyes.

I step in front of a mirror to see my reflection. I've never really been a girlie girl, but I must admit, knowing I was getting dressed up for Dalton made me want to put a little more emphasis into how I looked for the homecoming dance tonight.

"I'm sorry we couldn't get you a new dress." The pain is evident in her voice.

I grab her hand and give her a reassuring smile. "It's okay. To me, this is a new dress."

I glance in the mirror at the borrowed dress a cousin of mine wore a few years ago to her homecoming dance.

Mom takes a somber breath, then tucks a stray hair that came loose from my updo. "That's so cool that you all are going as a group. I wish your brother would go too."

HOW WE HATED

I can't tell her how happy I am that he's not going, but I try to hide that fact.

"He's never been into school functions like this," I say.

"I know. Doesn't mean I don't want to see him get all dressed up too." Her expression shows she's sad, not getting the chance to see her son this way.

I laugh at the thought. He's always wearing Ariat jeans and cowboy boots. Yes, he plays football, but I think that's more so he can crush people and take out his aggression than actually play the game.

The doorbell rings.

"That's Ashley and Susie," I say, picking up my purse from the dresser and leaving my bedroom.

By the time I get to the front room, my dad has already opened the door and welcomed them into our home.

"Don't you both look lovely?" he says as he hugs both of them.

"Thank you, Mr. Spencer," they both respond.

He grabs his phone from the entryway table. "Now, come here in front of the fireplace. I want to get a photo of you all together."

We do as he asked and smile for the photo.

"Here, dear," Pops says to Mom. "I want to get a picture with my baby girl."

He comes to stand next to me, wrapping his arm around me like a proud dad would. Instantly, I feel guiltier than ever.

I glance over at Susie, who notices my change in mood. I know she understands what I'm going through. She's my oldest friend, and she knows firsthand how lucky I am to have such a supportive, amazing dad. She's said so a few times that she wishes her dad were more like him. I really got lucky in that department. My dad is such a good, honest man, and I'm going behind his back like this.

After our photo, he gives me a big hug. "Have so much fun tonight."

I hug him back. "I will, Pops."

We head to the front door, where I hug my mom goodbye, and we walk out to where Ashley's car is parked.

Susie nudges me. "You good?"

I take a large inhale, my head fighting with my heart. "It's just not fair."

She purses her lips. "Totally not fair."

Hearing that she agrees makes me feel a little better, so I try to push all my feelings aside and get in a happier mood, hoping it doesn't ruin my night.

When we arrive at the school gym, Marcus, Dalton, and the rest of the crew are there, waiting for us, and we head their way.

Ashley runs into Marcus's arms while I approach the group, not wanting to make such a public scene with Dalton.

When our eyes meet, he mouths, *You look gorgeous.*

I feel my entire body flush as I try not to blush and mouth back, *Thank you. You look pretty good too.*

He stands just a little taller as he straightens his suit jacket.

Maya gives me a hug. "I love this dress!"

"Thank you. I love yours too." I notice that she and Ben match, yet they aren't standing with each other.

HOW WE HATED

"Did you guys plan that?" I point to the matching tie Ben is wearing that's not just the same fuchsia pink, but also the exact same pattern, like it was made from the same cloth.

She chuckles as she rolls her eyes. "Yes. He said he wanted us to match so we had pictures to look back on."

I laugh in surprise. "For homecoming? It's not like it's prom or anything."

"Lord, please tell me I get an actual date by then so I can match my date and not just my friend."

She shakes her head and rolls her eyes teasingly, but it makes me wonder even more what is up with the two of them. He dates. She doesn't.

It's not like our school has a ton of guys to choose from, but it is weird that when I think back, I've never heard of her dating anyone, and when you grow up in a small town, everyone knows everything, so even if I wasn't in their circle, it would have been discussed at some point.

I glance around the group. "No Eli tonight?"

Maya laughs. "No way. He'd never come to something like this. He's too cool for dances." She mocks his height and stoicism.

"Why is he so quiet?"

She shrugs. "He's always been that way. Just keeps to himself. Totally okay with being at home, alone. It's just him, but I respect that."

I nod. "Hey, you be you."

"Exactly." She places her arm around mine. "Shall we?"

She motions toward the entrance to the gym, and we all head that way.

Dalton stays behind for a few seconds so he's walking behind me.

I shiver when I feel him lean in and whisper, "I mean it. You look stunning. Most beautiful girl here."

I turn to face him for a brief second with a smile on my face, making sure he knows how thankful I am for his words even if only I can hear them.

The gym has been completely transformed into a wonderland with balloons and flowers lining the entrance and fairy lights strung from end to end, acting as the only lighting in the dimly lit room.

We all grab a table, and to my surprise, Dalton and I are able to sit next to each other without anyone making a big fuss about where everyone can sit. He leans back in his chair as I slide out the seat next to him, trying my hardest not to pay any extra attention to him.

Yes, I know everyone at this table knows what's going on between us, but no one else in the school does, and we need to keep it that way. Sitting together like this is going to have people questioning things as it is, but thankfully, we can blame it on Marcus and Ashley if anything comes up. Anyone who sees them together knows they're absolutely a couple, so I'm hoping all they see is two groups sitting together for the sake of their mutual friends.

Susie is itching to go dance and grabs my hand. "Please come dance with me?"

I slyly grin at Dalton over my shoulder and love when he raises his eyebrows at me in interest. He might not be able to dance with me, but nothing says I can't put on a little show for him to enjoy.

I hop up, and Susie squeals her appreciation as we

HOW WE HATED

head to the dance floor. "Body Like a Back Road" by Sam Hunt plays, and I sway my hips side to side, facing Dalton for a brief moment before turning around so my back is to him.

Knowing he's watching me, I start to move in ways I never thought I could. As I run my fingers down my hips, I drop my head to the side. As I raise my arms over my head, I shimmy my ass, making it pop to the music. When I turn to face him again, I make sure my chest is on full display, pushed forward.

Our eyes meet, and it's obvious what I'm doing is working.

His lips are slightly parted as he stares at me like I'm the only one in the room. When he licks his lips, tingles spread throughout my body as I imagine what his tongue would feel like on me.

I continue to dance around while our eyes stay locked on each other until Susie disrupts us by sliding in front of me with her eyebrows raised. She takes me by the hand and spins me around so I'm facing the other way.

"Obvious much?" she whispers to me, making me tense up. "Are you not trying to keep this a secret anymore?"

My stomach turns, and I cover my mouth as I head off the dance floor and to the girls' restroom.

I assume Susie's following me, so when I hear the restroom door open, I don't think anything of it until I turn and see Dalton standing there.

"You can't be in here." I panic.

He steps up to me, pressing me against the counter. "I locked the door."

His hands grip my face while his lips crash into mine. I instantly melt at his touch. All panic leaves my body, and I all I want is more. More of him. More of this.

He lifts me up onto the counter and nestles in between my legs. I wrap my arms around his neck, my legs around him and pull him closer to me, rubbing my core against him as our tongues dance in a forbidden language we've become very good at speaking.

There's a knock on the door, and I freeze in fear until I hear Susie's voice.

"Okay, don't push your luck."

We touch our foreheads together as we both laugh until he backs up and takes a deep breath while adjusting his pants.

"You stay here, and I'll sneak out first." He gives me one more quick kiss, then exits the restroom.

I turn around and am hit by my reflection—slightly swollen lips, my disheveled hair from where he ran his fingers through, bringing me closer to him, and my flushed skin from the heat he caused to race through my body.

Susie enters the restroom, whistling when she gets a look at me. "Damn … sorry I had to interrupt the party."

I laugh as I cover my face in embarrassment. "What is he doing to me?"

She begins to fix my hair. "I don't know, but something tells me it's very good for you, and I'm super jealous. Stop stressing and enjoy it! He's obviously a mess over you. You should have seen how concerned he was when we met in the hallway."

HOW WE HATED

"Really?" My voice is laced with hope that I know I shouldn't have.

She levels her eyes with mine. "Really. Now, let's go continue to put on a show that will drive him crazy."

I bite my lower lip, loving how mischievous all of this makes me feel. "Okay."

We walk out of the restroom, arm in arm, only to be met by Trish, standing at the door like she's guarding it with her life. Her arms are crossed, and her eyebrows are raised when she locks eyes with me.

"Oh, this is good," she says as I internally panic.

Thankfully, Susie is quick on her feet, acting like she didn't see Trish standing there and completely blowing her off.

"Excuse us," she says with the same glee as when we were inside the restroom.

Trish grabs my arm and stops me as we walk away. "Don't think I didn't see Dalton leaving this restroom a few minutes ago while Susie was standing guard."

I look at Susie, who tries to release me from Trish's grip.

"I just had to see who his latest conquest was. Because that's all you are ... a conquest to him." Her smug expression makes my stomach turn. "Never thought I'd see you walking out though."

I rip my arm from her grip. "I don't know what you're talking about."

She lets out a harsh laugh. "Oh, but you do. And I really wonder what your brother would think if I shared this little tidbit of information with him."

"There's nothing to share, so back off," Susie demands.

Trish steps back and holds her hands up like she's surrendering. "Okay. You keep believing that, and we'll see just who has the last laugh."

We turn and walk away trying to act unfazed by her even though I'm internally freaking out.

"Don't listen to her," Susie says.

I can't help but relive every word she said on repeat in my head.

I'm so screwed.

I head back to the table, where Dalton is sitting, looking as cool as a cucumber with his legs sprawled out in front of him. When our eyes meet, he tenses up, knowing something isn't right.

What's wrong? he mouths.

I shake my head, blowing him off, and grab a sip of my water from the table, trying to give my attention to anything in this room but him.

He lightly kicks my foot under the table, and I close my eyes, taking in a big inhale before I look at him.

What happened? he mouths.

I close my eyes again, praying the tears that are stinging my eyes go away. Susie has been watching our interaction and decides to take the bull by the horns when she walks over to him, whispering something in his ear.

Without even giving me a second glance, he stands, throwing his chair back in the process, and marches over to where Trish is with a bunch of girls.

Susie comes over to sit with me as we try our hardest to not make it so obvious that we're watching their every move.

HOW WE HATED

Dalton is sly about his emotions and words with the way he's trying to be friendly with her and not make a scene, but you can tell she's not buying it.

With every second that goes by, my chest becomes tighter, and my stomach feels like it's doing somersaults inside me.

I'm caught staring when Trish looks my way, and instead of flinching to turn my attention elsewhere, I just close my eyes, feeling even guiltier than before and owning up to my betrayal.

He walks away from her and heads back to our table. I'm amazed he can keep his composure the way he is. Seemingly unaffected by the conversation he just had.

After he sits down, he grabs his phone and sends me a text.

It's taken care of.

I don't respond, just throw my phone back on the table and try my hardest to get out of my head and enjoy the rest of our night.

The dance committee gets up on stage saying it's time for the homecoming king and queen to be announced, and I try my hardest to change my mood and be present. When they call Ben and Maya as the winners it hits me even more. Not only can I not be with Dalton, I can't even cheer for my new friends because up until a few weeks ago, I hated them too, and everyone in this school knows that.

I think about what I would have done back then and roll my eyes, trying to come off as bored, but it just hurts me even more. I want to be cheering for Maya, she deserves this, and I was too blind to notice it before.

Not able to take it anymore. I get up and leave, sending a text to Dalton:

Don't follow me.

CHAPTER 30

Natalie

I wake up with my stomach in knots, thinking about Trish. If there's ever anyone who I would think would tell on me, it's her, especially when it comes to Dalton.

After that encounter, I kept my fair distance from Dalton, never going back to the table, making sure if anyone she might have told saw us, they would think she was crazy, and any rumors would stop there.

My phone dings with a message. I close my eyes and take a deep breath when I see it's Dalton. His texts used to make me so happy, but now, I'm even more confused.

Morning.

Morning.

I'm sorry I didn't get to kiss you good night.

HOW WE HATED

Chills rush through my body at the thought of his kiss. It's better than any kiss I've ever had, but I can't keep doing this. Even though it kills me to do so, I text back.

We need to talk.

Instantly, he replies.

No we don't. Everything will be fine.

I let out a sigh. I love that he's willing to fight for me and knew exactly where I was going with that, but it doesn't change anything.

You don't understand. My family is my everything.

You're right. I don't understand. My family doesn't give a crap about me.

My heart breaks for him. I can't believe we were raised so differently.

This is our lives. Not theirs. Don't forget that. I really like you. And I know you like me too.

I can't take this feeling inside me anymore. I've never been so torn in my life. I text back.

I have to go. I'll call you later.

I don't wait for his reply when I put my phone on silent and walk out to my living room, leaving it on my bed, face down.

The smell of bacon wafts through the air, which doesn't help my emotions one bit. I wonder if Dalton has ever woken up to Sunday morning breakfast. It's a tradition in our household, without fail. It's something I've grown to treasure, and I know I'll miss it when I go to college.

I turn the corner to see my mom swaying her hips slightly to the music that plays overhead in our kitchen.

"Morning, Mom," I say as I slide onto a kitchen stool and pull my foot up next to me.

She drops the spatula and walks toward me with a big grin on her face. "Good morning, sweetheart." She kisses my forehead and gives me a hug. "How was the dance?"

Thankfully, they were in bed when I got home, so I got to slip in with just a simple good night from both of them.

My heart hurts that I can't tell her what happened. My entire life, I've told her everything, sometimes in too much detail, so not being able to talk to her now kills me.

So, yet again, I lie, "It was fun."

She walks back to the stove. "Just fun? Nothing else?"

I get up to get a glass of water, more so I don't have to face her as I talk with my head in the cupboard and grab a cup. "Yeah. Nothing special. We all just hung out."

"Well, I'm glad you had fun. Go wake up your brother and let him know breakfast is almost ready."

HOW WE HATED

Guilt riddles me, so I walk up behind her, wrapping my arms around her and giving her a hug—my silent apology for something she knows nothing about.

I leave to go wake up Thomas before I start to cry from all the emotions running through me.

Dalton

I texted Natalie back, asking her to hang out with me today. It's been two hours, and she hasn't gotten back to me yet.

Wanting to get some things off my chest, I pick up the phone and call the only person I've ever really been able to talk to—my sister, Leslie.

She picks up on the second ring. "What's up, baby bro?"

I take a few seconds to think about what Natalie has said about her family and how close they are. I guess that's how I am with my sister. We've always joked that we only had each other. I've just never really thought about it that way.

"Hey, you got a second?" I ask.

"Sure. What's up?"

I lie down on my bed, taking a big inhale, ready to spill all my thoughts. "I've been seeing someone," I admit.

"Oh! So, that's where this is going. Do tell. Do I know her?"

I chuckle to myself. Leslie is two years older. Though she knows of the Spencer family, she never really grew up with them the way I did.

"You know of her."

"Okay," she says slowly. "Who is she?"

"Natalie Spencer," I blurt out.

She laughs instantly. "You're joking, right?"

I grin to myself, thinking of how our relationship progressed. "I wish I were."

"How the hell did that come about? I'm guessing her family doesn't know."

"That's the problem. We were forced to do a school project together, and one thing led to another, but she's all freaked out about her family."

"Rightfully so."

I throw my arm in the air in frustration. "Why?"

"You don't know the whole story then."

"What story?" I ask, exasperated.

"You do know our dad, right?" she asks, all snarky.

"All too well," I say with a huff.

"Look out your window, toward their property."

I get up and look out my window.

"Do you see that old barn that was burned down years ago and never fixed?"

Funny how I've never paid it any attention until now.

"Yeah," I respond.

"Dad did that."

"Shut the fuck up."

I stare at the dilapidated building, shaking my head. "Do I want to know the rest of the story?"

"You need to know to understand why she's so worried."

HOW WE HATED

I lie back down and rub my hand over my face. "Okay, give it to me."

"Dad has always hated Natalie's dad. They were big rivals in high school, I guess. My thoughts are, he hated that Randy was rich."

"And Dad wasn't," I say barely above a whisper.

My grandpa was an honest man, a prideful man. Even when TimeLand took off, he refused to change his lifestyle. He still lived in the small home my dad had grown up in until the day he died. He used to talk about how money changed people and not for the better. Something I absolutely agree with now.

"Bingo. Then, add in that Dad had a thing for Tracy."

I let out a small laugh. "Dad and Natalie's mom dated?"

"They sure did. And you can say Randy kind of stole Tracy from Dad—at least, that's the way he saw it. They were already broken up though, and she was ready to move on, but Dad wasn't. I guess he never really got over it."

"But Dad married Mom, so obviously, he did."

Now, it's her turn to laugh. "Who do you think I learned all of this from?"

I inhale a deep breath and roll my eyes.

"You know Mom and Dad have never had this amazing relationship. Mom married Dad for his money. Plain and simple. Mom knew he moved his entire company here because of some girl, but she didn't care."

My blood starts to boil through my veins. I've never understood the two of them, and after hearing this, I'm even more frustrated. I try to wrap my head around what I'm hearing, and then I remember. "But, wait, go back to the barn. What did he do?"

"The night before he moved to California, he poured gasoline all over the barn, which had tons of animals in it. It devastated the farm for a while. That was the beginning of the downfall for them. The stress got to be too much, and Randy's dad had a heart attack and died."

I grip my chest at the sudden pain racing through my heart. So, this is why Natalie never knew her grandpa.

"Mom said there was something weird with their insurance that wouldn't cover it. She didn't know the details, and of course, no one could prove it was Dad who had started the fire. It's not like Grandpa could have covered the damage anyway. Six years later, when Dad moved TimeLand here, the Spencer's still hadn't fully recovered. Sounds like it's just gotten worse from there."

"Natalie kept saying they moved the company here to purposefully ruin the ranch."

"Oh, one thousand percent," she says without hesitation.

"What the fuck? Why would Dad do that?"

She laughs again. "You've met our dad, right?"

I let out a sigh. "Yes ..."

"He came back with this notion of wanting to help the town, and blah, blah, blah but it's all bullshit. He's a vindictive man, and he wanted to prove to Tracy that she should have chosen him.

"I guess there was a big blowup when we were little about Dad buying the land to build our house. Don't think that location wasn't purchased on purpose. He

HOW WE HATED

wanted to look down on their property like some kind of trophy case as he watched it go to shit."

"God! Fuck him!" I sit up, not able to lie there anymore. "I knew he was an asshole, but this is too much."

"Welcome to our lovely family," she responds sarcastically.

I close my eyes and think. "What do I do?"

She laughs. "I don't think there's anything you can do. It's already been done." She pauses, then asks, her voice laced with surprise, "You really like her, don't you?"

I nod before I respond, "I really do. She pushes me like no one has before. In a good way."

I hear her let out a breath, but she doesn't say anything for a few seconds.

"Then, you'll have to prove to her family that you aren't our dad. That you're different."

"And how do I go about doing that?" I ask, feeling helpless.

"I don't know, but I do know you'll figure it out. You always do."

I plop back down on my bed. "Gee, sis ... I called you to help me feel better and ..." I let my thoughts trail off.

"And now, you know the truth. Hopefully, you understand Natalie's thoughts more. If there's one thing I've heard about her dad, it's that he's genuinely a really good man. He's very liked in our community. I know it doesn't faze us one bit to go against our parents' wishes because of the assholes they both are, which we know firsthand. But that's different for her. You have to respect that. Shit, we should be jealous of that."

I nod even though she can't see me. "Yeah, I hear that."

"Sorry, little bro. I hate to say you're stuck between a rock and a hard place, but …" She trails off, obviously trying not to laugh.

"But I'm fucked."

"Yeah, pretty much." She finally lets out her laugh.

"Well, thanks for your help," I say sarcastically.

She laughs harder. "Happy to help ruin your day even more."

"Talk soon?" I ask.

"Of course. Love you, bro."

"Love you too, sis."

I hang up, feeling even worse than I did before I called her.

How can I convince Natalie's dad that I'm not like my dad and I shouldn't be judged like I am?

CHAPTER 31

Natalie

"Hey, Ashley," I say unenthusiastically as I answer her phone call.

"Girl, what's wrong?"

I sigh as I plop down on my bed, exhausted from the thoughts going through my head. "Everything."

"Then, it's a good thing I called. I'm coming to pick you up. I want to go get some lunch."

"Okay…"

"Uh-huh. I need a little more enthusiasm out of you."

I grin even though she can't see me. "Fine. Yay!" I say, faking excitement.

"That's better." She laughs. "I'll be there in ten minutes."

I make sure I look at least a little presentable and head out of my room. "Mom, I'm going to get something

HOW WE HATED

to eat with Ashley," I say as I enter the kitchen, where she's canning some jam.

"Okay. I have money in my purse if you need some," she responds.

"I've got it. Thanks though."

She steps away from what she was doing and comes closer to me. "Hey." She places her hand on my shoulder. "Is everything okay? You seem a little off."

I force a smile, though all I want to do is cry. I can't let her see that because then there'll be no holding back and I'll have to tell her. I'm not ready to tell her. I have to decide if this is even worth upsetting my family over.

"Yeah. Just tired. Maybe some caffeine at lunch will help me."

She eyes me, and I know she knows I'm lying, but thankfully, she lets me go without questioning me more. We've always had a great relationship like that. She knows I'll talk to her when I'm ready—I always do. I love that she gives me the space to work it out in my head first though.

Ashley texts me, saying she's here, so I grab my purse and give my mom a hug. "See you later."

She returns my hug. "Love you, so much."

"Love you too, Mom."

I walk out the door and head to Ashley's car, where I plop down in the seat with a huff.

"Hey." She slaps my leg with the back of her hand. "I told you I'd need more enthusiasm from you, none of this moping crap."

With my head lying back on the headrest, I turn to her with a sigh. "Sorry. It's just that I'm a wreck over this Dalton thing. How did I get myself in this situation?"

"By situation, do you mean, how did you end up dating one of the hottest guys in school? Because I don't really see the problem there."

"You don't. But they will." I point back to my house, then reach for the seat belt and click it into the buckle as she drives away from the curb.

"What would they really do?"

I look down and fidget with my phone. "I've never disappointed my dad. He'd probably feel like I was betraying him." I look back at her. "I don't want him to ever feel that way. My dad is the most amazing man I've ever met. He's already been through so much, all basically because of Dalton's dad."

"But it's *your* life."

"But he's *my* dad." I glance back at the house. "He deserves a daughter who respects him more. Mike Wick ruined my dad's life in more ways than one. He'll never be okay with us dating."

"Then, end it with Dalton," she states so bluntly that my eyes pop out of my head. "Ha! Your reaction says everything I need to know about that option." She grabs my hand. "You really like him, don't you?"

I nod, biting my inner lip.

"Don't you think your dad would understand then?"

I drop my head back on the headrest again. "I just don't know."

When she makes a left turn instead of a right toward the downtown area, I ask, "Where are we going?"

She gives me a half smile. "To Ben's. Dalton asked me to come pick you up. Looks like you two need to talk even more than I thought."

I'm not sure if I should be mad that she lied to me

HOW WE HATED

or happy that she's taking me to see him. All of it just adds to the jumble of emotions that are flying through my head.

We pull up, and Dalton is waiting by the curb for us.

Seeing him doesn't help my emotions because, right now, I'm overjoyed he's here even though I know I shouldn't be.

He opens the car door for me, and when I step out, he takes my head in his hands and kisses me softly yet so passionately that I melt in his grasp.

"I'm glad you're here," Dalton says as he places his forehead on mine.

"Me too," I admit.

Standing here with him is the best I've felt since we were together in that restroom last night. He's this missing part of me that I never knew existed, and now, I can't let him go.

"You two have fun," Ashley says, waving at us as she heads toward the barn, where I assume the whole crew is.

"Thank you, Ashley," Dalton says.

"Yeah, thanks for dragging me out here," I respond.

"You know I got you, girl." Ashley grins, then walks into the barn.

Dalton turns back to me, his hand still on the nape of my neck, his eyes burning into mine. "I want to figure out a way to make this work."

I place my hands on his arms, making sure he knows I'm serious. "Me too."

He steps back and holds my hand in his as he walks me to the curb, the area that is seemingly turning into our spot.

We sit down, and he stares forward, almost like he's collecting his thoughts. He looks so intense in this state that I allow him to do so and wait for what he has to say.

"I talked to my sister," he finally says, but I'm not following.

"Okay … what did she say?"

"We didn't grow up like you. Our parents were never the loving, *wanting to be with their kids* parents. My grandpa, on the other hand, he was my everything. Since he passed, it's just been Leslie and me."

I place my hand on his shoulder. "I'm sorry you didn't get to experience life like I did, growing up," I say sincerely.

He looks at me through the corner of his eye. "I didn't understand why you cared so much about what your dad thought. I didn't understand what that might feel like to let him down in any way." He stares off into space in front of him again. "I couldn't care less what my dad thinks. He's trying to rule my life in ways I don't want. Anything I can do against that is a win for me."

"But—"

He stops me by turning to face me fully and grabs my hands in his. "But your life isn't like that." He lets out a somber breath. "I had no idea what my dad had done to you guys."

I drop my chin and close my eyes. He places his finger under my chin and lifts it up until I meet his eyes.

"My sister told me everything. I can't believe he was that vindictive of a person." He pauses and shakes his head. "Actually, I can believe it, which is why I hate him so much. That's not me though. I—*we*—shouldn't be punished for his sins."

HOW WE HATED

I grip his hands tighter. "I know that. But my dad will never see it that way."

"Then, we need to prove it to him. Prove that I'm worthy of you."

"How?" I plead.

He wraps his arm around me, pulling me closer to him. "We'll figure it out. Until then, we'll be more careful. I promise. No more close calls, like with Trish."

He turns his head to face me, and I lean up and give him a kiss. I might not know how this is going to work, but I do know I feel best when I'm in his arms.

CHAPTER 32

Dalton

It's been a week since homecoming, and Natalie and I couldn't be better, except for the whole *sneaking around* thing. The more time that goes by, the more we both realize this is real and we need to figure some way for us to be together in the open, for everyone to know.

After school, I see Thomas with a group of guys, so I go up to him. "Hey, man. Can we talk?"

Thomas looks at me like I threw manure all over him. "Fuck off."

I grit my teeth. There is a reason I've never liked this guy, but knowing the truth now, I can't really blame him.

"I'm serious. Just a second. I need to talk to you about something."

With a huff, he turns and walks a few steps away from his group so we can talk in private. I've practiced

HOW WE HATED

this speech over and over again in my head, so here goes nothing.

"I know you've never liked me, but I want to make it clear that whatever horrible things my dad has done genuinely had nothing to do with me."

He squints his eyes and wrinkles his forehead, obviously wondering why I'm telling him this now.

I continue, "I need you to know that. I'm not my dad. And take away all those things and think about it. You don't even know me."

"Why do I care?" he asks bluntly.

"I want to squash everything between us. I don't know you just as much as you don't know me. We were raised to hate each other for no good reason."

He glares at me. "Oh, I can give you a good reason."

I hold up my hands in surrender. "And I fully agree you could. I just found out everything, which is why I'm standing here. I didn't understand things the way I do now, so I'm coming to you, so you know that's not me. I don't want to be lumped into that entire situation anymore."

"But you are. And honestly, I don't give a fuck about you either way. You've been dead to me for years, so, no, this changes nothing."

He walks away and joins his group of friends. I know it might seem like that didn't go well, but it went down exactly as I'd expected. Gaining his trust won't happen overnight. But I know if I can get in with him, it will put me one step closer to being able to date Natalie freely.

The next day at practice, I keep my eye on Thomas. On the field is where I can gain his trust the most.

I see him sitting on the bench, catching his breath after some drills, so I go sit a few feet away from him, where no one is in between us. I don't say a word, so he seemingly doesn't even know I'm there as he wipes away the sweat dripping off his brow.

I grab a bottle of water, squirt it in my mouth, and set it down, taking another deep breath to calm my heart from racing after those drills. Before I get up, I grab a towel from the container next to me and toss it his way before leaving without saying a word.

As I get back to my position, I see him wiping his face off with it. Him not throwing it on the ground just because I gave it to him is a win in my book.

When game time rolls around on Friday, I do the same thing. All week, I've tried not to make my intentions obvious by doing things I do for my other teammates all the time. Before, I just purposely never helped him that way.

Eli calls off the play, and we both go running. I turn right and catch the ball just before going out of bounds. I look back and see Thomas untangling himself from the guy he tackled to the ground so I could make that catch.

I jog over and offer my hand to him to help him up. To my surprise, he grabs it, and I lift him back to his feet, slap his back, and say, "Great block." Then, I jog back to the line to get ready for the next play.

HOW WE HATED

I stay after practice on Tuesday to get some extra reps in the gym and really stretch before I head home. Natalie can't meet me tonight, so I plan on just skipping my run and getting some homework done.

I'm driving out of the mostly empty parking lot when I see Thomas with his truck hood up, so I head his way.

Putting my truck in park, I hop out, leaving it running. "Need a jump?"

He stares at me, and to my surprise, I don't get the normal *fuck you* glare I've gotten for so many years. Now, don't get me wrong; he's not happy I'm here to help him, but he doesn't look like he wants to kill me either. Progress.

"Yeah, I can't tell if it's the battery or if the alternator is going dead. I just called my dad to come help me. People with fancy, new cars don't know shit, and most of them can't even jump this old beast."

"It's all good. I have jumper cables and an old beast, just like you. We'll see if we can get it going."

I jog back to my truck and reposition it so the cables will run between both trucks.

I toss him the cables to hook them up to his truck as I pop the hood of mine. He hands me back the other side of the cables, and I connect them to my battery, then walk back to my truck and crank the engine. My truck roars to life in a sound I've come to love more than any of my favorite songs.

Thomas hops in his truck and cranks the engine. It takes a few tries, but it eventually turns over, so I unhook the cables and put them back in my truck. When I shut the passenger door, I see his dad pulling up next to us, his expression not hiding his disdain that I'm standing here.

"Everything okay? Looks like you got it started," Randy says.

I walk up to him, man to man, and offer my hand to him, just as my grandpa taught me.

He used to always say, "A man's handshake says a lot about him."

Thankfully, Randy does the same, and we shake hands.

"Yes, sir. We got it jumped."

He looks a little perplexed, which I take as a good thing. If I'm going to change his mind about me, then I'm on the right path.

He doesn't say anything, and really, there's no need for him to, so I head back to my truck, shouting over my shoulder, "See you, Thomas."

"Yeah, thanks for the jump," he replies.

"Anytime."

I put the truck in reverse, pull out of the spot, and drive away, giving them a friendly wave as I do so.

A couple of days later, I'm leaving practice when I see Thomas a few feet in front of me in the parking lot, walking with another guy.

I decide to try to talk to him, so I yell, "Hey, Thomas. You got a minute?"

I don't get the same glare I have in the past, but his body language says I'm still on his shit list. He hits the

HOW WE HATED

guy's shoulder with the back of his palm, motioning that he'll talk to him later. Then, he waits for me to get to where he's standing.

"Yeah, what's up?" he asks.

I continue walking toward him and as I get close, he starts again keeping my same pace as I ask, "How's the truck?"

"It was just the battery. Got a new one, and she's good as new."

"Glad to hear. I wanted to talk to you about something else."

He doesn't say anything, so I look at him, and he raises his eyebrows, like he's waiting for me to say something. We stop walking when I get to my truck, and I turn to face him.

"Your sister," is all I say, and I'm pushed up against my truck so fast that I feel the beast shake behind me.

"Don't you fucking touch her," he growls in my face.

I've known Thomas to be a mean son of a bitch, but this takes it to a whole other level.

I hold up my hands in surrender. "I just want to—"

He places his forearm into my chest. "You want to nothing. You hear me? Nothing. She is absolutely off-limits to you."

He pushes himself off of me and turns to walk away with a huff.

That did not go well.

CHAPTER 33

Natalie

I'm sitting in my room, doing homework, when Thomas bursts in.

"Please tell me there's nothing going on between you and Dalton Wick."

I'm speechless as I stare at him and blink.

My expression must answer his question because he steps closer. "You have got to be shitting me."

I stand up, knocking my books to the ground. "How did you find out?"

His eyebrows rise so high that I think they might fly away, considering I just solidified what he'd thought was happening.

"How could you?"

I grab his arm. "It just happened. Believe me, neither of us meant to fall for each other."

He pushes me off of him. "End it."

I wrap my arms around myself in a hug as tears

HOW WE HATED

sting my eyes. "I don't want to. I like him. I'm happy with him."

"You're happy, sneaking around, because you know our father will lose his shit?"

I reach for him again, but he quickly moves his arm away from me.

"You can't tell him!"

"You're right. I can't. Because there's nothing to tell. You"—he glares at me—"will end it with him."

He stomps out of my room in the same way he entered. I plop down on my bed and cry for the first time since all of this started. I cry for my family, but I also cry for Dalton. I don't want to lose him.

Five minutes later, Mom calls out that dinner is ready. Knowing I have to put on the show of my life, I get up and fix my face only to see my eyes are all puffy and red.

There's no hiding this.

I do the best I can and head out of my bedroom to the kitchen table, where Thomas is sitting directly across from me, staring daggers into my soul. Dad pulls out his chair to sit, and the tension between Thomas and me is so intense that I feel like I could burst.

Mom places the last of the dishes on the table, and we all jump in.

"Sweetheart, how come your face is all red?" Mom asks.

Of course, she noticed. After learning of Dalton's parents, I should be happy that she cares enough to ask, but right now, I really wish she hadn't.

"It's nothing." I try to blow her off. "I was watching a show where the girl died, and it made me cry," I lie, making myself feel even shittier.

Thomas lets out a huff, and I purposefully get up to get something to drink.

"Do you want something other than water, dear?" Mom asks, considering she already had a cup of water sitting in front of me.

"Yeah, if that's okay?" I respond.

"Sure, get whatever you want." She dismisses me, and I hide my head in the fridge, taking a few breaths to calm my nerves.

"Thomas, how was practice today?" Dad asks.

My chest tightens, and I close my eyes, praying he doesn't say a word as I grab a Bubly sparkling water out of the fridge and head back to the table.

"I got to knock Dalton Wick on his ass, so that was fun," he states.

"I hope that wasn't intentional for any other reason but the game of football," Mom states, surprising me.

We've never really talked about the Wicks this way. I shouldn't be surprised though. Mom doesn't want Thomas to physically hurt Dalton—she doesn't want to hurt a fly—but hearing she has at least a little compassion for him gives me some hope.

Thomas lets out a hard laugh. "Yes, it was very intentional. And, no, it had nothing to do with football."

"Thomas," Mom sighs.

Thomas looks at Dad for help, and he just shrugs.

"I mean, as long as he didn't get in trouble for doing so, I don't see why a few blows to knock him over would hurt."

Thomas directs his attention at me with his eyebrows slightly raised in a *told you so* manner.

HOW WE HATED

I open my drink and force myself to take a bite even though I have zero appetite.

Thankfully, the subject is changed to what happened on the ranch today, and I keep quiet while I try not to throw up with every bite I take.

After dinner, we all help Mom clean the kitchen. Of course, Thomas and Dad are the first to bow out, always leaving the last few items for Mom and me.

"Everything okay?" Mom asks. "You sure were quiet during dinner."

I wipe the counter for the second time just so I don't have to face her. "Yeah, I'm fine."

She still doesn't pry, which I appreciate.

I clean the rag and place it on top of the faucet. "Thanks for dinner."

"Hey." She stops me and looks in my eyes. Instantly, I feel tears well up, and she pulls me to her. "I love you."

I wrap my arms around her. "I love you too."

She holds me like that for a few seconds, giving me her love unconditionally because she knows I need it right now even though she has no clue why.

She pulls away from me, and I grin in her direction. "Thanks, Mom."

"Anytime."

I head back to my room, so thankful for a caring mom who doesn't pry. She knows I'll come to her when I'm ready.

My phone fell to the floor when Thomas was in my room, and when I pick it up, I see I have a few texts from Dalton.

Are you coming?
Everything OK?

I text back.

> **No. Everything is not OK.
> Thomas knows.**

He replies instantly.

*I know. I'm sorry. I thought we could
get him on our side.*

> **Are you crazy? You knew he'd
> never go for this.**

*I'm sorry. I fucked up. I'm just sick
of having to hide. I want to be out in
the open with you.*

Tears roll down my face again. My heart is absolutely broken, but I know there's nothing I can do. I have to end this. I type out:

> **I'm sorry, but we need to put
> a stop to this.**

Then, I sit on it with my thumb hovering over the Send button, my stomach turning so much that I feel like I'm going to throw up.

He must sense my hesitation because before I can hit Send, he texts.

*We'll figure this out, I promise.
It's worth it. We're worth it.*

HOW WE HATED

Tears stream down my face. *Is it worth it though? Is breaking my father's heart worth saving my own?*

When I put it that way, it's an easy choice. I've hated Dalton basically my entire life. How can I go against my family's wishes for someone that I like now, but I have no clue if it will be forever? Family is though. Trust is. Honesty is.

I close my eyes and do the one thing I don't want to do, but I must. I hit Send.

I'm sorry, but we need to put a stop to this.

Then, I turn off my phone, not wanting to see his response because I know I'll cave and change my mind. My heart is broken, but I need to accept this and move on. We can't be together. We'll never be able to make this real. I'm sure his father wouldn't accept me the same way.

I've lived this long without him. I just need to remember what life was like when I hated him and go back to that.

Knowing there's always things I can do at the school FFA, I yell to my mom, "I'm heading to FFA for a little bit," then head out the door toward my brother's truck. Technically, it's supposed to be both of ours that we share, but since he's turned sixteen, I allow him to drive it all the time since I can normally grab a ride with Ashley or Susie anywhere I need to go.

The truck roars to life, and I peel out on the gravel road in front of our house before he can stop me.

The school is empty, but I know the code to get

back to the FFA area, so I hop out of the truck, enter the code, then get back in as I wait for the gate to open so I can drive back there.

I get right to work on cleaning up and getting lost in the music that I have playing through a laptop we have sitting in the main area. I left my phone at home so I wouldn't be tempted to check Dalton's response, so I'm thankful the laptop is here, or I'd be lost in my head for sure.

I've completely lost track of time when I hear someone open the gate behind me and see my dad's truck driving through. My breath hitches when I see my dad and my brother staring back at me.

My brother hops out of the truck, and to my surprise, my dad puts the truck in reverse and leaves.

"What the fuck, Natalie?" Thomas says when he knows Dad's out of hearing range and it's just the two of us. "You can't just take my truck. Dad had to take me to pick up a school project that I needed to work on tonight. Your phone is off, so we couldn't get ahold of you."

I'm so not in the mood to put up with him, so I have no problem barking back. "First, it is *our* truck, and you're lucky I've always let you use it and not made you share with me, and, two, I left my phone at home on purpose all because of *you*," I spit out.

"Why would you leave your phone at home because of me?" he asks, dumbfounded.

"Don't act so smug. I broke it off with Dalton. Are you happy? That's why I left my phone at home and why I'm here."

He smirks as he crosses his arms over his chest.

HOW WE HATED

"Yeah, actually, I am. You shouldn't have even been talking to that guy, let alone dating him."

"You don't even know him!" I yell.

"And neither should you!" he yells right back. "Our entire life, we've been told how they are the enemy, the sole reason why our family's ranch is struggling. How could you do that to Dad?"

"I know, but that's not Dalton. Dalton has nothing to do with that. It was his dad. That's not fair that we should hate him for things that happened before he was even born."

Thomas shakes his head with a smug expression. "Doesn't matter. Guilty by association is still guilty."

I huff and get back to work. Obviously, there's no point in arguing with him, as he'll never change his mind, which is exactly why I had to break it off with Dalton.

"Come on. Get in the truck."

"No." I get back to what I was doing before he got here.

He grabs the rake from me. "Dad said you have to come home, so get your ass in the truck, or I will tell him why you're really here."

I clench my teeth and grab the rake back from him, putting it back where it belongs before heading to the truck with a huff.

Thankfully, he keeps his mouth shut during the drive home and blasts his music, like normal. When we pull up to the house, I head straight to my room and shut my door, not wanting to talk to anyone else for the rest of the night.

CHAPTER 34

Natalie

I didn't get a lick of sleep. The thought of having to sit in front of Dalton in class was making my anxiety sky high. I still haven't turned on my phone from last night. Not knowing what he might have texted back is killing me, but I really don't think I'll be able to handle anything that he said.

To say I'm a mess is the understatement of a lifetime.

"You ready to go?" Thomas peeks his head into my room.

I don't say a word, just grab my bag and walk past him with a huff.

"It's like that, huh?" he says under his breath.

I just ignore him and head to the truck, thankful that my mom was nowhere to be seen.

It was hard enough to try to act normal around her this morning while I ate breakfast and got ready. I guess

HOW WE HATED

I should be glad I don't have to fake it with Thomas because I'm not sure just how much more I can take.

I'm able to sneak in and out of first period without having to see Dalton, but now that second period is about to start, I know my luck has ended.

I walk into class, and my heart skips a beat when I see Dalton sitting there, slumped down in his seat, staring at his phone.

He looks up, and when our eyes meet, I can't breathe. His expression of hope just about kills me.

We stare at each other for a second before I close my eyes and head straight to my desk, sitting in my chair with my back to him and begging myself not to turn around.

"Where's your phone?" he whispers, making me blink away tears at the sound of his voice.

I dig in my bag, holding it up and showing that it's turned off.

He huffs and tosses his phone on the desk a little too loudly, making the class turn his way. Thankfully, Miss Hernandez ignores him and goes on.

I don't know how, but I make it through the class without completely losing it.

When the bell rings, I grab my things, but before I can get up, Dalton walks past me, saying, "Turn it on."

I stay seated in my chair, taking a deep breath and gathering my thoughts as everyone else leaves the classroom. I take my phone out of my bag and stare at it like it's some puzzle that could solve the problems of the world, but no one seems to be able to figure out how to turn it on. At least, that's how it makes me feel inside.

When I notice I'm the only person left in the

classroom, I grab my things and race out of the room, heading straight to the restroom and into a stall. My heart is racing as I turn on my phone and wait for whatever Dalton had to say to pop up.

As the dings come in, I feel like my stomach falls to the ground.

Please don't do this. We can figure it out.

Natalie, I mean it. I want to be with you.

*You mean more to me than anyone
I've ever known.*

Natalie, please talk to me.

*I'm going down to our spot. Please
come meet me so we can talk.*

I'm here. Will you please come?

I'm going home, but I'm not giving up on us.

The last text came through past midnight. Knowing he waited that long for me out there breaks my heart even more. I don't want to hurt him this way, but I really don't have a choice. I have no doubt that Thomas will tell my dad, and if he does, my dad will put a stop to it right then and there.

The warning bell rings, and I clench my phone in my hand, inhaling a deep breath and willing myself to go to my next class.

HOW WE HATED

I exit the stall and leave the restroom, praying I can make it through the rest of the day. As I enter my third period class, I take my seat just when I feel my phone buzz in my hand. I didn't even realize I was still clenching it.

I look down at it to see Dalton's text.

Please meet me tonight.

Tears well in my eyes. This is exactly why I turned off my phone last night. I knew I couldn't tell him no. And I still can't. So, I reply.

OK.

After school, I hop into Ashley's car for a ride home since I didn't feel like working on the FFA stuff while I waited for Thomas to get done with practice.

"Okay, we're alone. What's going on with you today?" she asks with zero hesitation once the doors are closed.

I let out a harsh laugh. "Is it that obvious?"

"Hell yes, it is. I can only imagine it has something to do with Dalton and the way he couldn't keep his eyes off of you at lunch and you looked like you wanted to crawl in a hole and cry."

I drop my head back on her headrest. "Thomas knows."

"Oh … yeah … that's not good."

"No. He made me end it."

"I'm sorry, but that's an asshole move. How did he find out?"

"Dalton tried to get him on our side."

Now, it's time for her to laugh out loud. "That's an even more asshole move."

I turn my head to face her. "He thought he was helping. I know he knows why my dad feels the way he does, but I don't think he truly gets it. My dad is a prideful man, and his dad has ruined so many things."

She places her hand on my arm. "I'm sorry. It was fun while it lasted, I guess. How is Dalton taking it?"

"He's not. I had to shut off my phone last night so I wouldn't give in to anything he said."

"And today?"

"I gave in."

She laughs again and cranks the engine. "Of course you did."

CHAPTER 35

Natalie

I sit through dinner, not saying a word. I can't. My anxiety is through the roof at the idea of meeting Dalton tonight. I have to end it, but I'm afraid I won't have the strength to do so when I'm with him.

I push around the little food I put on my plate, knowing there's no real way I'm going to be able to consume it.

Thomas gets up to put his empty plate in the dishwasher, so I do the same.

Once my dad and Thomas are gone from the kitchen, my mom places her hand on mine. "Don't worry about anything else. I'll get the rest."

"Thanks," I say, trying my hardest not to look her in the eye.

"Hey." She stops me as I walk by. "I'm here if there's anything you want to talk about."

HOW WE HATED

I give her a hug. "I know. Thanks, Mom. I'm going to go take Brandy for a ride."

"Okay. Have fun."

I go to my room, change into something that's more comfortable to ride Brandy, and head out to the barn.

When I open the barn door, Brandy lights up my world, just like she always does.

"Hey, girl." I run my finger down her soft brown mane. "Thanks for always being there for me."

She huffs, almost like she understands what I said, which puts a small smile on my face.

"I wish I had your life right now," I say with a sigh. "Life choices can be hard sometimes. I wish I didn't have to choose, but I know I do."

She nudges her head into my palm, almost like she's hugging me, so I wrap my arms around her and hug her like I have a thousand times before, but needing it even more now.

After I get a saddle on her, I hop up and start my journey out to the end of our property to meet Dalton one last time.

I take my time riding out there, going over in my head a thousand times what I'm going to say and wondering how this is going to go. Even though we're meeting at the same time we always have, I can tell the seasons are shifting and the darkness is falling faster than it did at the beginning of the school year.

By the time I get out to meet him, the sun is making its final descent behind the hills that surround us. Though it's not as bright out, there's no missing the guy I've gone from hating to—dare I say—loving, standing there, waiting for me to arrive.

What surprises me is the setup he has going on. He laid a blanket on the ground with some food already there, like a picnic.

I don't say anything as I dismount Brandy and tie her to the fence, then walk in silence to where Dalton is standing.

"Hi," he says.

I haven't been able to look up, so I stand here, staring at the ground, focusing on my breaths. He takes his finger and places it under my chin, lifting it until I meet his eyes.

I instantly close mine, willing the tears that are threatening to appear to stop.

"Open your eyes," he whispers.

I do, and one tear falls down my cheek, which he wipes away with his thumb.

"Don't cry."

I swallow and inhale a deep breath.

"I know this isn't what you want. That's obvious. But I get it. I understand. So, you know what? I'm willing to wait. To wait for you. You won't live at home forever, and neither will I. We can go away to college—together— away from here. Away from any drama of Leighton River, where no one knows us and we can be together like we want to."

Is that even possible?

He nods like he heard my thoughts. "We can make it happen. I have no doubt. I can basically play football wherever. I'll let you know all the colleges that I've talked to and who have made offers. You tell me which one you want to go to, and we'll go there together."

HOW WE HATED

A few more tears fall down my face, only now, these are tears of relief. Out of all the things that have gone through my head since yesterday, this is not one that I even considered.

"I respect that you want to honor your father. I wish I had that kind of relationship with mine. We'll have to figure out how we'll tell him in a few years, but we can deal with that then. Hopefully, by then, I will have been able to separate myself from my father, and we can prove to your dad that I'm not like him."

I don't know how this will work, but knowing we have a chance rips the dread I've felt for so long away, and for the first time in a while, I feel like there's hope.

He lowers his body so he's looking right into my eyes. "What do you think?"

I wrap my arms around him and kiss him like I've wanted to do more than anything since the second I saw him in class today.

Our kisses turn intense, and when he lowers us to the ground with ease, I let him until we're lying together.

With all the stress running through my body for the last twenty-four hours, the relief he gives me pushes me to want even more from him.

With one leg propped up, I run my fingers under his shirt while he lies on top of me.

He reaches up behind him, removing his shirt with one hand, then nestles back on top of me. As I run my fingers down his muscular back, he slips his fingers under my shirt, sending chills throughout my body just with his touch.

When he moves my shirt up, I lift my arms so he can remove it completely. Feeling his skin against my stomach brings a warmth I've been dying to feel for too long.

He pulls back and looks in my eyes as he says, "I want you, Natalie. I know I said I'd wait for us to be together, but I want this. I want it so bad."

I lean up and meet his lips with a kiss. "I want it too."

The sexiest grin I've ever seen covers his face as he moves down my body, slipping my bra to the side and sucking my nipple into his mouth. Instantly, I buck my back off the ground from the sensations that he sent flying through me.

I run my fingers through his hair as he kisses my stomach.

"Are you sure?" he asks as he fumbles with my waistband, teasingly placing his fingers under the fabric.

"Yes," I say breathlessly.

"Oh, thank God," he responds as he slides my pants down my legs.

Leaving my panties on, he moves his palm down my stomach and over my core, moving in slight circles, bringing my arousal to full force.

"Dalton," I whisper.

He moves up my body so he's face to face with me. "Natalie," he whispers back, sending a zing of thrill to rush through my body.

He reaches for his bag and grabs a condom from the side pocket. Holding it up with a grin, he moves back down my body, taking my panties all the way down to my toes and tossing them to the side. Standing up, he stares from above me as he unbuttons his pants and removes them completely.

His erection sticks out through his boxer briefs,

HOW WE HATED

making a ripple of excitement of what's to come race through me.

I had sex last year with my ex, but I never felt about him the way I do about Dalton.

Everything about him is different.

The way he makes me feel is different.

I know this will be different too—in the best way possible.

He pulls his boxer briefs down and drops to his knees before me, ripping the condom open with his teeth.

After he slides it on himself, he slowly positions himself between my legs, placing his hand on my face. "I'm falling in love with you, Natalie. I know this will be worth the wait until I get you again."

He positions himself at my entrance as he slides into me for the first time.

I lock eyes with him as immense pleasure radiates through me.

How did this happen? How am I here, falling head over heels for the one person I never thought it would happen with? But it has, and being here in this moment is the best I've ever felt.

He kisses my lips, then begins to push in and out of me slowly, gripping my shoulders to hold me tighter as he does.

Dropping my head back, I moan from the sensations building inside me so deep that it's driving me wild. He moves faster, and the intensity builds stronger.

"I want to feel you," he whispers, bringing me to an edge I didn't even know existed.

I knew it would be different with him, but this is

unimaginable. Now, I understand the lure of sex. Now, I understand just how amazing this is, and I have no idea how we're going to wait until next year to be with each other again.

He slows for a second, and it's like he just pushed me over the ledge when he pulls out slightly and pushes back in, causing my body to convulse around his.

"Yes." He pauses, feeling me squeeze around him.

Two seconds later, he grunts as his release pours inside me.

He kisses my lips as we come down from something so magnificent that I'm not sure if I'll ever recover.

"Thank you for not giving up on us," he whispers, kissing my lips between every word.

After he pulls out of me, he curls to my side and holds me close to him. The night sky has fallen all around us, the stars and moon our only light source.

I sigh happily in his arms, feeling so content that I could float away on a cloud of pure glee.

Everything that's amazing in this moment is ripped away when I see headlights heading directly our way.

CHAPTER 36

Natalie

I tense in his arms. "Dalton."

"What the fuck?" he whispers. "Who could …"

He doesn't finish that sentence when we both realize we're here, naked and about to get caught by either my dad or my brother, both of which means we're completely screwed.

We jump up and race to get dressed as the truck comes closer and closer.

With the high beams shining directly on us, I slide my shirt over my head, and Dalton stands, buttoning up his pants as the truck screeches to a halt and the door flies open.

The sounds of the roaring engine and the cocking of a gun are all that surrounds us when my dad comes rushing up to Dalton, shotgun pointed in his direction. Thomas must have told him I've been secretly seeing

HOW WE HATED

Dalton. I told mom I was riding Brandy so he must have figured out I'd be back here with him.

"Get the fuck off my property!"

"Dad!" I yell, running toward him.

"Natalie, get in the truck," he bites out.

"Dad, stop. Don't do this."

Dalton holds up his hands as he stares down the barrel of a Remington shotgun. "Sir, I'm sorry. But I love your daughter."

"You have three seconds to get off of my property, or I'll shoot you with my daddy's gun. We'll call it retribution after all these years," Dad says firmly yet as calm as he could be.

"Daddy, stop! I'm sorry, but he's not like them. I love him!" I plead.

He doesn't take his eyes off of Dalton. "Natalie, I said, get in the truck. One."

Dalton looks at me, wondering what he should do.

Dad holds the gun steady, pointed right at Dalton. "Two."

"I'm sorry, Natalie," is all Dalton says before turning and racing across the creek.

Dad drops his gun and stomps back to the truck.

"Dad, talk to me. You need to understand. He's different," I beg.

"Get in the truck." He walks to Brandy, untying her knot and hitting her side. "Head on home, Brandy."

With tears rolling down my face, I hop in the truck, terrified about what just happened.

Dad puts the truck in drive and skids the tires as he flips the truck around to head back to our house. I've never seen him drive so erratically. Seeing him grip the steering wheel so tight that his knuckles are white frightens me, but the way he's staying silent downright terrifies me.

"Dad—" I say, but he cuts me off.

"Not a word, Natalie. Not now."

He practically flies through our ranch back to our house, the truck sliding and bumping with every dirt pile we hit. When we get there, Mom is standing at our back door, worry written all over her face.

Dad kills the engine and gets out, slamming the door before rushing past Mom, still staying completely silent.

Mom races to my side.

"Mom!" I cry out, reaching my arms open for her to hug me.

Thankfully, she does, and I bawl into her shoulder as she holds me tight.

"Well, now, I understand what's been going on with you the past few days," she says caringly.

"I'm sorry, Mom. I tried to stop it."

"But the heart wants what the heart wants …" she says, trailing off.

I cry even harder as I nod my head.

"Thomas told me he found out and made you put a stop to it."

I nod again. "And I was. I was putting a stop to it."

She rubs her hand over my hair. "Sweetheart, I have no doubt you were, and that's why you were so miserable. I knew something was going on."

"We were just saying goodbye. We were ending it. He told me he'd wait for me. We'd go to college, where we could finally be together."

"Sounds like he really likes you."

"He does, Mom. Believe me, neither of us planned on this happening, but when we did …" I can't finish that sentence as more tears fall.

"When you did, it was magical."

I cry out even more.

"I know, baby. I know. I've been there, remember?"

"But Dad and Thomas, they'll never allow it."

She sighs, knowing I'm right.

We sit there, holding each other for a few minutes longer.

"Don't worry about that right now. Let's get you inside and get your face cleaned up."

She turns me toward the house, where we walk together, her giving me the strength to do so.

She goes to the bathroom to grab a washcloth as I curl up in my bed.

How did the best night of my life turn to the worst night in the blink of an eye?

When she returns, I lie on her lap and cry as she runs her hand down my hair and comforts me in my time of need.

Dalton

I burst into my dad's study. "Why are you such a vindictive asshole?!"

Of course, me calling him an asshole doesn't go over very well, but I don't give a shit.

He throws back his chair and stands up. "What did you just say?"

"You heard me. Do you get a kick out of ruining people's lives?"

"Listen, you little shit, I don't know what you're talking about, but watch your tone with me. I'm your father."

"You might be my biological father, but you've never been a real father to me. You've never given a shit about me. How can someone care so much about ruining the Spencer ranch, yet not give two shits about their own flesh and blood?"

"Is that what you're bitching and moaning about? The Spencer ranch? Why do you care?"

I slam my fist against my chest. "I just had a gun pointed at my face because I was with Natalie on their property. All because of you."

He stands up straight and raises his eyebrows, a sudden calmness coming over him. "You. Had a gun pulled on you. By Randy Spencer?" he asks, all spaced out, almost happy to hear the news.

"Yes, because of you. I love her, but we've had to hide our relationship because of the horrible shit you've done to them over the years."

"Why would you want to be with someone from that poor trash of a family?" he asks like they're the scum of the earth.

"I guess the apple doesn't fall that far from the tree after all. Us Wick men are helpless when it comes to Spencer women." I cross my arms over my chest. "Don't

HOW WE HATED

think I don't know about how she turned your ass down when you were younger."

Enraged, he races toward me. "You don't know what you're talking about."

"I know all of what I'm talking about. You loved her. She didn't want you. So, you came back here to prove she should have chosen you. How can you live with yourself?"

He raises his arms to the sides. "Last time I checked, I've done a lot for this town. Way more than the Spencer's have done with their ranch. This town loves that I brought TimeLand here. People love us."

"You're sick."

"Yeah, well, I also have this town at my beck and call." He walks back to his desk and picks up the phone with a clear smirk on his face.

"What are you doing?" I ask, suddenly afraid of just what this man is truly capable of because he obviously has an idea in his head, and I have a feeling it's going to start even more shit.

He dials someone and waits for them to answer, staring at me like the disgusting human being he is.

"Hi, Sheriff Townsend." He waits for his reply, and my stomach drops. "Yes, I'd like for you to go arrest Randy Spencer. He just pulled a gun on my son."

"Dad, no!" I scream as I jump to grab the phone from him, but he pushes me away.

"Yes, he came onto my property and pointed a gun at him. Once he crossed that line, he broke the law."

"No, he didn't. I was on their property!" I scream out, hoping he hears me.

I can't hear what the sheriff is saying, but I pray

to God he's telling my dad he can't just go arrest Mr. Spencer.

"Well, I hear what you're saying, but I want you to hear me." He pauses for effect. "I can have a recall ballot drawn up by morning, and you know all it takes is my recommendation to change this town's feeling in a second. Now, I would hate to have to do that, but I would hate it even more if Randy did not get in trouble for breaking the law by pointing a gun at my son while on my property."

I wrestle for the phone some more, but my dad fights harder than I knew he even could.

"I'm glad you see it my way. Have a good night." He hangs up the phone and smiles at me. "It's done. He'll be arrested, all thanks to you. I'm sure your little girlfriend will just love that. Do you think they have money to afford a lawyer who could beat the attorneys I already have on retainer?"

"I'll testify. He wasn't on your property, and there were no other witnesses."

He laughs. "No need for witnesses. There's no way to prove he wasn't. All I'll need is a jury to see how, of course, you are willing to lie to save your girlfriend's dad. I'm just the protective father who is looking out for his son."

"Fuck!" I yell out loud. Then, I run out of the room while I scream, "I hate you."

"Love you too," he yells back, making me sick to my stomach even more.

I race to my room and slam the door while picking up my phone and calling Natalie. "Pick up. Please, pick up," I say under my breath.

HOW WE HATED

She doesn't, and my next three calls go unanswered as well.

Our football team has a text thread with all the players, so I scroll through the names, looking for Thomas, and hit Call once I find his name.

"How dare you fucking call me after what you did!" he answers.

I don't bother with any of that and just get straight to the point. "Your dad. Go get your dad. My dad called the sheriff, and he's having your dad arrested, saying he pointed the gun at me on our property."

"You have got to be shitting me."

"No!" I yell out. "Go get him."

He hangs up, and I pace my room, wondering what I can do. Then, it hits me. My dad can lie all he wants, but if I'm there to fight, saying I was trespassing on the Spencer's property, then maybe it will go on official record.

I grab my keys and race out of my house and straight to my truck. After I crank the engine, I peel out, racing down our long driveway. Our properties might back up to one another, but to drive from one house to the next, I have to go all the way down the hill and around this side of the ranch, which has never felt so big in my entire life.

When I get to their house, the sheriff is already there.

I put the truck in park and hop out, racing to their door when I'm stopped dead in my tracks by Sheriff Townsend escorting Randy out in handcuffs.

"No! Stop!" I plead, grabbing Sheriff Townsend's arm. "I was trespassing on his property. He thought I was going to burn down his barn, like my dad did. He had every right to protect what was his."

"Sorry, son. The law is the law. I was told he was on your property. The justice system will have to sort it out from here."

I look at Randy, who is hanging his head, completely defeated by my dad once again.

"This is bullshit!"

"Damn right it is!" Thomas comes up from behind me. Grabbing my arm, he turns me to face him and coldcocks me right in the jaw.

I fall to the ground, but don't get up as I rub my face.

"Get up and fight me!" Thomas yells.

"No! Stop!" Natalie screams from the front door, her mom right behind her.

"Natalie!" I yell out, getting up to go to her.

"Don't you fucking dare," Thomas growls, pushing me back toward my truck.

"Natalie, I'm sorry," I plead.

"Get your ass off my property. With your truck here, there's no way to say you weren't on my property, and I will personally kill you myself."

I look over to where Sheriff Townsend has already loaded Randy into the back of the patrol car, and he's getting in the car himself.

What's done is done. I need to find another way to help him before something really bad happens and this family loses everything.

"I will make this right, I promise," I state, looking Thomas in the eye.

"You've already done enough. I never want to see

HOW WE HATED

your fucking face for as long as I live," Thomas spits out. "Now, leave."

"Natalie, I'm sorry," I say one more time before jumping in my still-running truck and leaving, having no clue where I'm going to go.

There's no way I can go home, so I go to what I consider my second home—Ben's place.

On my way there, I dial his number.

"Ben, I need your help."

"What's up?"

"Natalie's dad has been arrested. It's a long story, but I'm on my way to your house."

"No shit?"

"Yeah. It's been one fucked-up night. I'll be there shortly." I hang up and drive like a maniac through the streets of Leighton River to get to Ben's place.

When I arrive, Ben is already standing outside.

"What's going on?" he asks.

I fill him in on everything. Rehashing it makes me fume all over again.

"What are you going to do?" he asks.

"I have no clue, but I know I can't go home. Can I crash here tonight?"

"You know you can."

He heads back to his house, and I follow him, knowing tonight is going to be the worst night of sleep I've ever had in my life. I've never felt so helpless, so guilt-ridden, and so heartbroken, all at the same time.

How could I fuck things up any worse?

CHAPTER 37

Dalton

The last thing I want to do today is go to school, but I'm hoping Natalie will be there so I can at least talk to her. When she doesn't enter our first period class, my blood boils. When she's not in second period, I get up and walk out of the class, knowing I can't sit through another hour of pointless nonsense.

Of course, the gossip of Natalie and I and what happened spread like wildfire through the rumor mill, and everywhere I go this morning, people are whispering and staring at me, so I'm done.

I hop in my truck and leave the school parking lot without looking back and head straight to her house.

I shouldn't be surprised that when I get there, Thomas has his truck blocking their entrance and is sitting there with a shotgun, most likely waiting for me to show up. I guess he's right.

HOW WE HATED

When he sees me approach, he hops out of the bed of his truck. I keep my strut, making sure he knows I'm not afraid of him. That is, until he grabs the gun sitting next to him and cocks it. Even though he keeps it pointing down and not at me, the thoughts running through my head don't know the difference.

When Mr. Spencer pointed the gun at me, I wasn't afraid. Deep down, I knew he'd never shoot me. But Thomas … he's got nothing to lose, and he's just young and dumb enough to actually do something.

"I'd advise you to stop right there," he bites out making my heart pound uncontrollably.

I hold my hands up in surrender, praying he knows I really don't want any trouble with him. "I just want to talk to Natalie," I plead.

"Yeah, well, she doesn't want to talk to you."

"Please. I need to know she's okay."

"No!" he shouts, lifting the gun slightly, making my breath hitch. "She's not okay. Our dad is in jail because of you. Our mom had to drive to Billings to a bail bondsman after the bank denied the loan she needed to bail him out. What part of that don't you understand?" His voice is so loud and strong that it makes me flinch in fear.

I've had my dad yell at me many times, but this is different. This is a crazy man, one second away from snapping, and I know if I push at all, that might be the end of it for both of us.

I drop my head in shame. "I'll fix this."

"Yeah, like you've fixed things so far? Now, get the fuck out of here before I go to jail for what, in my mind, would be justified, and I wouldn't feel a lick of guilt for it either."

I sigh and nod, turning to head back to my truck, trying to figure out what I can do. I want to talk to Natalie, but I fear if I push this right now, it will absolutely make things worse.

I head downtown to where a local attorney's office is located next to my favorite diner. After my encounter with Thomas, I need to calm my breath. I take a few minutes to work out in my head what I need to say before I walk in.

Once I'm ready, I hop out of my truck and head into his office, trying to be as adult about this situation as possible so he'll take me seriously.

"Dalton?" his receptionist asks.

Of course everyone in this town knows who I am.

I try to hide my disdain. "Hi. I'm hoping I can talk to Mr. Diaz."

Her expression tells me she's confused, but thankfully, she doesn't question me. "Sure, let me see if he's available."

She walks back to his office, then comes back out to me. "He said you can come on in."

I guess being known in this town does have its perks. I doubt he'd see just any random kid who walked in off the street.

I walk through his office door, and he stands.

"Dalton Wick." He holds his hand out to greet me. "How can I help you?"

He motions for me to take a seat, and I do.

I explain the situation with every detail, making sure he understands our parents' history and why Natalie felt

HOW WE HATED

so strongly that she had to hide our relationship. Most importantly though, I explain how this is all wrong and how, really, it's my dad using his power in this town to get Randy in trouble.

"Okay, so how can I help? I'm a little confused as to why you're here," he asks.

I sit up straight in my chair. "I want to hire you to represent Randy and help get him out of jail."

"Now, son, I appreciate your willingness to help, but I'm sure Randy has his own attorney."

"Has he contacted you?" I ask.

"Well, no, not yet."

"Who else would he contact? I know they are strapped financially. I don't want him sitting in there until a public defender gets him out."

"And you want to pay for his counsel?"

I take a deep breath. "Yes, but there's one catch. I have a trust set up that I got access to when I turned eighteen. I can do whatever I want with the money, but it takes a few days to process the paperwork. You know I'm good for it, so I'm asking that you take on this case now and I can pay you by next week."

Mr. Diaz sits back in his chair, steepling his fingers. "I appreciate your gusto. I've known Randy Spencer for years, and I know he is well respected in this community. Let me make a call to the judge and see what I can do. Then, we can discuss things moving forward from there."

I stand up and hold my hand out to him. "I'd appreciate that. Please keep me posted if there's anything I can do to help."

He shakes my hand. "I will. Make sure you give

your information to Linda, my receptionist, and I'll be in touch."

"Thank you, sir."

"You're welcome, son."

After giving Linda my phone number, I leave and send Natalie a text message.

I'm trying to figure this out, I promise.

I don't expect her to answer. Shit, I don't even know if she'll ever talk to me again, but at least I'm letting her know that I'm not just walking away. I will make this right.

I go home, only because I know my dad's gone and my mom's off doing whatever she does all day. There's no way I can just sit here, so I do the only thing I know how to do—I run.

As I head out the door, thoughts of these last few months wash over me, and all I can think about is how it started with this run. I loved the way she pushed me to go harder and faster and how she pushed herself to keep up. She challenged me in all the ways, and it opened my eyes to the idea of what a partner in life really meant.

I run so long and so hard that by the time I get back to my house, my legs are shaking, but my mind is still a jumbled mess.

As I slam a bottle of water, my eyes drift over to the fireplace, and an idea hits me. Without overthinking it, I rush to the drawer to grab a book of matches, then to the garage to grab a bucket. If my dad wants me to prove I was on his property, then I'll take a page from his book and prove I was there.

HOW WE HATED

Once I'm down at our property line, I cross the river and fill my bucket with water. I walk about ten feet up onto their property and dump the water on the dry brush that covers the property. After doing that a few times and making sure a circle about fifteen wide and long, coming out from the river, is nice and damp, I fill my bucket one more time to have it sitting next to me and stand back to take a breath.

I turn to look at the ranch that's empty land as far as I can see. Then, I notice the barn that sits dilapidated with burn marks, which I now know came from my father. I guess I am more like my dad in this case. The only difference is, I'm doing it to help the ranch, and he did it to destroy it.

"Thanks for the idea, Dad," I say under my breath as I strike a match and light the brush on fire.

I watch it intently, making sure it moves only toward the river and nowhere else. With very little brush to light on fire, it never gets any taller than a few inches, but that's all I need to prove my point.

As the fire burns, I think about how evil my dad must have been to stand here all those years ago and inflict that kind of damage on purpose. What kind of human being would be so evil to want to cause that kind of harm?

"Funny how it's all about to backfire on you," I say to myself as I watch the last of it burn out.

I take my phone from my back pocket and take pictures as my proof, making sure to include the ranch in the background so there's no question where these photos are taken.

Once I have my shots, I send Natalie another text.

LAUREN RUNOW

Keep your faith. I'm working to get him out.

I stare at my phone, hoping she responds, but after a minute of standing there, willing it to show me those three little bubbles on her side, I give up and walk around the land I burned, making sure the fire is all out. Then, I walk back to my place to hop in the truck and head straight to the sheriff's office.

I fly through the city, not paying attention to anything but the mission I'm on. I've never been so sure about anything I've done in my life, and pure determination is the only thing leading my way.

Parking my truck in front of Sheriff Townsend's office, I hop out, slamming my door shut. I walk in, adrenaline racing through my veins. If I thought scoring touchdowns was the biggest high, I was completely wrong. Justice tops that in spades.

The old building the sheriff is located in is one of the original buildings in this town, and it has more history than any other place. Mainly because it's the one place my father hasn't bought to completely renovate and make new, erasing everything that was Leighton River at one point.

I catch the receptionist, who's sitting behind a tall desk, off guard, and I'm sure my expression doesn't help as she questions, "Dalton? How can I help you?"

"I'd like to turn myself in. I was trespassing on the Spencer ranch. Everything my father said to Sheriff Townsend was a lie, and I can prove it. I'm the one who should be in jail, not Mr. Spencer."

Her eyes open wide as she stands and stutters, "Let—let me get the sheriff."

HOW WE HATED

Seconds later, Sheriff Townsend comes out. "Dalton? What's going on?"

"My dad lied, and I'm here to turn myself in. I was lighting the Spencer ranch on fire. Just like my dad did all those years ago. I was just trying to finish what he'd started. Mr. Spencer saw me doing it and pointed the gun at me to get off his property." I pull out my phone, swipe it on, and hold it out to him. "I have the pictures to prove it, and you can go check for yourself at the back of the ranch, where our property lines meet. He stopped me from getting very far, but you can see here what I lit on fire."

He steps closer to me. "Son, do you realize what you're doing right now? Does your father know you're here?"

I stand up straight. "I'm eighteen years old. I'm an adult. I don't need him here."

"What about counsel? You shouldn't be putting yourself in this situation without proper representation," he states clearly.

"Please call Mr. Diaz. I've already hired him."

"Does he know you're here? Without him?"

I shake my head. "No. I'll sit right here and wait for you to arrest me. If you want to call him first, that's fine with me."

I turn and sit in one of the chairs they have waiting along the wall.

Time goes by as I sit up straight, my fingers steepled in front of me on my lap with my gaze locked forward, not wavering one bit.

Expecting Mr. Diaz, I'm not surprised when the

door opens, and someone storms in, but I am surprised when I see it's my dad.

"Dalton!" he chastises.

I don't respond.

"What the fuck is going on?" he yells.

Sheriff Townsend exits his office. "Mike, I'm glad you came."

Thankfully, Mr. Diaz walks in right behind him, so I stand to greet him.

"Thank you for being here."

"I wish you had called me before you came to turn yourself in," Mr. Diaz says to me with his hand outstretched to greet me.

I shake his hand firmly, hoping it tells him I'm not scared one bit, and this is what I need to do.

"I didn't call you. Why are you here?" Dad asks Mr. Diaz.

"I'm here for my client, Dalton," he responds, unfazed, looking at my dad fiercely, making sure he knows he's not afraid of him.

Makes me like and respect him even more.

"Your client?" Dad asks, shocked.

"Yes, he hired me to represent him earlier today." Mr. Diaz holds his head slightly higher.

I'm thankful he goes along with my plan though he had no clue I was going to do this. It makes me wonder what his true feelings are of my father that he would take my side like this.

Maybe everyone doesn't love my dad after all like he thinks...

"And you let him turn himself in? Without you here?" Dad chastises.

HOW WE HATED

Mr. Diaz turns to me. "No, I did not advise him to do this, but I'm here to support him in any way I can."

"Your services are not needed, Alex." Dad spits his name out like it's trash. "My attorneys are on their way."

"No," I state. "Mr. Diaz is my attorney. I don't want anything to do with you, Dad. I'm here to turn myself in for setting fire to the Spencer ranch, just like you did all those years ago. That's the real reason why Mr. Spencer held that gun on me. He had every right to do so, and I'm man enough to admit that I was wrong. Unlike you."

Dad steps up, getting right in my face. "What does that mean?"

I stare right in his eyes. "It means, I know you started the fire that caused so much damage to the ranch years ago. I was just trying to finish what you'd started. You know, put my own mark on the Spencer-Wick battle."

"What are you talking about? What fire?" Dad tries to deny it.

I get more in his face. "Don't lie. Soon, everyone will know the truth of what you did and who you really are. And now, thanks to you turning in Mr. Spencer for pulling a gun on me, I'm forced to be the better man and take responsibility for what I did. I guess I just wasn't as good as you, and I got caught. Looks like I'm going down for the both of us."

He grabs my arm. "We need to talk."

I push him off of me. "There's nothing to talk about." I turn to face the sheriff. "Sheriff." I hold out my wrists to him.

Sheriff Townsend looks at my dad, then Mr. Diaz. When Mr. Diaz nods his head like he's approving his client to be arrested, Sheriff Townsend walks through the swinging door, standing between Mr. Diaz and us, and turns me around to put me in handcuffs.

"Dalton Wick, you're under arrest for trespassing on the Spencer ranch and setting fire to it." He goes on to read me my Miranda rights, then guides me through the swinging door.

When my dad tries to follow us, Sheriff Townsend stops him. "I'm sorry, but you're going to have to stop right there. He's an adult, and only his counsel is allowed back here while we process him."

Mr. Diaz walks through the half door, and we all walk back to the processing room. I know I should be scared about what I just did, but as I stand here, giving my fingerprints and taking a booking photo, I'm positive this is absolutely the right move.

CHAPTER 38

Natalie

Darkness covers our land as I sit on our porch, waiting for any news about my dad. It's gotten so late, but I can't go to sleep until I hear anything. My dad has already spent one night in jail, and I can't believe he's about to spend another one.

All because of me.

When my mom drives up our dirt road, parks, and walks up the stairs, looking absolutely deflated, I rush to her.

"Were you able to get him out?"

Tears roll down her face. "No. We have to wait for a public defender to go before the judge."

"How long will that take?"

"They said a couple of days."

I wrap my arms around her as we both break out in sobs. Sobs for the leader of our family, who's sitting behind bars.

HOW WE HATED

"Mom, what have I done?"

"Hey." She pushes me back to look me in the eyes. "Don't talk like that. We'll figure this out."

"But it's all my fault. I knew I shouldn't be seeing Dalton." I break out in more sobs.

"Sweetie." She pulls me back into a hug just as her phone rings.

We both jump, and she hurries to grab it from her purse.

When she doesn't recognize the number, she answers in a rush, putting the call on speakerphone. "Randy?"

"No, Tracy. This is Alex Diaz. I have some news about Randy. Can you meet me at my office?"

"Really? How did you know?" Mom asks, confused.

"I'll fill you in on everything when you get here. I'll see you soon."

He hangs up, and we both look at each other, not having a clue what's going on.

"I'm going with you!" I state, and she holds up her hands.

"No. I want you and Thomas to stay here. The last thing you need is to see your father behind bars."

"But you're going to Mr. Diaz's office. Let me come."

She places her hand on my face. "Please. Just let me be the adult here and you be the kid. I know you're just as worried as I am, but I really don't want you or Thomas to be any part of this."

I nod. "Okay. You'll keep me posted as soon as you know anything, right?"

She hugs me again. "I promise." She lets go of me

and grabs her keys from her purse. "I'll talk to Thomas as I leave. He's still standing watch at the gate."

I tilt my head to the side. "Is that really necessary?"

She sympathizes with me. "He just wants to protect us. Protect you."

"Dalton isn't who we need protection from."

"I know. Just let him do what he feels he needs to do as the current man of the house, okay?"

I nod, wrapping my arms around myself as I watch her walk back down the stairs and back to her car, having no clue how I'm going to survive sitting here by myself with so much guilt and worry that I feel like I'm going to be sick.

How did the best night of my life turn into this absolute nightmare?

Dalton

Sitting in the holding cell for the past eight hours has given me a lot of time to think. I asked where Mr. Spencer was being held and was told since he was already processed, they moved him to the county jail. I hate to say that's a good thing, but it's better than us being the only two people in this holding cell. I guess I never really thought about how the criminal justice works in this small town.

I definitely never thought I'd be sitting here—ever.

A deputy sheriff walks to the sliding gate that locks

HOW WE HATED

me in here and sticks his key in the door. "Dalton, you've been bailed out."

I stand, confused. "By who?"

"Mr. Diaz. His assistant, Linda, is out front, waiting to take you home."

Home.

I guess I don't really have one of those anymore.

Closing my eyes and trying to push out the thoughts of what will happen next, I walk out of the holding cell, ready for whatever is going to happen.

"Hello, Dalton," Linda says as I come into view.

"Hello. Where's Mr. Diaz?" I ask.

She looks at the deputy sheriff. "Is he good to go?"

He hands me a bag with my belongings, including my phone, wallet, and keys. "Yep. You're all good. Have a good night," he responds.

We both reply, "You too," and walk out of the sheriff's office to her car, which is parked next to my truck.

"What's going on?" I ask.

"Mr. Diaz asked that you follow me back to his office."

I nod, and we get in our separate vehicles. When the music turns on, I reach over and turn it off. Music has always been my savior, my calming force in life, but right now, all I need is silence.

Once we're there, she walks me back to his office. "You can wait in here. He'll be here shortly."

A few minutes later, Mr. Diaz walks in with, to my surprise, Randy Spencer right behind him.

I stand instantly. "Mr. Spencer." I hold out my hand to him.

He pauses, obviously just as surprised to see me here. When he doesn't shake my hand, I pull it back and retake my seat at Mr. Diaz's desk. Randy takes out the chair next to me and does the same.

"Randy," Mrs. Spencer says as she walks through the door with her arms open wide.

Randy stands and races to embrace her in a hug; even I feel their love from a few feet away.

"How did you get out?" Mrs. Spencer cries. "I couldn't get the money to post bail. I promise, I was trying."

"I don't know yet. Alex"—he pulls back from her and points to Mr. Diaz—"came and got me. He hasn't told me what's going on, and when I arrived, he was here."

They turn to me, and Mrs. Spencer's expression doesn't hide her confusion. "Dalton?"

I stand to shake her hand. "Hello, Mrs. Spencer."

"Please, call me Tracy." She shakes my hand, then turns to Mr. Diaz. "Alex, what's going on?"

I offer Tracy my chair and stand next to the wall.

"Thank you," Tracy says as she takes the chair and scoots it next to Randy so they can hold hands while Mr. Diaz speaks.

"Dalton came to me, explaining what had happened in full detail."

I speak up. "I love your daughter, Mr. and Mrs. Spencer. I never meant for any of this to happen, but I'll make it right."

Tracy reaches out her hand to me, and I grab it. She grins at me, and I smile back. Randy, on the other hand, stays stoic as a statue.

HOW WE HATED

"He was asking for my help to bail you out of jail," Mr. Diaz says.

"He paid my bail?" Randy's voice deepens a few notches in anger, his question directed only at Mr. Diaz, like I'm not standing right here.

Mr. Diaz holds up his palm to Randy, trying to calm him down. "No, he didn't. I was able to talk to the judge after Dalton here proved that he was there, lighting your property on fire, and that he was the one who should be arrested."

Randy stands so quickly that his chair knocks to the floor, and he rushes toward me. "You did what?"

I stand in shock, staring at a man so angry that I genuinely fear for my life.

Mr. Diaz rushes around his desk, grabbing him by the shoulders to stop him. "It's okay. I've been out there to see for myself. There was no damage. He did it to prove he was on your property, so you had every right to point a gun at him."

Randy looks at him, then back at me, confused. "What are you talking about?"

"Dalton turned himself in as the guilty party here. Which got you out of jail," Mr. Diaz responds, his grip on Randy lessening and his hands just resting on his shoulders now.

Randy's tension softens but only slightly. "Then, why isn't he in jail? Why is he here?"

"I explained everything to the judge." Mr. Diaz looks right at me. "Everything."

I hold my head high. Still not ashamed or wavering from my decision.

He turns back to Randy. "The judge decided to let both of you out, knowing now that nothing really happened to warrant you both being in jail. Dalton is here because I wanted to make sure you knew his side of the story and, more importantly, that he was willing to take the fall for everything."

"Fine. I heard you. He can leave now," Randy bites out.

"Randy"—Mr. Diaz sighs—"I've known you a long time. I think you need to listen to the boy."

I watch as Randy closes his eyes for a brief moment, then looks up at me.

I stand up straight with a plea for forgiveness. "Please know I am nothing like my father. I don't blame you one bit for hating him. I now know the truth, and I completely understand why you wouldn't want me with your daughter. I will prove to you that I am the man she deserves."

"He is," a female voice says from the doorway.

Natalie enters, her face red and stained with tears, and I instantly rush to hold her, trying to wash the pain away.

When she allows me to wrap her in my arms, all the stress I've been holding disappears for a breath—until I hear Randy yell, "Get away from her!"

As I glance his way, Tracy reaches out and holds him back. "Randy, hear them out."

Natalie grips me closer, her head lying on my chest as she confesses, "Daddy, we never meant for any of this to happen, I swear. Dalton's proven to me he's not like his father, and I know he'll prove it to you too."

HOW WE HATED

"I want to help, sir," I say. "We all know you had every right to think I was trespassing on your property, and you had the right to protect that property. I made sure the sheriff knew that too."

"He proved it too. In a way I would *never* recommend anyone to do, but it made the case pretty open and closed," Mr. Diaz says. "You both are free to go, and all of this is behind us."

Randy takes a deep breath, and I watch the last bit of stress that he's been holding on his shoulders melt off completely.

He faces Mr. Diaz and holds out his hand to him. "I really appreciate your help, Alex."

"Don't thank me. Thank Dalton here." Mr. Diaz nods in my direction as they shake hands. "I wouldn't have known if he hadn't come to me for help. Please know that I'm always here for you. For anything."

Randy nods his head in agreement. "That means a lot."

Tracy stands and walks around Mr. Diaz's desk to give him a hug. "Thank you, Alex."

Watching the interaction between adults who have an obvious longtime connection fills me with a hope I didn't know I needed. I've never seen my parents act this way toward any other adults. Shit, they don't even act this way toward each other.

My dad has always had this *you're on your own in this world* attitude and doesn't trust anyone. Not even with his business partners. It's a horrible way to live.

I want to be more like Randy and Mr. Diaz. I want to be there for people I know and help them in any way

I can. That's what life should be about. Helping each other.

I look down at Natalie, who's still in my arms, and kiss the top of her head.

"Sweetie," Tracy says.

We both turn her way, and Natalie releases her grip from me and falls into the arms of her mother. Sounds of their tears fill the room, making my eyes well up too.

"Dalton." Tracy reaches her arms out to me, too, and I come closer to her, embracing the two of them in a hug. "Thank you for your help."

My eyes meet with Randy, whose expression reads nothing but hesitation. I take a deep breath and move out of their embrace and head toward him.

I reach my hand out to him. "I'm truly sorry for all the trouble my father has caused you. Not just now. But for everything."

He stares at my hand, and then after a few seconds, he grips it firmly with a nod, not saying anything in response.

I know he's not going to like me right away, so I take this as a win for the moment and head back to Natalie, who instantly wraps her arms back around me. Being able to be so open like this is the best feeling in the world.

We all head out of Mr. Diaz's office and to the street, where my truck, Tracy's car, and Thomas's truck are.

"Where's Thomas?" I ask.

Natalie smiles. "He went to the restroom back home, and I took off. There was no way I was sitting at home, waiting to hear what was going on."

HOW WE HATED

I laugh and grab her in a hug again. "That's my girl."

"I didn't know you would be here. Mom got a call, saying to come down. We didn't know anything else."

"I told you I was going to make it right."

"That you did," Tracy says, placing her hand on my back. "Thank you for contacting Alex."

"It was the least I could do. I'm sorry my dad got us in this mess to begin with," I say.

"No, I'm sorry," Randy says with a big sigh. "It wasn't right of me to point a gun at you. It's just—"

I cut him off, "She's your daughter. You don't have to tell me how special she is. To be honest, now that I know everything that happened with my father, if I were in your shoes, I probably would have done the same thing."

He nods his head, pursing his lips. "I've turned into the cliché country song about getting my gun to fight away boys from my little girl."

We all laugh, and I smile at Natalie.

"She's worth every cliché in the world."

"That she is," Randy says with a grin, then looks at me again. "That doesn't mean I'm okay with this." He moves his hand back and forth between the two of us.

"Randy," Tracy admonishes with a slight slap of the back of her hand on his chest.

I hold my head high. "I don't expect you to be right away. I'll prove myself to you, and I know, over time, I will have your blessing to be with your daughter."

He nods again. "Only time will tell." He turns to Tracy. "Let's get home."

Tracy hugs both of us one more time, and Randy

comes over to hug Natalie. When I offer my hand out to him, he gives me a firm handshake.

"Thanks again," he says.

"Glad to help."

They hop in Tracy's car, and once they're out of sight, I bring Natalie close to me.

"God, I've wanted to kiss you so bad."

I pick her up in my arms and kiss her with every part of my soul, knowing she's finally mine, in the open, for the entire world to know, and I'm never letting her go.

CHAPTER 39

Natalie

Dalton wanted to make a statement, so it was clear to everyone that we are, and have been, together. So this morning I'm sitting on the front porch of my house waiting for him to arrive to pick me up for school.

I hear his tires roll over the gravel entrance into our ranch and I stand up, excited to see him.

When the door to the house opens behind me, I look to see my dad standing there with my mom by his side. Knowing he's here, not only allowing me to date Dalton, but coming outside to greet him himself fills me with so much joy I can hardly contain it.

Nothing needs to be said as to why he's here right now, so I walk to him and hug him. "Thanks, Daddy."

Dalton parks the truck and exits, walking up to my family with his head held high. "Morning." He holds his hand out to my dad.

HOW WE HATED

When they shake my mom wraps her arm around my back, just as proud to be seeing their interaction in front of us as I am. I know she's always felt a layer of guilt for their feud with the Wick family so this moment is just as big for her as it is for me.

"Thanks again for last night," Dad says.

"I wish none of it would have happened, but I'm glad we got it resolved. I love your daughter, sir," Dalton says, then turns and gives me a smile.

"I know you do. You're a good man, and I trust you'll do right by her."

"You know it."

Dad nods his head in my direction as if he's giving his permission for him to go greet me. A grin spreads across Dalton's face as he heads my direction and gives me a hug with a kiss on the cheek and turns his attention to my mom. "Mrs. Spencer." He holds out his hand to her.

"Oh please, call me Tracy and give me a hug." She opens her arms wide to Dalton.

He smiles as they hug.

Thomas exits right then. "You know I'm still not okay with this, right?"

Dalton turns to him. "I know. You'll come around."

"I doubt it." He looks at all of us then holds out his hand to Dalton. "But we can be civil at least."

They shake. "I'll take it."

"That is, unless you let me drive that truck." Thomas motions toward Dalton's 94 Chevy.

Dalton laughs. "I'll let you drive it. As long as you don't dump it in the marsh like your sister did."

"You did what?" both Mom and Dad say at the same time.

I laugh out loud and walk up to Dalton, putting my arm around his waist and tell everyone, "Long story. He deserved it though."

Dalton leans in to kiss my cheek. "I probably did. Just don't do it again."

He gives his attention back to Thomas. "We're good though, right?"

Thomas sighs. "Yeah. We're good. Doesn't mean I like your dad though."

"That makes two of us," Dalton states matter-of-factly.

It breaks my heart that he doesn't have a relationship with his father. I can't imagine not having parents who care about you and always standing by you.

Last night he stayed at Ben's to avoid any interactions with his dad. His plan is to get a place of his own, but we'll see what happens.

"I'm sorry to hear that, son," Dad says, placing his hand on Dalton's shoulder.

Dalton shrugs. "We both know he's not going to change."

Dad sighs with a shake to his head. "Unfortunately, not."

"Okay, you three. Time to get to school," Mom says.

We say our goodbyes as Dalton and I head to his truck and Thomas walks toward his.

"See you there," Dalton says to Thomas.

To see Thomas nod his agreement and be okay with me getting in Dalton's truck is the best feeling in the

HOW WE HATED

world. For so long I was terrified of what would happen if my family knew I was dating Dalton, and here they are more than okay with it, they're accepting it.

We hop in the truck and Dalton reaches over to squeeze my hand with an expression happier than I've ever seen on him.

We head to school where he parks in his normal spot. When his crew, along with Ashley and Susie, see me jump down from the passenger side they all come over to greet us, obviously happy to see we can finally be out in the open with our relationship.

Ashley, Susie and I pull up to our last football game of the season, and of our time at Leighton River. Dalton asked that I meet him at the back of the school so we all exit the car and head to where he said would be best.

After a few minutes, the team exits the locker room and he heads straight to me.

"You have what I need, Ashley?" he asks.

Ashley grins from ear to ear as she hands him a black paint pen. "Sure do."

He takes it from her then turns to me. "May I?" he asks, holding up the pen for my permission.

My heart flutters as I nod, trying to hold back tears of joy.

He has a cheesy grin on his face as he paints his number, 81, on my face. Ashley and Susie cheer behind me and even Marcus, Ben and Eli hoot and holler when they see what's going on.

"Finally, we get to tell the world," he says before he kisses me.

"Finally," I respond, loving the fact that I'm able to be his out in the open, for everyone to know.

ACKNOWLEDGMENTS

A few years ago, a fellow author contacted me asking if I would be interested in participating in a group series about a small town in Montana. I wasn't sure if I could fit it in my schedule, but when I found out the town would be called Mason Creek, I knew I had to do it. You see, my oldest son is named Mason, and this author had no clue that was his name. I'm all about the thought that there are signs everywhere, and I felt this was a neon blinking sign saying I should participate.

After releasing *Fumbled Past* my amazing PA, Autumn Gantz with Wordsmith Publicity, said I needed to keep within that high school realm, and she wanted it to be a series of at least three books.

Since Mason Creek included my older son's name, I decided to name my next series after my youngest son, Leighton. From there, the town of Leighton River was born.

The series was supposed to release on his birthday,

but I decided to push it back so that the books would release closer together.

Once I had the rough draft done, I sent it to Chelle Lagoski Northcutt, Jeannine Collette, Stefanie Pace and Ginger Scott to help round out the story as beta readers. Then, after adding their suggestions, Courtney DeLollis beta read for me to fill in those last little gaps. I can't thank them all enough for their help in completing this story.

A huge thank you to Sarah Sentz with Enchanting Romance Designs for the beautiful cover, Jovana Shirley for her amazing editing, and Courtney DeLollis who proofread for me.

And thank you! You, who is reading this sentence right now. I couldn't follow my writing dream without you. Thank you for reading my words!

ABOUT THE AUTHOR

Lauren Runow is the author of multiple Adult Contemporary Romance novels, some more dirty than others. When Lauren isn't writing, you'll find her listening to music, at her local CrossFit, reading, or at the baseball field with her boys. Her only vice is coffee, and she swears it makes her a better mom!

Lauren is a graduate from the Academy of Art in San Francisco and is the founder and co-owner of the community magazine she and her husband publish. She is a proud Rotarian, helps run a local non-profit kids science museum, and was awarded Woman of the Year from Congressman Garamendi. She lives in Northern California with her husband and two sons.

www.LaurenRunow.com

Sign up for her newsletter at http://bit.ly/2NEXgH1

Check out her books on Goodreads:
http://bit.ly/1Isw3Sv

Follow her on:
Facebook at www.facebook.com/laurenjrunow
Instagram at www.instagram.com/Lauren_Runow/
BookBub at www.bookbub.com/authors/lauren-runow
Twitter at www.twitter.com/LaurenRunow
BookandMain: www.bookandmainbites.com/LaurenRunow

Join her reader group on Facebook: Lauren's Law Breakers

Made in the USA
Las Vegas, NV
16 January 2024

84459437R00187